RUNAWAY QUEEN

A DARK MAFIA ROMANCE

MADE OF MAYHEM DUET
BOOK TWO

MILA KANE

WELCOME TO MILA'S WORLD

Join my newsletter for deleted scenes, polls, and character inspiration at Mila Kane.

AUTHOR'S NOTE

Welcome to Mila Kane's New York. It's not the city you know, and here the Kings and Queens of the Underworld reign supreme.

Along with life or death love, darkness and mayhem rules this corner of the book world. If that's your thing, read on.

If you're not sure, check out my website for a full list of TWs.

1

NIKOLAI

"It's better to die than do nothing."
– Nikolai Chernov.

I caught the man's eyes across the crowded cafeteria. First, they skittered from mine, and then they returned. I pinned him with a mocking gaze. That silver stare was the first nail in his coffin. I made sure he realized that from my expression.

His name was Gerald, and soon, he'd be dead.

He shuddered and shuffled out of the room, head down.

"He's probably running back to his cell to cry into his stuffy," a lilting voice said beside me. Bran lounged against the cafeteria bench like he owned it. A displaced Irish prince giving his time to the unwashed rabble.

"I'm going to make him eat that thing. Every single bite." I smirked, gripping my plastic fork in the only way that made the damn thing work. I scooped the tasteless white mush on the plate into my mouth. "Food is fuel" was a mantra that really came into its own in prison.

Powdered mashed potato made with water. My favorite. It must be Wednesday. I'd had seven years of mashed potato Wednesdays. Proof that people can get used to anything. I didn't just survive in prison. I ruled it. I'd almost miss it, and the predictability of the meal schedule, when I finally got out. One month from now.

Bran laughed, rubbing a tattooed hand across his gold stubble, and nodded, his green eyes fastening on the place where the man had disappeared. "I heard that's how he took them, you know? Chloroform on a stuffy, held it to their faces and…" Bran trailed off, his eyes hardening.

I knew how he felt. I felt it, too. The same white-hot sense of rage that a man like that got to live another day, at the state's expense. We might all be criminals in the maximum-security prison where I was currently an honored guest, but even felons have a code. That man had none. He didn't deserve to keep breathing. Unfortunately, New York state didn't have the death penalty for men like him.

But they had me.

There was no bleeding-heart committee or protest groups that would save him from me. Especially not when we were locked in the darkness together. The monster that stalked the halls of my empty chest hungered for his blood.

Bran whistled under his breath. "We've got company."

The chair beside him jerked out, and a large body filled it. I knew who it was without looking up.

Ramirez had only been inside for a month, and he'd already signed his death warrant by cooperating with the guards to get better privileges. His gang wasn't happy with him. So, he was coming to me.

The Executioner. *Palach*.

"Well, Chernov, did you think it over?"

I continued to eat, scooping the liquid mash from the plastic partitioned plate with ease, before I settled back and played with the plastic knife. Ramirez's anxiety radiated across the table.

Bran tutted. "You should know better than to think that the *Palach* would be interested in your cause. Bending over for the guards won't keep you safe in here. It's too late for that now, though."

"When you get out, I can make sure you have a real good time. All the coke you want, girls, the best week of your life. That has to be worth something."

Ramirez was sweating. I could smell him from across the table. I was tired of male sweat and desperation. The smell was one of the worst parts of prison.

"You have nothing I want, Ramirez. Besides, I wouldn't take anything from a rat. Run back to your gutter and say your prayers. You'll need them where your old friends are sending you."

"Fuck you, man, you could fix it, you could help. Instead, you want more blood on your hands?"

A laugh left me at that. One unhinged peal after another. Ramirez flinched, looking to Bran for an explanation. There wasn't one. There was no reason to laugh at the very realistic thought that this man would be dead by morning, and yet, laughter was all I had for him.

I looked at Bran and jerked my head toward the unwanted guest. "This fuck thinks I'll care if his blood is on my hands."

Bran chuckled. "He clearly missed his calling as a comedian."

Ramirez's face turned red. He was feeling embarrassed. Eyes were on us. He lost what was left of his sanity and swore at me, reaching into his jumpsuit.

The homemade shiv was out of his pocket and through my hand before I could pull it back. He pinned my left hand to the scarred cafeteria table and spit at me.

"Laugh now, bitch."

So, I did.

The pain was nothing to write home about. It barely registered. I lifted my hand. The shiv hadn't penetrated that far, bouncing off the metal of the table. Now, I held my hand up before Ramirez, my smirk still firmly in place.

"Come on, Joey, it's like you're not even trying. Did your guard friends teach you how to play 'just the tip?' I prefer much, much more."

With that, I pushed the knife further into my hand. The silence in the cafeteria was deafening. It was boring as fuck in prison, so when someone did something interesting, you drew quite the crowd.

Ramirez went pale, his eyes riveted on mine. He was clearly rethinking his life choices right now. "I'm sorry, man, I shouldn't have done that."

I grinned at him. "No, you probably shouldn't have, but everyone makes mistakes, isn't that right, Bran?"

My friend grinned widely, settling back and resting his hands behind his head. "Where are your pals now? The ones you bend over for?"

Ramirez licked his lips. "They don't mess with the *Palach*."

Bran laughed. "That's right. They don't. I guess they're smarter than you."

"It's fine, *bratan*. No big deal. I don't have scores to settle with a soon-to-be-dead man. You can go." I gestured benevolently toward the doors, dismissing Ramirez.

The sound of the chair scraping back punctuated the silence.

I glanced down at my plate, under my dripping hand, and sudden annoyance flickered through my broken mind. My other fist banged on the table. Ramirez froze, glancing fearfully at me.

"That being said, I wasn't done eating, and now it's ruined." With a fluid motion, I pulled the shiv from my hand and swept the plastic plate with the blood-spattered mash onto the floor, standing to tower over Ramirez.

"That's unforgiveable." Bran stood beside me. "Mash Wednesdays are his favorite."

There was a gathering tension in the air, like the crack of electricity before a storm.

"What game are you in the mood for today, brother?" I aimed the question at Bran, although my eyes never left Ramirez.

"Hmm, maybe whack-a-mole?" Bran laughed and picked his tray up, just as another inmate, an idiot who'd just arrived the day before and was poor at reading the room, wandered past.

Bran cracked him over the head with the tray, a signal for all hell to break loose.

I launched myself at Ramirez when he tried to turn and run. The lunchroom exploded in thrown food, followed by punches. Blood spattered across the tiles, and the sound of screams and an alarm blaring in the distance was a comforting lullaby for my fractured mind. Prison might smell like shit, but sometimes, it was entertaining as hell.

THE MAN in cell 3H actually slept with a stuffed animal. I had no idea what psychiatrist had fought for him to have it, considering who he was and what he'd done, but I had half a mind to put them on my shit list as well. The list of people who needed killing when I got out of here grew longer day by day.

He barely made a peep when we took him. I watched my men carry him out of the cell. It was dark, and the guard shift change was purposefully delayed. Bran hadn't even had to twist their arm that hard. No matter what kind of man you are, if you have even a scrap of humanity in you, you didn't mind turning a blind eye to some good old-fashioned justice for a man like this one.

We took him to the shower block. It was only polite to make the cleanup easier.

He whimpered when he was tossed to the floor.

"Hello, Gerald," Bran said, approaching the cowering man. "That's your name, isn't it? Gerald Townsend. Local coach and do-gooder. I heard you clocked more hours of voluntary work this year than anyone else in the city. What a hero," Bran chuckled, but there was nothing warm in his tone. "Though, I'm not sure the kids at the different foster homes you volunteered at would agree, would they?"

"I never—they lied," he fumbled out.

Bran was quiet, and I knew he was fighting the urge to rip Gerald's throat out.

"You're telling me over thirty kids lied? And they all had the same details? Wow, that's some bad luck for you, isn't it, Gerald?"

Bran moved away, getting too worked up. I got him. Men like Gerald made me enjoy killing. I'm sure there were plenty of men like Bran and my brother, Kirill, who could be detached and unemotional, and end a man like Gerald out of necessity, so he could never hurt a child again. They'd never enjoy inflicting pain like I did. They'd never linger and watch the life drain. They didn't have a twisting fun house of chaotic horror inside their chests like I did. The world had started its carnival spin the day I'd found out Sofia was dead, and nothing had ever had the power to stop it since. It was like being drunk, when the world blurred and your heart raced, but it never went away. The vestiges of my shattered sanity held on for dear life, as the merry-go-round spun its never-ending circles inside me.

Round and round the mulberry bush... pop goes the weasel.

I spoke from the doorway as I lounged against the wall. "I'm afraid your streak of bad luck is set to continue. Do you know who I am?"

Gerald blinked at me, paling further. He licked his thick lips. "Yes, you're the *Palach*. The executioner."

"Wow, Niko, you're famous," Bran laughed.

"I'm flattered, but in this case, flattery will get you nowhere, Gerald." I crossed the room toward him, pulling the stuffy from my pocket. The sad-looking rabbit was missing an eye.

"Here, you forgot something in your cell," I murmured, passing it to him as I crouched to his level.

He took the rabbit and held it close, huddling in a horrifying parody of his victims.

"Since you're new here, let me be the one to explain to you how this place works. You're in here with hardened criminals, violent psychopaths… and that's just the guards. In here, there's no one small and meek who you can victimize. In here, you're the prey."

Gerald whimpered.

"Do you know what most criminals have in common, Gerry boy?" Bran chipped in. His grin chilled even my blood. "They have families, kids, little innocent nieces and nephews, godchildren. Even the *Palach* has them."

Gerald turned his terrified face back to me.

I smiled at him, unsettling him even more. "That's right. Two, actually. I've never met them, but that doesn't mean I wouldn't kill for them, in their honor. A man who likes to hurt little kids needs to learn to play with boys his own size. What do you say, Gerald? Do you want to play with me?"

Gerald wet his lips, his gaze darting fearfully around the place, at the men watching us silently. My loyal devotees.

"What kind of game?"

Bran laughed, and I smiled.

"What kind of game would you like to play? How about… hide-and-seek? Or tag? Truth or dare?"

Gerald wet his lips. "Hide-and-seek."

"Ding-ding-ding, we've got a contender here." I stood and stepped back.

I nodded to one of my men by the door, and the lights went out suddenly, plunging us into unrelenting darkness. My natural habitat.

"Hide, Gerald. I'll give you until the count of ten before I look for you."

His stumbling steps made him easy to find in the dark.

"One, two, three," I trailed off, moving easily toward Gerald's lumbering shape. I was used to the darkness. I'd lived inside for seven years. Seven years of darkness and horror. Seven years to forget the starry skies of my childhood.

Seven years to forget *her*.

I'd found that I could forget a lot of things in seven years, but I hadn't forgotten her. Every single second we'd spent together was tattooed on my memory, etched in blood. As permanent to me by now as the madness that plagued my mind.

I closed in on Gerald from behind. He opened his mouth to scream, and I shoved the rabbit inside it, enjoying every second of his fear.

"Ten."

Then I pulled Ramirez's shiv. It fit my hand like an old friend.

Now, came the fun bit.

2
NIKOLAI

*T*he next week, I was doing push-ups in my cell when a guard rapped on the bars. Exercise helped to numb the boredom, and my body was a temple honed by hard discipline that made my former, younger self look sloppy and weak. Now, I was truly strong.

"Chernov, a visitor."

I got up, toweled the sweat off my neck, and passed by the guard without acknowledging him. I had learned how to play the prison game in Russia. I didn't cooperate with the authorities and had taken plenty of beatings for it. Me and authority still didn't mix.

A shriveled figure sat at a scratched table in the waiting room. Age and a hard life had turned Artur Golubev into a gnarled hump of a man, but I knew he could still beat down the newest bratva recruit when he needed to. Artur would never need to prove his physical strength. Besides, his talent with discreet explosives was renowned.

He was *vor,* and no Russian in jail would ever challenge him.

"Nikolai, *malchik,* you look well, a difficult thing considering what they feed you in here." Artur smiled at me. His gold teeth flashed under the fluorescent lights.

"I've gained a taste for it." I grinned at him and relaxed back in my seat.

Artur had been an inmate two separate times while I was incarcerated. The sight of the old man was a strange comfort. He was the only person I'd ever met who had as many tattoos as I did, but his were infinitely more valuable.

He had the marks of the *vory v zakone.* He kneeled for no man.

"Of course you have. Prison suits you, Niko, like it suited me. I saw your brother last week."

That caught my interest. Kirill was *pakhan* of the Chernov bratva, a brotherhood who claimed New York and ruled from Brighton Beach, a historically Russian seat of power. Still, a single bratva in the scheme of the countless number of brotherhoods in the vast territory of North America was a small thing. Kirill was smart. He knew his position, and he'd have known to show respect to a man like Artur. *Vor* status is a mark of the deepest respect, and the *vory v zakone* wasn't an organization to fuck with.

"I trust he was welcoming," I said.

Artur nodded. "As he should be. Your brother is a smart man, and a good *pakhan.* New York is a difficult territory to hold, and he does it well. The *vory* hasn't had to intervene in there since your father and his troubles in the nineties."

He was talking about a particularly bad few years when a bratva based in Boston and the Chernov bratva had clashed spectacularly. The streets in both cities had run red with Russian blood, until the *vory* had intervened.

"I guess the apple fell far from the tree when it comes to Viktor and Kirill, unlike me."

Artur raised an eyebrow. "Meaning?"

"Meaning my father was an ignorant Russian thug, and I'm pretty sure he attended school more often than I did. Kirill is the brains in the family." I shrugged like it didn't bother me, which it really didn't. I had no illusions about who I was.

"You sell yourself short, Nikolai. I've been impressed by you. There are book smarts, and then there are street ones. More than that, not every man understands the code."

The code. Artur was talking about the code of the *vory*. *Vory v zakone* roughly translated to "thieves in law" and had its own rules. Above the petty squabbles of rival bratvas, the *vory* knighting a man with the title was a sign of ultimate respect. It was an old system, and while it had changed and adapted in many ways, it remained a powerful accolade.

"I've seen how you reign in here, your effortless understanding of rules that aren't written anywhere. The *vory* needs men like you."

Now it was my turn to stare.

Artur's gaze shifted over my prison overalls. "I hope you have space on that scribble board of a body. I'm making a case for your stars."

Stars. One of the many symbols imbued with meaning in the intricate system of the *vory*. When inked in different places, they marked different stations in the organization.

"Stars? I'm too young."

"You're old for a man with your experiences."

"Fine. I'm too unstable."

Artur laughed. "Knowing that makes you not."

I smoothed a hand down my shaved head. Stubble prickled my palm. "It's too late for me, old man. I just want to watch the world burn."

Artur stared at me for a long time.

"And your brother, and his wife, his children? Having a *vor* in the family would make the Chernov bratva stronger and safer."

I let out a tired sigh. "Kirill can more than take care of himself. I don't want to be bothered with bratva shit. That life ended a long time ago for me."

Artur stared at me, a critical look in his eyes. "You don't get a nickname in prison like *Palach* if you're done with bratva life."

"Being the executioner has nothing to do with bratva business."

"What's it about then?"

"Feeding the beast."

I smiled at Artur, and the old man flinched. That seemed to happen more and more these days. I was the abyss that no one wanted to look too deeply in to.

"Here." Artur passed me a book. "For your collection." *The Brothers Karamazov* by Dostoevsky. "I thought it fitting."

I smiled and took the volume, rubbing my finger over the title. A classic I'd read before but would happily read again.

"Thank you. I'll pass on your *vor* recommendation, but thank you for your consideration," I said quietly.

Artur sighed loudly. "You sound like a fucking politician. Well, I'll see you when you get out. Surely you can make time between burning the world down and going back to prison to take an old man for a drink."

"I have my scores to settle. I'll find you after."

Artur frowned at me. "Why do I doubt that's going to happen?"

Because you know me too well. I simply shrugged, watching the old man lever himself up and head out. I turned my gaze around the rest of the visiting room.

It hadn't changed in seven years. The table by the window was the one where my brother had delivered the killing blow to my sanity.

"It was quick if it helps at all. She's gone, Nikolai. Sofia De Sanctis is dead."

He'd stabbed me deep and left me to die. Like a truck blindsiding me at an intersection, I was lying at the scene, bleeding out. I was stuck in that moment, and I had no idea how to come back to the world. I hadn't lied to old Artur. I didn't care about the world anymore. I had no interest in having a fresh start or turning a new page, like the thera- pists droned on about inside. If they could see inside my head, they'd never let me out.

I was going to watch the world burn and warm myself in the blaze.

Hell was waiting for me, and I couldn't fucking wait to go home.

BACK IN MY CELL, I added the book to my prized collection. Every single paperback on the small shelf I'd read countless times. Every word was etched in my memory. The characters in the books sometimes felt more real to me than the people I had once known. Except for her. She would always be the most real thing to me, even if she was only a ghost.

The thought of becoming *vor* played through my troubled mind. It was a surprise to be considered. It was the highest accolade a man like me could ever aspire to. An uneducated, violent felon with a track record that read like a serial killer's rap sheet. I swung myself onto my bed and stared at nothing. Bran was gone, released a few days ago. I would follow in a few weeks. It was too fucking quiet in the cell without him. I didn't like the quiet anymore. It only made the screams in my head louder.

I stared at the ceiling, where several things were taped up. My treasures, if such a word could apply to such a meager collection.

A photo of Molly Chernova, my sister-in-law, with two young children. My imposing brother stood behind his family, his hand lying on Molly's shoulder. They were the only remaining family I had in the world.

Then a black-and-white newspaper clipping. An obituary. I hadn't bothered to keep the words beneath the photo.

Antonio De Sanctis couldn't have written an obit for his daughter if his own life had depended on it. He'd never known her. He'd never cared enough to try.

Sofia. *My lastochka.*

The picture quality was terrible. It was far too grainy to make out, unless I let my eyes unfocus a little. She wasn't smiling in the picture, merely staring a black hole through the camera lens, right at me. Every single night, I stared back, for hours on end, and let my mind wander the halls of the past.

My little swallow with the clipped wings, who had died inside her cage, after all.

Her death had ripped away what little sanity I'd had left. Everything had stopped making sense in that moment, and it had never gone back to normal.

I'd always known I was a damned man. I hadn't been enough for my mother to live for, and I hadn't been strong enough to protect my *lastochka*. Life was a horror, a sickening freak show.

I wanted it to end. I would soon.

First, I had my scores to settle.

First, I'd have my vengeance. It was the only thing that brought me a measure of calm.

Violence was all I had left. The whirling chaos inside me had only quieted once in my life, around her, my little *lastochka*, and now she was gone. It'd never be still again.

I'd learned to live with the storm inside me. People had learned to fear it, and that made sense. The part of me that had been sane and rational had died with her. All that was left were the flames of madness.

There were the only thing that kept me warm.

The only thing I had.

3

NIKOLAI

*T*he day of my release was anticlimactic. My lawyer, Ronan Black, came to oversee the paperwork.

Ronan was the kind of man who liked to dress up in suits and pull a veneer of civility over his brutality, but he was just the same as the rest of us. His stepfather, Brian O'Connor, had made sure of that. Despite going by a different name, Ronan Black was known in our circles as a man you didn't want to cross. Luckily for me, Kirill employed him on behalf of the Chernov bratva. Funnily enough, he was Bran's stepbrother. He didn't go by the surname O'Connor in his professional life. The name was too notorious. Instead, he took his mother's maiden name and played pretend that he wasn't the son of a mob boss and his clients weren't all criminals. Many a man had disappeared who dared to go against Ronan Black, and even the odd, irritating coworker. In the last few years, I'd enjoyed seeing him make the trek out to the prison sporadically to see me. He had hated every second.

"Well, today's the day, Chernov. I finally get to see your ugly face for the last time."

"Sure, until I get arrested again." I smirked at him.

He shot me a glacial look. "Here, I have a cell phone for you. My number is in it. Do not call me for any reason, other than getting arrested again, and for fuck's sake, Nikolai," Ronan warned, his voice firm, "stay out of trouble."

I took the phone from him, turning it over in my hands. "Even phones have changed," I muttered.

"Congratulations. You're a time traveler. All your favorite things will still get you in trouble, however, like violence, murder, and general mayhem. Try to not do them too quickly, or I might just kill you myself, instead of representing you again." His clipped, polished voice sounded at odds with his words.

That accent was as fake as the friendly smile he shot the guards. Ronan had no respect for the police or legal system. He simply enjoyed playing with it, pulling people's strings to his advantage. I was pretty sure he was a sociopath. Suffice to say, I enjoyed his company.

He'd brought me clothes to wear. A gray suit and shirt. It didn't feel like me at all, and the material felt odd and too soft after years of rough overalls.

Leaving the prison after many checks, I stopped to collect my belongings, before realizing that, of course, I didn't have any. I'd left my dog-eared books to the prison library.

The first step outside, onto free land, felt stranger still. I looked around the scrubby car park and the deserted road beyond. A shiny car was sitting at the curb, in the no-parking zone. I approached, knowing only a few assholes who would flaunt the rules right outside a prison. Ronan came out of the building behind me, having dealt with the last of the paperwork. I had Ronan to thank for getting out of jail so quickly. His reduction of my sentence to self-defense had been a masterclass I was sure they'd teach in hell.

"That your car?"

"Sure is. Hop in, I'll give you a lift into town."

He took off toward the vehicle without a backward glance. He got into the front passenger seat, which was odd.

Someone was in the back.

I approached, and the window slid down. The sight that met my eyes sent a reluctant grin to my lips.

"Well, well, Mallory Madison, you're a sight for sore eyes, princess."

"It's Molly Chernova, which you know, and don't call me princess. Kirill might send you back inside if he hears it," Molly quipped as the door opened.

She pushed herself along the long cream leather seat in the back of the town car, and I ducked in beside her. I inhaled the scent of her perfume. Fuck, it was good to smell something other than male sweat and agony for once.

"Right, and where is your uglier half?"

"Russia. He's back next week."

I noticed three more black cars pulling in behind as we left the prison grounds.

"So, Kirill isn't around. Is that why you've got a security battalion following us? Why Russia?"

Molly sighed. "He's building a goddamn castle in the woods, complete with a crocodile-filled moat." Her tone told me this was a contentious subject.

I looked out the window, watching the changing landscape as we headed into the city. It all seemed so mundane. Everything had continued on just as before, while I'd been outside of the world for seven whole years. "Of course he is. Kirill can't help but be extra as fuck."

Molly tutted. "He's lost his mind."

"Why? Every *pakhan* needs a retirement plan. I like it. Kirill and Mallory, the great star-crossed lovers, growing old, safe and sound in their snowy Russian castle. You'll keep the east wing for me, of course, so I can be the monster who lives in the shadows up there and scares the kids. You didn't bring them?"

"No. They're in school."

"School?" I sucked a breath through my teeth. *I missed it all. Seven years. An entire childhood.* "For the record, I also think the PTA at Kira's new school sounds like a satanic cult."

Molly smiled. "So, you got my letters? I guess my replies got lost in the mail."

"You didn't want to hear from me. You're the kind of fucked-up, pathetic bleeding heart who would have worried for me, and there wasn't any point. I enjoyed reading them, though, for what it's worth. I liked not being forgotten."

Molly laughed, a sound like silver bells. "Like anyone could forget the great Nikolai Chernov."

I clenched my hand in my lap as Sofia's name seemed to float in the air between us.

"Does Kirill know you're here?"

Molly slid a slideways glance at me. "What do you think?"

"I think he has no intention of letting me anywhere near his family until he can be sure about my mental state. He's not an idiot."

"And how is your mental state? You look well. Terrifying but healthy." Molly looked me up and down.

"And you're still a terrible judge of character, clearly."

Molly turned to me, one eyebrow cocked. "So, you're not well?"

I watched the world pass by outside the car. "Isn't that what my brother warned you? Isn't that why you didn't bring the kids?"

Molly was quiet for a long moment before rallying. "Kira wouldn't be scared of you anyway. She has a way with monsters."

"She gets that from her mother," I noted. "And Ruslan?"

"He's protective, but he'll love you. You're his uncle, and he's heard all about your escapades."

"Don't scare the kid."

Molly was quiet for a long moment. "If you're going to haunt the east wing, you need to be alive."

She finally broke a chuckle from me. "Oh, princess. My ghost will haunt your fortress of Russian solitude just fine. Don't worry about me. Nothing good ever happens to people who worry about me. It's safer not to risk it."

"OKAY, I changed my mind. I didn't want to come. This is a total downer," Bran complained, a few hours later, when we pulled up at the ornate gates of Silent Grove, a cemetery in New Jersey.

He'd called me just as Molly and Ronan had left me at some faceless hotel downtown. I'd only been in Manhattan a few hours and was already itching to leave. I'd been waiting seven long years for this moment, and I couldn't fucking wait one more second.

"Like you had anything better to do."

It was a dry fall day. Perfect weather really. I left Bran at the car and pulled my cap low over my face, grabbed the stuff I needed from the trunk, and headed through the marked graves in the general direction of the De Sanctis family plots. The graveyard was well tended and full of fresh flowers. Well, it seemed that way until I reached my *lastochka's* grave. It was bare of adornment. Even in death, Antonio's daughter was an afterthought.

I knelt on the wet grass, setting aside my supplies and laying a bouquet of lilies against the green grass that covered the woman I loved. I might have always been fucked up, but that I loved Sofia couldn't be denied. She was my ghost, haunting my days, always just tantalizingly out of reach. The inscription on the headstone made me itch to visit Antonio De Sanctis this second and even our debts.

Here lies Sofia Leonora De Sanctis,
dutiful daughter and beloved sister.
May she find the peace that eluded her in life, in death.

"DUTIFUL DAUGHTER?" I snorted into the still air. "Fuck you, Tony. I'll get you for that."

I backed onto a bench, positioned to look at the boring patch of ground that now held my little swallow's cage. A prison she'd never escape. A bird flew from the underbrush right then, and I gazed upward, following its flight. Maybe I had it all wrong. Maybe in death, she'd escaped. Maybe she'd finally flown far, far away.

"I'm sorry he buried you here. You'd hate it." I looked around the place. There wouldn't even be a good view of the stars with all the trees overhanging her grave.

"They didn't let me come to the funeral. We weren't family, well, not in the way the penal system can understand." I opened my palm and stared down at the S carved into my skin. It was a light scar now, silvery, but still there. If it ever disappeared, I'd cut it back in.

I eased a hand over my shaved head, the stubble bristling against my palm.

"I'll be visiting your father soon. I hope you can forgive me for the things I'm going to do to him, but even if you wouldn't, that won't stop me. I'll ask for your forgiveness, instead of your permission, prom queen, when I see you again." I stood then, feeling cold through and through. "In the next life, or the one after. I'm a man of my word, after all, and I promised you I'd always find you. Wait for me."

I pushed myself to my feet. The chaos inside my chest was screaming at me, louder than ever. It hurt. It really fucking hurt.

"First, *lastochka*, since I know how much you'd hate it here, I brought a little 'fuck you' to your father, so he understands that I'm coming for him. Nothing is better torture than fear, and I want him to be afraid. I want him to understand that his end is near. I'll see you soon."

Turning from the silent grave, I looped around the other De Sanctis family plots and found the small church on the grounds and went inside. It was reserved for the De Sanctis family alone, a place where Antonio could come and not worry about getting shot, apparently. It seemed he didn't come too often, as I hadn't seen more security than CCTV cameras. Antonio had always been sloppy, and now he'd only gotten worse. It'd would only make terrorizing and killing him easier.

There were a few chairs for prayer, an altar with flowers on it, and not much else. The chairs were padded and opulent-looking. Even when praying, Antonio thought a lot of himself. I couldn't wait to teach the arrogant bastard the ultimate lesson.

I uncapped the gas can I'd brought with me and poured it liberally over Antonio's chair. I could tell exactly which one it was, since it was the most obnoxious. I was surprised he hadn't had it bedazzled with his initials or something equally tasteless.

When I flicked the lit match at it, it went up in a whoosh, and I enjoyed the sight.

I watched it burn, the air growing thick inside the incense-scented room, before leaving.

Soon, De Sanctis, I'll be doing the same to you.

I strode from the graveyard, with only more darkness dawning inside me. I'd thought I'd feel closer to her there, but I didn't.

There was no hint of Sofia in that dreary place. Bones and decomposing flesh wasn't people, and my *lastochka* had been in the ground long enough to be both.

She wasn't here. Not even a trace remained.

She was gone.

4

NIKOLAI

"*P*lease, don't… don't!"

The sound of the gunshot echoed around the warehouse, accompanied by laughter.

Mine.

"I asked you for Antonio's routine… his death is on you." I crouched before the man I had tied up.

He was sweating bullets, and his eyes were bulging out of his ratty face with fear.

I had three men tied up total. One had just died, and two were left. The one I was focused on was the one before me, the dirty accountant who scrubbed the De Sanctis family books. He was a man of power in the family and the first one I'd gotten my hands on. In terms of underling men, I had to be closing on nearly fifteen deaths so far. They made it too damn easy. One week after I'd gotten out of jail and I was really finding my rhythm.

The man beside the accountant grunted.

I turned to him, lowering his gag for a second. "Yes?"

"I know he goes to the golf club every Monday morning." The man panted.

I nodded, impressed. "Now, that is real info. Well done. What's your name?"

"T-Tommaso."

His stutter was irritating me. I turned back to Mr. Accountant.

"Now, Tommaso has just proved that he will rat to stay alive. That means that you might be surplus, unless you give me something right now."

I stared at the bookkeeper. His lips stayed closed in a firm line. It was fucking annoying.

I tapped my lip with the warm end of my gun, contemplating. "I know. I have a great idea."

I jumped to my feet, and both men flinched.

"Let's play a game, shall we? I love games, and believe me, you don't want to be the loser of this one."

Luckily, I had just the right gun for it. I shook out all the bullets but one and grinned at the waiting men. "You guys must be big gamblers, considering how much time you spend in Atlantic City. Let's play... you give me something interesting, or we see how lucky you are... I always loved roulette."

Snapping the gun closed, I spun the chamber. "Now, since Tom gave me something, we'll start with you, Moneybags. You want to tell me something, or do you want to take your chances?"

The accountant stared at me silently.

I whistled. "You've got bigger balls on you than I expected. I can respect that, but it doesn't change the rules of the game."

I pointed the gun at him and pulled the trigger carelessly.

It clicked emptily. The accountant had gone deathly pale.

"Well done. Back to Tommaso. Anything for me, man?"

Tommaso licked his lips. "He has a mistress who lives in Trenton. He goes there three times a week."

"It's a good effort, but I'm not interested in the women in his life. It was a valid try, though. Now, back to you. Got something for me?" I swung the gun back to the accountant.

There was no defiance in his eyes this time. He just looked shit scared. The ravenous beast inside me devoured the man's fear, only growing stronger and stronger. I thrived off the scent of piss and blood in the air. It was honest. Fear was the most honest thing there was.

He swallowed, his throat bobbing, then shook his head.

I pulled the trigger again. Another click.

"Tom? Your turn."

Tommaso blanched. He looked about to cry. He was clearly out of titbits to share. That made sense. I hadn't taken him or his dead companion for their insider info. The tail of the snake never knows what the head is up to.

"No? Tick-tock goes the clock."

"I-I don't know," he mumbled.

"Too bad." I pointed the gun at him. The sound of the shot followed my words.

"Oops. Looks like his luck ran out."

Tommaso's chair toppled back and hit the floor; the man in it was already dead.

I put another bullet in the gun and approached Mr. Accountant. He was completely still now.

"It's just you and me now, Bob. Do you mind if I call you that? You look like a Bob."

I spun the chamber of the gun and then pressed the tip point-blank against his forehead. "Tell me something I don't know about your capo."

Bob wet his lips. "He prefers cognac to scotch."

"Very good, but not enough to skip a turn. Don't fuck with me. You know what I want." I pulled the trigger, and it clicked against his head.

He was shaking so hard I had to press the barrel tightly against his skin to keep contact.

"I can't tell you the details of Antonio's routine. If you hurt him, if he finds out I told, he'll kill me and my family."

"So, you'd rather die here. You think I won't kill your family?"

He swallowed hard. "I don't know if you will. I'm certain he would."

I blew out a breath. "That puts me in a tricky position. I guess we're done here, and you know what that means."

I pulled the trigger again. The click was deafening.

Mr. Accountant was openly crying now. I almost pitied him, but not quite. He was part of Antonio's inner circle and had no doubt been witness to the way his boss had treated his only daughter all her life. He deserved everything he got.

"Wait! I know something." His sudden cry broke through his sobs.

"If it isn't about Antonio, I'm not interested. I don't want him investigated by the IRS."

"Not Antonio. Sofia. It's about Sofia."

I stilled, everything inside me contracting to a point of controlled violence. "I don't want to hear you say her name. You're not worthy of it." I ground the barrel against his forehead. I wanted to end him now, but I had to find out what he was going to say.

"What about her?"

"She… she…"

Bob was stuttering so hard now he was hard to make out. Still, it felt like the world had slowed for a moment. Like every pivotal moment in my life, I felt the weight of the seconds pass.

"Spit it out, for fuck's sake," I growled at him.

The world stopped turning as he spoke.

Bob looked up and finally met my eyes. "She's not dead. Sofia De Sanctis didn't die. She's alive."

5

SOPHIE ROSSI

"Ms. Rossi, we're ready for you."

The voice tugged at the edge of my consciousness.

"That's you," a voice reminded me.

I jerked my head up and focused on the nurse standing in the doorway.

Right. Sophie Rossi. That was my name. That was me. Sometimes, it was hard to remember.

I stood on shaky legs. "Yes, that's me."

"The doctor is ready to see you now." The nurse turned around and bustled up the hallway, leaving the door to the consultant's room gaping wide behind her. Everything would change when I walked through that door. Every single thing.

"Come on, we've got this," Chiara muttered in my ear and tugged me forward.

"Miss Rossi, please come in."

Inside was a regular old doctor's office, and yet, it had been the scene of some of the most terrifying events of my life. Considering the life I'd led, that was an impressive feat.

Chiara pulled me forward, and I sank into a chair, feeling numb.

I stared at the same poster over the doctor's head that I'd looked at three years ago, when I'd first sat in this office, and my little, hard-won life had fallen apart.

"Good morning, Dr. Evans. We're a little nervous today," Chiara said, still gripping my hand hard.

Dr. Evans was a beautiful older woman. She had that motherly energy that was entirely comforting, even when delivering the hardest news.

It's renal failure, I'm afraid. A transplant is the only long-term fix.

I shook the voices from the past from my head and tried to focus on the present. My mind often drifted, too burned out and traumatized from the way life had thrown me back and forth.

"I understand." Dr. Evans smiled. "But I think today will be a better meeting than you expect."

Hope, too huge to contain, blossomed in my chest.

"Better than we expect? You know what we expect, Doctor."

She smiled again and nodded. "I know, so I don't take that lightly. There's good news and bad news."

"We'll take the bad news first, on the chin," Chiara declared. She might sound breezier than me, but she had my hand in a death grip.

"The bad news is that you're going to be seeing a lot more of me, and a lot more of this place."

I couldn't speak. Tears burned behind my eyes.

"The good news is that we have a potential donor. A donor has been found who might be a perfect match. Subject to tests and checks, of course. We'll need to start the admittance procedure shortly to carry out the tests and observe for a few weeks before we make the final call."

"Holy shit." Chiara breathed into the silence that the doctor's words left.

Dr. Evans laughed. "Holy shit indeed."

"Say something," Chiara said, and nudged me.

I opened my mouth, trying to scrape my scrambled brains together enough to say thank you or ask follow-up questions. Something, really, anything.

"You... I..." I trailed off, those damn tears burning behind my eyes. *"Per questo, ti devo la vita."*

Chiara wrapped her arm around me. "For this, I owe you my life," she translated for the doctor.

I never heard her answer.

The side door to the consultation room opened, and a tiny figure appeared, ushered in by the nurse.

"Mom! I didn't cry at all this time!"

I turned and stared at the small boy who had changed my life completely. I still couldn't speak, so I simply held my arms open.

Leo started forward, throwing himself into my embrace. I breathed in the smell of his hair, and the raging storm of emotion quieted for a moment.

He was small for his age. I held him tightly.

He was speaking to the doctor, but I couldn't focus on what he was saying.

"Mom, why are you crying?" Leo asked, and leaned back to look up at me.

His silver-gray eyes stared into my soul.

"I'm just happy, Leo Lion. I'm just really happy."

"You shouldn't cry when you're happy, silly!" Leo dissolved into giggles as Chiara tickled him.

"I know, right! Silly Mommy," Chiara laughed.

"Leo, do you want to come and stay in the children's ward for a few weeks?" Dr. Evans asked.

Leo shrugged and screwed up his little nose. "Does that mean I'm having my operation?"

"Possibly."

"After, will I be able to go ice skating?" He turned his excited eyes to me, making me laugh.

"Maybe one day, when you're all recovered." I patted his hand.

"Yes!" Leo turned to Dr. Evans. "One day, I'm going to play for the high school team, where my mom works."

"Are you?"

"Yes. I'll be good at skating when I finally get to do it." Leo stretched out the word finally. The room filled with laughter.

I smoothed his hair back. "I'm sure you will be. First, though, let's work on getting better. Second, world ice-hockey domination."

"Mom, can we have burgers for dinner?" Leo was holding my hand as we walked through the parking lot half an hour later. The late fall afternoon was crisp. Maine weather was best described in those kinds of terms I'd found over the years. Crisp, bracing, mysterious. In the seven years I'd lived in Maine, I'd gotten familiar with all its faces.

"I'll see if we have the ingredients at home."

"Or, we could go to a diner, like everyone else does?"

I gripped his little hand. "Are you telling me you don't like my cooking, mister?"

Leo shook his head adamantly. "No. You just look tired, that's all."

My heart swelled for the little boy who always thought of me before himself. I didn't deserve him. No one did.

"I'm never too tired to cook for my best boy."

"Okay."

I pulled Leo tightly to my side as a fancy car swung into the lot right before us. It was a small hospital and one our insurance barely stretched to. For that reason, our car was always the most beat-up one in the lot. I didn't care if the high society of Hade Harbor thought I was a charity case. When it came to Leo, I had no pride. There was nothing I wouldn't do for him. If I had to, I'd crawl on my hands and knees and beg.

Thankfully, my job as an art teacher at the local high school got me medical care for Leo. It could be a lot better, but it was the most I could hope for. I'd been lucky to get the job when I'd escaped to the tiny coastal town, six months pregnant and terrified, nearly seven years ago now.

"Here, strap in," I instructed as he got into his car seat in the back.

The sound of a car door slamming shut behind me raked along my nerves, and I twisted to look over my shoulder. No matter how long I lived a normal life, far away from the dark and dangerous lifestyle of my childhood, I couldn't lose the instinct that an attack might come from anywhere, at any time.

"Sophie! Nice to see you," a deep voice called to me.

I spied the luxury car that had pulled in and the man now striding away from it toward me.

Ugh. Edward Sloane. Local golden boy, billionaire playboy. Since he'd fucked his way through the entire eligible female population of Hade Harbor, excluding Chiara and me, he'd seemed to have set his sights on me. Of course, I didn't have a terrifying husband like Angelo threatening to crack his skull if he looked at his wife a second too long.

I was alone, and painfully aware of it.

"Mr. Sloane, good morning."

"How many times have I asked you to call me Edward?"

"You're paying me to do a job for you, so I'd really prefer not to."

He leaned his hip against my car, crinkling his thousand-dollar suit.

He had commissioned me for a custom art piece a month ago, and I was slogging my way through it. It wasn't a labor of love. I was doing it purely for the cash. He had adored his recently deceased mother, his only redeeming feature, and was having me paint her portrait from a photograph.

In my free time, I painted, but rarely portraits. Well, that was a lie. I had plenty of portraits, but they were of one person. No one had ever seen them. He was my ghost with the silver eyes.

The man who I had betrayed. The one who'd never forgive me.

Nikolai Chernov.

The rest of my paintings were landscapes. They were unfailingly dark and ominous. Why, exactly, Edward had chosen me to paint his mother's portrait, I had no idea, and didn't want to look too closely at. If he was doing it to get in my pants, he'd be sorely disappointed.

"If I'd known that we couldn't even be on a first-name basis while you were working for me, I'd have asked you out before starting the painting."

I smiled uncomfortably, grateful that Leo was already in the car. "And I'd have had to say no. I don't date, and I'm not interested in starting."

"You have your hands full with Leo." Edward nodded, like that could be the only reason I wasn't interested in going on a date with him.

"Yes, and I'm just not interested in meeting anyone."

Edward's eyes flickered down to the simple silver band on my ring finger. "Even widows have to move on sometime, Sophie."

"Not this one."

My absolute tone only made Edward smirk. Declaring myself a widow had seemed the fastest way to avoid awkward conversations, I'd decided early on. Even more, there was a piece of my heart, deep down and secret, that felt like one. I'd lost the love of my life and could never see him again. I felt like a widow.

"I won't stop trying to change your mind. I think we could be great together. One day, you'll agree," he said. It sounded like a threat.

"I should have the next stage of the painting by the weekend, if you want to look at it," I said firmly, crossing my arms over my chest.

A slight tic of irritation in Edward's jaw was the only sign that I'd pissed him off. He was one of those men whose fragile egos couldn't take the slightest knock, like being interrupted or refused. He reminded me of my father and Silvio.

"Sure, that would be good. I'm not paying you the big bucks for nothing, am I? Can you bring it by the house? I want to see it in the right light, in the place where it would hang."

"It's not at that stage yet," I protested mildly.

He grinned. "What about the customer always being right? I'm sure you'll indulge me." There was something slimy about the way he lingered on the words.

"Mom?" Leo asked from inside the car.

"Hi there, buddy." Edward poked his head just inside the door.

I fought the urge to pull him back. I didn't like anyone except myself, Chiara, and Angelo getting too close to Leo. Even a simple cold was hard for him to fight off sometimes.

Leo stared at him. "Hi." He sounded as enthusiastic as I was when dealing with the local hotshot.

"Wouldn't it be nice for your mommy to get dressed up and go out with a grown-up and have fun sometimes? I bet if you told her that, she'd stop feeling guilty about wanting to do grown-up mommy things."

Leo looked at me, confusion etched on his little face. Anger filled me, white-hot. These days, I had a hairlike trigger and was hotheaded as hell. I was always walking a fine line between being okay and completely losing my shit. Angelo told me it was anger. A deep-down fury at the way my life had turned out. Resentment at my father, rage at how everything in my life had only trapped me and hurt the few people I cared about. He was probably right. Maybe one day it would overflow my tired heart, and I'd knife Edward Sloane to death on the hood of his fancy damn car and cackle maniacally while they arrested me.

Sometimes, it felt like the only thing stopping me from that fate was Leo.

I had to hold it together for him.

He needed me.

I shoved between Edward and Leo's open window.

"Please don't speak to my son like that. You can't manipulate me into dating you. I'm not interested. If that's a problem, I can stop work on your mother's portrait, and we can go our separate ways."

Edward raised an eyebrow at me, looking amused at how I'd pushed myself against him to stop him from talking to Leo.

"You misunderstand me, Sophie. I'm not interested in seeing less of you, only more, and I'm a man who always gets my way."

He reached out and attempted to tuck a stray lock of my dark hair behind my ear. I knocked his hand away before he made contact.

He rocked back on his heels, his eyes narrowing. I knew exactly what his problem was. He was good-looking and rich, and no one in Hade Harbor said no to him. I was just a poor high school teacher, and the single mother of a sick kid at that. I should fawn over him, gobbling up scraps of his attention and begging for more. It drove him crazy that I didn't care about him. Truthfully, I found his all-American blond Ken-doll looks boring and generic. He was the kind of man who looked like a hero but was cruel and selfish beneath it. He had mean eyes. I was familiar with them. I'd grown up with those eyes, watching my every move. He had Silvio's eyes.

I turned to check on Leo and met his gray stare. I always found solace, and pain, a double-edged knife, in those steady gray orbs. They reminded me of his father, a man who had been the opposite of Edward Sloane. Nikolai Chernov had looked like a walking nightmare and yet had only ever protected me. A demon with a code. My villainous savior. Go figure.

"You're making me uncomfortable."

Edward sighed. "Don't be dramatic. Come by the house with the painting, and let's see how it's getting on."

He turned away and took two steps before turning back to me. "Do you know what wing of the hospital Leo is being treated in? It's the Sloane wing. You might not like me, but you'll make use of the advantages I've given this town, won't you?"

I didn't know what to say to that. Was it a threat? Maybe it was. I was well versed in the power dynamics of men who liked to throw their weight around. He didn't want an answer from me, so I didn't give him one. If it was a threat, with a donor in the works for Leo, I couldn't afford to piss him off.

"I'll see you this weekend, Mr. Sloane."

He smirked. Maybe he thought he looked roguish. He looked like an ass.

"Yes, you will."

6

SOFIA

We drove home slowly through downtown Hade Harbor. The main street was filled with overflowing flower boxes and tiny, busy independent stores. It was discreetly wealthy, and also felt safe in a way I'd never experienced before. Not that it didn't have its darker elements, it certainly did. Just the other week, there had been arrests during a fight between two rival gang members. Drugs flowed through Maine from Canada and down into Boston and New York, and where there was drug money, there were people who wanted a piece.

Still, the darkness of my former life had never touched Leo's. No matter what else happened in a day, as long as I had kept him from that, I'd achieved something.

"Okay, little lion, let's get dinner started."

My house sat on the outskirts of town, overlooking the water. It was isolated and small, but I loved being between the woods and the ocean. Leo jumped out of the car almost as soon as I'd stopped and raced for the door.

I followed behind him. Inside the house was a mix of old, and even older. I'd done what I could to repaint, repair, and upcycle the furniture that the aging house was stuffed with. It might not be picture-perfect, but it was made with love. Leo kicked his dinosaur sneakers off and went upstairs. I headed to the kitchen.

It was quiet. Outside, I watched the little boat that Leo liked to play around on bobbing in its tether to a small dock. I turned the tap, and cool, fresh water flowed into the sink. The tattoo on my wrist called my attention.

A little bird, in a cage, with the door open. The bird hovered by the edge, unsure whether to fly free. It was my only tattoo. An homage to the man I'd lost. Nikolai wasn't dead to the world, only to me. I couldn't visit his grave, and I didn't have any pictures of him to frame and show Leo. Instead, in his memory, and in recognition of the way he'd changed my life, I had this tattoo. It might be only skin deep, but the mark he'd left on my heart was deeper. I could never get him out. The only man who'd ever risked everything for me. The one who had never let me fall.

As always, when thoughts of Nikolai crowded my head, I stuffed the heartache and guilt into a tiny box inside myself and turned my mind to other things.

I poured a glass of water and sipped it, looking out at the view of the ramshackle garden that sloped toward the water. Mist hung heavily over the water. The sky was a churned gray, a shade that never failed to make my chest ache. The pain was like an old injury that flared up in certain conditions. The sea when it reflected that gray was one of the triggers. The sight of an innocent roll of duct tape sitting on a counter at the post office. A tourist group walking past, speaking in a rapid torrent of Russian. Leo's eyes. Those were always the most precious and most painful reminders of the past.

The news about the donor swirled in my head. It changed everything.

Leo had been born eight months after Nikolai got sent to prison. I'd already been in Maine. I'd just run away from Casa Nera, with my father's threats still fresh in my ears. I'd been dirt-poor, with only a burner phone to call my own. My brother, Renato, had pressed it into my hand as I'd fled on a bus. Antonio De Sanctis hadn't only wanted his only daughter to run away and lose everything she'd ever known. He'd wanted me to crawl away, and suffer a hard life, as the ungrateful child who'd defied him.

Since that night, I'd spoken to my brother only a handful of times. I'd called him to ask him to get tested for compatibility with Leo. At this stage of his illness, only a kidney donation would drastically change his quality of life. No more hospital visits. No more dialysis. No more missing school.

Renato hadn't been a match. He'd gotten the tests in secret. My father was as hell-bent on revenge as ever, and my older brother hadn't dared to let him know that I'd reached out. I was supposed to be dead, after all, and my father wouldn't allow anything that might reveal the ruse. Antonio De Sanctis was determined to control my life, even if I never saw him again.

Personally, I wasn't a match, and neither were Chiara or Angelo. As Leo's renal failure had progressed, a rare genetic defect that hadn't become apparent until he was four years old, I'd considered the only other person who could be tested.

His father.

Of course, testing his father involved a lot of obstacles that I had no idea how to overcome. First of all, it would risk all our lives. Still, despite the danger and the pain of reaching out to Nikolai, I had been considering it. Maybe his brother, Kirill, and his brutal bratva could protect us, until Nikolai got out of prison? The thoughts had plagued me, keeping me up at night, rehashing the past again and again. The very real factor that I had no idea how to predict, was how Nikolai would react to knowing it had all been a lie, and not only that, but I'd hidden his son from him, too. It was unforgivable, and yet, there had been no choice. Protecting Leo meant accepting his father's hate, if he should ever find out. The paradox hurt my heart, every single day since I'd run from Casa Nera.

Now, though, there was a donor on the horizon. It changed everything. If this worked out, there was no reason to endanger Nikolai, Leo, and myself, by telling the truth to the one man I'd ever loved.

I could continue my quiet half-life, dreaming of a man who had once tried to burn the world down to save me, and he'd never know I was alive. We would all live, free of my father's threats.

I could leave all of it in the past, now that there was a donor.

I should be relieved. I should just be grateful. There shouldn't be any part of me that dreamed of finding Nikolai, dropping to my knees in front of him and confessing my sins, every single one, and taking any punishment he gave me.

It was too dangerous. It was selfish.

I should let go of the past, as no doubt, he already had.

I would try to do it.

Any day now… or maybe tomorrow.

One day, for sure.

7 years earlier

"Don't touch me," I snarled at my father's goon, who had dragged me through the house and dropped me in his office like I was a bag of rocks.

"*Basta!*" Ren shouted, his face contorting. He'd only been back from Italy a few days, when all the shit with *Zio* Franco had gone down. I'd been right. Franco and Silvio had been planning a coup, but their plans had gone to hell when Ren got home, Silvio died, and the police had descended on the house.

Now, it was a few weeks later, and my father, making miraculous progress, was still cleaning his brother's blood from under his fingernails as he stared at down at me with disgust. His influence had swept away all the problems with that bloody day, the last time I'd seen Nikolai. Except for Silvio's murder. My father had no intention of getting Nikolai out of jail. He wanted him to rot in there.

I'd been more of a prisoner in Casa Nera than ever before. I had no phone I could access, no laptop. I wasn't allowed to see anyone, and Antonio was angry that I wouldn't answer questions about Angelo and Chiara.

Worst of all, my condition had become obvious. I was the kind of person who was going to suffer from morning sickness, clearly, as I'd been throwing up nonstop for weeks, so long the doctor was called. I'd had no choice but to endure his tests.

Pregnant.

I was pregnant with Nikolai's baby. Despite taking my contraceptive religiously, except for those three days on the run. It seemed that was enough to do it. I still hadn't gotten over the shock of it.

"So, Sofia. What do you have to say for yourself?" My father's voice was silky with threat.

I pulled myself into a chair and glanced at Ren. He was standing beside me, his hands curled into fists.

"Did he force you?" Antonio continued.

I shook my head.

"Are you sure?" My father pressed.

"He didn't force me," I mumbled, with as much dignity as I could manage. My face was flaming with embarrassment, and I wished the ground would swallow me up. Discussing my sex life with my father and brother wasn't something I'd ever wanted to do.

I felt Ren's hand land on my shoulder, reassuring me. He was there, at my back. I wasn't alone.

"You stupid whore. Even after I tried to teach you to be respectable, you run off at the first chance and fuck our enemy," Antonio sneered at me.

His word bounced off of me. I didn't care what he thought. He didn't know anything, least of all what love was.

"You're just like Leonora, your mother. She was stupid, too," he said, turning to stare out the window. His hands looked like gnarled old tree roots, balled up on his lap. "So, here's what's going to happen."

As he turned back, there was a look in his eyes I recognized well. It was the look he gave me when he was about to dispense his discipline, but now he wasn't able to smack me around. I was stronger than him. Instead, he looked satisfied enough with whatever he'd dreamed up to torture me.

"You get rid of the bastard as soon as possible, quietly. We don't speak of it again. You marry Moroni, as planned, someone who understands the code and our way of life. This way, you might still be of use and fulfill part of your role to the family, instead of being completely useless."

"No." The word left me with quiet conviction.

"No?" Antonio repeated, his neck turning red.

At this rate, I'd give him another heart attack, and not be the least bit sorry.

"What do you mean, no?"

"I won't have an abortion, and you can't make me."

"We'll see about that," he suddenly shouted.

"Father, she said no," Renato interjected.

He was still standing right there behind me, and his weight behind my refusal gave it weight. I might not be able to do a damned thing on my own, but Ren was the heir, and if he disagreed with Antonio, then he could protect me.

Antonio sneered at both of us, disdain dripping from his words when he spoke. "How weak my children have become. Weak and softhearted. No heads for business, or survival either, for that matter."

He looked out the window for a long moment, his mind working so furiously I could practically hear it.

"I won't have my daughter bear an illegitimate Chernov son," he said finally. "If you do that, it means you are no longer my daughter."

"You were happy enough to marry me off to Kirill Chernov not too long ago," I reminded him.

"Marrying the heir to a powerful family is one thing. Getting knocked up by the black sheep brother is another. I get nothing from this match, and that little fuck, Nikolai, gets everything. I won't allow it. I'll see him answer for it in prison. He won't live to be released."

I found myself on my feet. "You won't go near him or pay anyone else to."

"And what will you give me in return?" Antonio pounced, waiting for my calm to break.

"What do you want?"

"You'll go away. You won't speak to Nikolai again, or me. You'll disappear, no, you'll die. Since I don't want Nikolai to know he has a child, you're dead as far as anyone else knows. That will be my revenge on the man who blew my fucking house up and defiled my daughter. To everyone except me and Renato, you're dead, including Nikolai. Talk to him, try to see him, or send him any kind of message, and I won't just kill him… I'll wait until you give birth and kill his bastard as well. Do you understand, Sofia? Don't think your brother could stop me. This family is mine more than ever, after I put down Franco. Don't test me."

The room swirled with horror. Antonio loved a good vendetta, and he liked to plan the perfect retribution. He was exactly the spiteful sort of monster who'd die with a smile, knowing he had fucked up everyone else's life. I had nothing to hold on to except my brother's hand on my shoulder and the urge to vomit right there on my father's desk. The hand that I'd pressed to my abdomen felt like an anchor. I wanted to scream and rage. I wanted to kill him, but Antonio had already expected that. I couldn't afford to be emotional. I had something else to think about. Someone else. A new purpose.

I would lose Nikolai; he would think I was dead. Just that fact was so painful, breathing hurt. But I didn't doubt my father. He was cruel and vengeful, and now I was on the receiving end.

"Tell me you agree, Sofia, or we have no understanding," he started.

"I agree." The words left me before I could consider them. Could I live without ever speaking to Nikolai again? It seemed utterly impossible, and yet, his life hung in the balance-his life, and his child's. *Our child.* With my hand pressed to my abdomen, where a tiny bundle of cells was growing, part of him, part me, I knew I had no choice.

"I'll do what I have to."

52

Now

"MOM?" Leo's voice called to me along the hall.

I was making my nightly rounds, where I wandered the house, locking up, picking up random socks and toys and returning them to their rightful places. These days, I valued the slow and predictable. There was comfort in numbing familiarity.

"Yes?" I poked my head into his room. "You are supposed to be sleeping," I reminded him.

We'd done the bathroom and teeth; we'd even done our story.

"I just realized that we haven't filled in that report about the book we read. It's due tomorrow." A little pinch of worry had settled between Leo's eyebrows.

"It's okay. Your teacher knows you had a doctor's appointment today."

"Maybe we can do it in the morning?" Leo wondered.

The things that other kids took for granted, or hated to do, like homework, Leo loved. It made him feel normal, just like the other kids.

I sat on the edge of his bed and stroked his silky hair. "Maybe. Let's see if we have time. Now, I'm turning out the lights."

"Okay. Turn off the lights and turn on the stars," Leo said, his favorite sentence to say, as he snuggled in his comforter.

I turned out the light and looked up. After a moment, the ceiling illuminated with stars. They weren't the stitched-on ones from my curtains at Casa Nera, and they weren't the real ones from his father's lonely childhood. This night sky was Leo's, and I'd do anything I had to, to make sure he had a better life than either of his parents had ever had. A life with choices.

I lay down beside him and wrapped my arms around him. I should really finish tidying up and go to my room. I should really plan out what was going to happen with the hospital in the next few weeks. There were a lot of tests that had to be done to determine if this donor was a real possibility. Leo was going to have to stay in the hospital to do it. He was more than comfortable with the staff at St. Mary's. He'd been there three times a week for dialysis for years. I couldn't afford to take too much time off work. Over the operation and recovery, I'd need to be on hand to help, though, I could count on Chiara's and Angelo's help as well. My mind whirled, going over scheduling and the impossible task of balancing a single-parent income with a very sick child. Tomorrow, I had class. Then this weekend would involve getting Leo settled in hospital and taking the damn portrait to Edward Sloane's house.

I closed my eyes, suddenly more tired than I could bear. For tonight, I let sleep carry me away. I'd figure out how to make it all work tomorrow. I always did.

After all, as a very precious person once told me, it's better to die than do nothing.

7

NIKOLAI

*T*he days after killing Bob, the accountant, were a blur. I'd lost count of the number of men I'd hurt, cutting a bloody swath through the De Sanctis ranks, trying to get to Renato or Antonio. In the end, it was Ronan Black, the devil's own attorney, who came through. I had in my shiny new cell phone the banking information for a one-off payment, made from a shell corp belonging to Renato De Sanctis, to a renowned forger, for a new set of identity documents.

Standing now, three days later, with a shovel in my hand, under a starless New Jersey sky, I stood on the cusp of finding out. I had to know, one way or another. I couldn't wait one more second to know.

"Crap. This isn't the kind of thing I had in mind for when we were out," Bran muttered. He was standing in the hole we'd been digging in the moonlight. He leaned on a shovel and sighed. "I still say we use the digger."

"No, it's too noisy, and besides, we don't know how deep to go. We might go too far."

Bran sighed and wiped a hand over his sweating brow. "This is really fucked up, you know that. I mean, even for you, digging up your ex-girlfriend's grave is macabre."

"She wasn't my girlfriend." There wasn't a word for what we were.

"That makes it even worse. And now the memory of her is a death wish. You want to bring the De Sanctis family down on your head?"

"They can't do shit. Antonio won't risk pissing off Kirill unless it's serious."

"I'd say fucking up half their men is serious."

"I've barely scratched the surface of the damage I'm going to inflict on them. I'm only just warming up. This is a diversion from the main event." I dug down again. The soil was deeper packed the lower we got, and it was working a serious ache up in my arms. I welcomed the pain. It kept me awake. The persistent feeling of being in a dream had dogged me since I'd killed the accountant.

"This is just a diversion?" Bran snorted, disbelief in his voice.

He knew me too well. This was just a diversion, unless she was really alive. Then, everything changed.

"I love throwing my back out for a diversion," he muttered.

"Less complaining, more digging."

We worked on in silence. The noise in my head was a muted roar. My bloodlust had been well and truly sated in the last few days, but even then, since this thread of intrigue had unspooled, nothing seemed to quench my need to break bones and inflict pain. I was restless, full of dark, twisted energy that had nowhere to go. Like a tiger pacing in his cage, tail lashing, temper simmering, I couldn't fucking wait to resolve this mystery.

A hard thud broke through my thoughts.

Pay dirt.

We uncovered the rest of the coffin quickly.

"Man, I don't know about this. If she wasn't really dead, why bury an empty coffin? It doesn't make sense."

"I'm looking inside this coffin, and nothing you say will stop me. Here, help me pry it open."

Grabbing the twin crowbars I'd brought with me, I tossed one to Bran and posed myself at one end of the long wooden box. Bran grimaced but caught the heavy metal bar and moved to the other end of the coffin.

"On three. One, two, three," I grunted as I leaned down on the crowbar.

After a moment of both of us pushing, the edge cracked open on one side. Bran stepped back, clamping an arm over his mouth and nose.

"Does it smell? I don't want to smell it."

I approached the gap and used my foot to push it wider. My heart was beating so hard, I couldn't quite catch my breath. The strange unreality of the last few days popped like an overripe bubble as I peered inside.

It was empty.

Bob, the accountant, had been right.

Sofia De Sanctis wasn't here, and she never had been.

She was alive. Just like that, I was painfully awake.

I COULDN'T SLEEP for days after the graveyard. I stayed awake, finding out what I could.

Seven years ago, Renato De Sanctis, through a shell corp, bought a new set of ID documents. The new identity was for a Sophie Rossi. Rossi was Sofia and Renato's mother's maiden name. I only had to pull out three of the forger's teeth to find that out. A light day's work. Once I had the name, it wasn't too difficult to find out more. There were a lot of Sophie Rossis in the country, and I needed to narrow it down. Luckily, one of the IDs that had been forged had been a Maine state driver's license.

Did you really think I wouldn't find you there, prom queen? Did you think a few states between us would save you?

Having the state really narrowed down the number of Sophie Rossis to look into. I was able to narrow further when I cross-searched by a couple of other names. It was only a hunch that the three of them would have stayed together, but I always trusted my gut. There were no hits for Angelo or Chiara in Maine, but I found a newspaper article about an Italian American who had started a boxing gym in some small town. It was a wide net to cast, and yet there was a photo of the front of the gym. Angelo wasn't dumb enough to pose in a photo, but his young wife wasn't nearly so careful. In the photo of the front of the gym, a car had just pulled up in one of the staff parking slots.

Chiara was getting out of the car, oblivious to the photo being taken. I scanned for more information. Andy and Cicci Salva were the registered owners of the gym.

It merited checking out, even if the very idea was still far-fetched. The truth was that Antonio De Sanctis had buried an empty coffin and told the world that his daughter was dead. It was a thread I'd never stop pulling until I had uncovered the truth.

THE GYM that Chiara and Angelo owned was in a small town. Hade Harbor, Maine, famous for its university and ice hockey team. A speck on the map, near the sea. I left the next morning, and Bran tagged along for "the story."

We stopped for dinner in some small diner. It smelled like grease and burnt coffee.

"Fuck, it's nippy up here." Bran hunched forward in his jacket, sticking his hands into his pockets.

"Aren't you from Ireland?"

"Fair enough. So, have you seen your brother yet? Is he back from Russia?"

I shook my head, taking a mouthful of the bitter black tar that the joint had the nerve to call coffee.

Bran pulled a face at the taste of it. "Does he know about this resurrection business? Ronan will probably tell him."

"I asked him not to. I don't want anyone to know, not yet anyway. I don't want him involved and I don't want anyone in her family to realize what I suspect." *I don't want anyone trying to save her from me.*

MILA KANE

"Right, that's why we had to fill the damn grave back in." Bran stretched his neck this way and that. "It still feels like shit, by the way."

"How about you? Seen your brothers yet?" I wondered how the O'Connor family worked. With a stepbrother like Ronan Black, it was a surprise that both Bran, and his older brother, Killian, had been inside so long. The only sibling who hadn't done time was Quinn, the youngest.

Bran grinned and shook his head. "Ronan sent me a message to stay out of trouble, but that's about it. I saw Quinn, though. She's all grown up and getting into trouble already."

"Must be an O'Connor trait. I'm sure she'll be a guest of the state before her twenty-first birthday."

"Fuck you. Ronan won't let that happen."

"Having a stepbrother who's a criminal defense attorney didn't help you, though, did it?"

Bran laughed. "I guess you're right there." He broke off as some burly trucker bumped into his chair from behind.

Bran twisted around to look up at the guy.

He was one of those local yokels, overconfident in his little pissing patch. He jerked his chin at my friend. "You got a problem, pretty boy?"

Bran shook his head slowly. "No, man. No problem."

"Good," Mr. Soon-to-Be-in-ICU grinned. He thought he looked tough, in his trucker cap, with his straggly beard. His plaid shirt was straining around his belly. He slapped the waitress's ass as he passed by her. A king in his shitty little kingdom.

I wiped my mouth on a napkin and set my fork down.

Bran was looking at me with amusement in his eyes. "What about not getting into trouble too quickly?"

The whirling chaos inside me chomped at the bit to get out. The beast I'd always tried to deny was frothing at the mouth for blood. It had become addicted. It demanded daily feeding.

"The man is clearly looking for a fight. Who am I to deny him?"

I pocketed the knife from my place setting and headed outside, already grinning in anticipation.

8

NIKOLAI

"*I* can't believe you let his friend get you," I muttered to Bran, steering his car into the lot of the Hade Harbor hospital, St. Mary's, a few hours later.

Bran grimaced. "It's not my fault. A fucker like him shouldn't have any friends."

I parked and opened my door. "Come on then. What road trip is complete without a trip to the ER?"

"You take such good care of me, man."

Bran's shit-eating grin was more irritating than normal. I didn't want to be going to the hospital and waiting around for him to have his leg sewn up. We were here, in the town where Angelo had settled, and where there was a Sophie Rossi living, according to public record.

Bran limped into the waiting area of the ER as I took the forms for him to fill out and dumped them on his chest.

"I'm going for a walk," I told him shortly, before leaving.

First, I hit the restroom. The trucker's blood was gummy under my fingernails, and I couldn't get it out. That had been reckless. Killing off De Sanctis men was one thing. Antonio wouldn't do shit about it. It was an unspoken rule of the underworld that we lived in that no one involved the cops. But killing a random rude trucker? One with friends? That had been a legal headache I shouldn't be inviting into my life.

I caught the wild expression in my eyes in the mirror.

I was losing control of the beast inside. The one that Sofia's death had finally freed. I didn't know what would happen if I found her alive. Something dark and twisted that smelled like impossible hope had rooted in my chest since I'd discovered her coffin empty.

I washed my hands again and dried them roughly. Looking in the mirror, I knew that when I found her, which I would, if she was really alive, that the way I looked would scare her.

Good. The damage life inflicted on us should show, so we'd know where to direct our vengeance. My eyes were shadowed pits. There was nothing inside. My eyes, more than my tattoos, shaved head, or predatory energy, made people nervous.

I'd really become the monster Sofia had once accused me of being, and people knew it. They stayed back. Except for Bran, apparently, and Molly, my brother's wife. Since she'd already married a demon, I guessed she was used to it.

I left the restroom and headed deeper into the hospital. I'd always found them fascinating places. A place where death walked the halls. Everyone knew it was there, but they tried not to look directly at it. Nowhere did the grim reaper walk with such acceptance. I, too, walked the halls without too many stares. Maybe people in the hospital are hardened to death, in whatever way it comes.

I found a cafeteria and grabbed a bottle of water, sitting in a secluded corner to stare out at the lights of Hade Harbor. It was dark already, and blackness seemed to yawn beyond the brightly lit cafeteria window. A long gulp of water wet my dry throat.

Is she really out there somewhere?

Then I heard it.

A voice ripped from the past. It was annoying, upbeat, and perky.

"I'm just grabbing a coffee for me and Sofia. We're all done here. I'll pick up dinner on the way home."

My entire body tensed. I listened without moving. The rest of the cafeteria was reflected in the window, highlighted against the dark evening outside. A short figure dressed like a gym bunny with waist-length, dark-blonde hair was walking past me, balancing her tray of two coffees with a bottle of water, and her phone.

Chiara, or Cici Salva, as she went by here.

She breezed past me, and I was on my feet and following in a heartbeat. She walked down the hall, totally oblivious to being followed. I prowled behind her.

Chiara headed downstairs to the reception area. I got close enough to hear her phone conversation.

"No, she's not coming for dinner tomorrow. She's got a date with Edward Sloane. Anyway, how's my little man? Are you guys having a nice boys' night?"

Chiara listened for a moment, nodding. So, Angelo and Chiara had a kid. Interesting.

"Good. Well, tell my little lion I'll see him soon. I have to go. I'll see you at home."

She was standing beside one of the chairs in the waiting area, and as she hung up, she tapped the shoulder of the figure sitting there.

A dark head was bent over a book and spoke without looking up. Her hair was short, and I could make out her slender stalk of a neck and the tip of one ear which she'd tucked her hair behind.

"It's not a date."

Her voice. *Sofia*.

Chiara rolled her eyes and perched on the opposite chair. I couldn't see the dark-haired woman as she was facing away from me. Even then, I knew. It was her. My *lastochka*.

Everything seemed to slow. Time lost its meaning. I forgot how to breathe, to think. All I could do was watch. That whirling blackness inside me returned tenfold. The cage around my heart, the one that meeting Sofia had shaken, finally cracked. My mind might have cracked, too, right then. I wasn't the man I was when she'd known me. Now, inside my chest, a gnashing, bloodthirsty monster, snarled at the world. That chaos had settled inside me, and I'd known that for as long as I lived, I'd live in the eye of the storm. It was the compromise my broken mind had found. I could function, talk, and eat and walk like a man, but inside, it was never still, never quiet. Inside, there were screams that never stopped.

I leaned against the wall, crossing my arms over my chest to stop myself from striding around the corner and hauling her to me. A handy floor-length information stand obscured me from their view, and anyone who thought it odd that a man was lurking just behind it received a death stare that sent them on their way.

"Sure, it is. Well, he wants it to be. I don't understand why you don't go for it," Chiara sighed dramatically.

Sofia sounded over it. "Not this again."

"Edward Sloane is rich, handsome. Everyone likes him, and pretty sure he's never killed anyone. I know that's not your usual type, but you shouldn't discriminate against nice guys."

"Very funny. Thanks for the coffee. All the paperwork is done, so let's go. I need to go and do some work on that portrait before my 'date' threatens to fire me again."

"Whatever, die alone," Chiara muttered, standing.

The dark-headed figure stood as well, stretching her lithe body this way and that, before picking up her bag. "I won't die alone. I'll come to your house to do it."

Chiara laughed and looped her arm around her friend's, turning her toward the doors.

I caught the first glimpse of my obsession's face. My ghost, made flesh.

Dark eyes, ringed by long lashes, smooth olive skin. Her hair was short, chopped at the chin. She had a dark coat on and a black scarf wrapped around her neck.

Her full lips were turned upward in a grin as she made her way outside.

Sofia De Sanctis. A ghost no more.

I followed them to the parking lot, sticking to the shadows. My natural place. Even if they looked right at me, they wouldn't see me. I didn't just hide in the shadows, I was the darkness.

She headed to a beat-up old wreck of a Honda and got in, waving goodbye to Chiara. Just like a magnet was tied to my chest, I found my feet heading toward Bran's ride. I still had the keys in my pocket. My eyes riveted on Sofia's car, I started my own, my mind oddly empty, and closed the door.

The Honda pulled out, and I was right behind it.

THE CAR HEADED NORTH along the shore. I stayed close behind. I missed call after call from Bran, but I couldn't answer right now. I couldn't think about anything at all.

Night had fallen, and I rolled down the windows to let the cool air keep me sharp.

The Honda pulled down a quiet, winding road toward the ocean. It pulled into the driveway of the lone house that sat at the bottom of the road. As the headlights died, I pulled to the side of the street farther back and killed the headlights. It was dark. I had to get closer.

I slipped out of the vehicle just as Sofia got out of hers. She had a shiny plastic bag in one hand and her handbag in the other. I ventured closer, sticking to the shadows for a moment, before stepping out.

I strode down the street, my hand checking my gun as I went. A simple reflex.

She disappeared into the isolated house, with the yard that backed onto the water on one side and the woods on another. It was quiet. The kind of quiet that let a man like me know that there was no one around for a good distance.

No one to hear her scream.

Go in there and take her, the voice inside me growled. Take her where? I'd only just arrived in town. I had no place to stay, no idea where to go, or even where I could take a woman, against her will, and keep her. No. I couldn't rush in, unprepared. Besides, I didn't want her to see me yet. I wasn't ready. I wanted to watch her. See her life. I wanted her to feel the jaws of her punishment slowly closing in, before they snapped shut on her.

A new game. A scrap for the beast inside, to soothe its mad hunger.

My prom queen, the only love of my wretched life, was alive.

I was relieved.

I was furious.

I was the happiest I'd ever been.

I was the angriest.

Above all, I was excited about something for the first time in seven years. A game finally worth playing.

I stood there in the dark watching for her, eyes trained for any sign of movement behind the shuttered windows, until a sharp ring cut through the night. It was my phone. I grabbed it out of my pocket and answered as I made my way back to the car.

"Dude, what the hell?" Bran sounded exasperated.

"I had to check something. I'm coming back for you. Sit tight. I'm on my way."

9

SOFIA

*F*all in Hade Harbor was beautiful. The temperature was pleasant, hitting seventy degrees most days, but the breeze from the ocean kept it manageable. The small town sat on the water, and I loved to walk by the harbor and see the boats come in.

On Saturdays, Leo went with Angelo to his beginner's boxing class. I trusted Angelo not to let Leo exert himself too much. Leo nearly always stayed at Angelo and Chiara's house on a Friday nights, and I worked on my commission paintings in my studio. The additional income was a big boost for my monthly budget. Today, given the clear weather, I was making the most of my free time, painting at my favorite coffee shop, on the huge outdoor deck that overlooked the water. Today was the day I had to present my work-in-progress to Edward Sloane, an appointment I wasn't looking forward to.

All the paperwork was done for Leo's admittance to the hospital later today. Just the thought of it, and the hope surrounding the donor, was setting me on edge. If there was anything I'd learned in my life so far, it was that hopes were usually dashed, dreams didn't come true, and it was best not to expect them to.

I was working on a landscape. Last night I'd made some progress on the commission, so my reward was working on something I liked. The landscape was darker than the paintings of the artists sitting around me, but that was my style. I loved the light on the water, but I loved the shadows more. My art was always dark. The students called it edgy, but I knew it was just reality, as I perceived it. I'd seen beyond the veil, to the other place, where people lived without rules or morals. After Silvio had died and my world had fallen apart, the darkness had never truly lifted.

Silvio had died? You mean after you'd killed him?

"Oh my god, that's beautiful," a voice called to me.

I turned. Chiara made a beeline for me through the tables. She was so stunning; several people turned and watched her make her way toward me. In tight jeans and a tight striped shirt, with her hair in a long braid, Chiara had really embraced the Maine aesthetic. She fit in here, with her sunny smiles and nautical chic outfits. I envied her. Once more, I was the odd duck. Despite living here for seven years, I still looked like a newcomer to Maine. Black was still my favorite color, and I still couldn't get used to Moxie or Allen's coffee-flavored brandy.

"You like it? I think the light is still too bright," I muttered critically, turning my head to see the painting from different angles.

"Girl, that is not a worry you should ever have. I've seen the stuff in your studio. Being too light isn't your problem,"

Chiara sighed as she noisily dragged a chair across the tile to sit beside me.

"How was class?"

"It was great, except I have a new student who I'm sure Angelo would flip his lid over if he saw him," Chiara smiled dirtily. She was a highly sought-after yoga instructor in town and ran a successful studio.

"Right, like that isn't exactly what you'd like," I teased her.

She smiled and wriggled her eyebrows. "You know that jealousy sex is the best. All the claiming, all the attempts to leave a mark."

She shuddered delicately, and I looked away. I could practically feel her anticipation for tangling with her husband, and I couldn't lie that it didn't make me jealous.

She nudged me with her foot. "You know you don't have to be a nun."

"I can take care of my needs just fine, thank you very much. I don't need a man to provide anything these days, not even an orgasm," I muttered, taking the cup of black coffee she'd brought me and sipped the hot liquid, enjoying the bite of it on my tongue. I still liked my coffee dark and bitter, like my soul.

"Honey, even battery-operated devices have their limits. A vibrator can't hold you down, spit in your mouth, and tell you that you're daddy's good little girl," she said.

The man next to us snorted his coffee out of his nose, as did I.

"Christ, take it down a notch in public," I muttered, wiping my nose on a tissue.

"I'm just keeping your day interesting, and random eaves-dropper's, too, apparently," she directed over her shoulder at the man who had clearly been listening.

Instead of flushing with embarrassment, the man turned in his chair and beamed at us.

"I apologize, ladies. I've been awfully rude. It's just that there's no one around here even remotely as interesting as you." His Irish accent was a pleasant surprise, and his twin-kling green eyes revealed he knew just how disarming it was. He grinned at us. "I don't suppose I could join you?"

"I don't suppose you could," Chiara said back sweetly. "My husband can pull the arms off a man without breaking a sweat. It's a risk you shouldn't take."

"I'm sorry to hear that."

"She's doing you a favor, believe me," I said, and attempted a smile at the man.

He was handsome as hell, and he knew it. A chiseled jaw and tousled blond hair framed those green eyes, and his navy T-shirt clung to an impressive chest.

"And here I was thinking a newcomer to town had finally found a couple of guides worthy of hanging out with. I'm sorry for interrupting you," he said and gave a small salute, withdrawing his attentions gracefully, before he became an annoyance. It was masterfully done, really.

Chiara turned back to me and tapped her lip, her eyes calculating. A wicked smile sprang to her face, and before I could tell her to forget whatever her devious mind had cooked up, she'd twisted around. "I'm married, but my friend isn't. Maybe she can be your guide."

"Excuse me," I started, and flushed horribly as they both looked at me.

"That would be great, as long as I'm not stepping on anyone's toes. I mean, I'm just looking for a local guide, where the hotspots are, good areas to live in, that sort of thing. We can work up to spitting and daddy stuff later," the stranger quipped.

Chiara laughed, and even I felt a reluctant smile touch my lips. The guy was charming, all right, and had somehow made it less awkward. Not that I had any intention of meeting up with a man for anything romantic. Those days were behind me.

"I wish I could help, but I'm really busy with work," I told him firmly.

Chiara sighed dramatically. "Unfortunately, that's true. She's a high school teacher, and she's always slammed."

"Hade Harbor High, is it? I heard they've a killer hockey team. Hade Harbor University is pretty famous, too, isn't it?"

"It is. This is a college town," I said.

The man pulled his phone out of his pocket and typed something in. "Well, I don't want to push you. If you have time, or if you could just answer a message, if I shoot one off about a neighborhood or something, while I'm with the realtor, that would be appreciated. I don't want to be a bother. I'll give you my number, then you decide," he said.

I nodded, feeling reluctant but not wanting to be an asshole to such a reasonable request.

He read out his number, and I typed it into my phone and then set it down.

"New number?" I mused as he tucked it away. It was odd to see someone read their number out by looking at it.

He grinned. "New phone." The cell in his hand rang, and he answered it.

"Hello! Now you have her number," Chiara said across from me.

I took a moment to realize that she'd called the stranger's number immediately.

I snatched my cell from her and gave her a death look that made her roll her eyes.

"Relax, what's the harm?"

"What should I save your number as? I'm Bran, by the way." He extended a big, long-fingered hand to me.

I shook it uncomfortably. Bran? The unusual name was vaguely familiar. I wondered where I'd heard it before.

"Sophie, and this is Cici."

"Sophie and Cici, nice to meet you."

Bran's phone chimed in his hand, and he glanced at it and then flashed us a brilliant smile. Yep, it was official. The man was charming as hell. He stood and gave us a better view of how tall and broad he was. His arms were inked with Celtic designs, and they gave me a pang. I hadn't seen someone with so much ink in a long time. Seven years, to be exact.

"I've got to take this," Bran said. He brought his phone to his ear as he started away. His eyes lingered on mine. "I hope I'll be seeing you again soon, Sophie."

DROPPING Leo off at the hospital was the worst part of the day. I hated when he was admitted and I was home alone, but this time, it was more important than ever. Ironically, he loved the vibe in the children's ward. He was together with a lot of sick kids he saw often. There was no staring or whispering about him and his spotty school record. He was with his own little community, and he treated it more like an extended sleepover than a hospital stay.

I said goodbye quickly, so I wouldn't get overly senti-mental and upset him, and headed toward Edward Sloane's house. It sat on a high cliff overlooking the ocean. It was a beautiful spot. I had to give him that. Huge gates surrounded his property, and I didn't feel like trying to drive my car inside. I parked out on the quiet street beyond the wall and got the portrait out of the car. I was on my way toward the gate when it buzzed open.

I stared up at the security camera mounted outside, taking in the entire street. I knew I was expected, but there was some-thing vaguely creepy about the idea of Edward waiting for me to arrive and buzzing me in before I'd pressed the damn bell.

As the enormous gate rolled slowly open, I felt an itching feeling on the back of my neck. The feeling of being watched. I turned and glanced back at the street, pressing the lock button on my car keys again, suddenly paranoid. No matter how long I lived away from Mafia life, I didn't think the unease would ever truly leave me. The feeling of phantom eyes crawled over me, and I turned back to the camera, realizing what it must be. Edward, watching me, waiting for me to enter. Understandable, but creepy.

I strode across the paved forecourt outside the vast house. It was all glass and wood, a real architectural dream. The view behind it was even better. The ocean rolling away, huge and uncaring about the petty problems of people. The salty air hit my nose and calmed me.

I headed toward the huge doors at the front of the house. They opened before I reached them.

"Good afternoon." Edward appeared in the doorway, smiling at me with that arrogant ease of a man who knows he can buy everything he wants in life.

"Hello. Where would you like the painting put?"

Edward smiled, even though that muscle kept ticking in his jaw. "This way."

He stepped back, allowing me into the house.

Inside was just as beautiful as the outside had promised it would be. Edward herded me through the long, arched corridors. We emerged onto a deck with a stunning view. Food was laid out on the table, salad and cold meats, bread and wine. I turned and stared at him.

"I thought I was here for work?"

"I never could separate work and pleasure." Edward smiled, as if there was something charming about what he'd said.

"Well, I can. I can't stay for lunch." I gripped the painting and stepped back. This asshole kept pushing at my boundaries, and I had no idea how far he was going to go.

"I insist. I'm going to eat before I see the painting, so if you don't want to, I guess I'll have an audience."

"Edward," I bit off, exasperated.

"Sophie. Stop fighting it. It's just lunch." He leaned a hip on the table, his arms crossed over his chest.

He would not budge, and he'd made it so I looked like a petty bitch if I protested more. I had no problem being a petty bitch, but I hadn't eaten, and I wasn't going to sit around and watch him eat before he deigned to give me his attention.

He pulled my chair out as I sat. I leaned forward to avoid his touch when he pushed me back in.

"Relax. You're so flighty. Such a city slicker. I never found out where you lived before you came to Maine."

Edward sat opposite me and picked up the wine.

I covered my glass. "None for me, and I don't think I mentioned it."

He smirked. "I'm aware. I was asking where you lived before you came here."

"Around, mostly the East Coast. We moved a lot."

"You and your late husband?"

I nodded, the lie feeling like it was branded across my forehead. Edward's gaze fell to my wedding ring. I'd bought it as soon as I could afford it and put it on the very day Leo had been born. I might not be able to introduce my son to his father, but I'd always wanted him to know that his parents had loved each other once.

"What was it he did for work?"

"A little of this, a little of that. He was a jack of all trades." The evasive answers were the best I could come up with right now.

"And a master of none?" Edward smiled like it was a nice thing to say about a dearly departed loved one. "Anyway, it's been a while, but you still wear the ring."

"I'll always wear it. I'm not interested in dating. I've told you that before."

"Yes, you have. These things change with enough time."

"Not for me."

Edward chuckled. "You really have a knack for that, don't you?"

"For what?"

"Making me want to prove you wrong."

Instead of answering, I looked out at the garden below us. The cliff was a good hundred feet away from the wall of the property. As I looked out at the rugged beauty of the coastline, I felt the same creeping sensation of eyes on me that I had at the front of the house.

"Do you have cameras all around your property?"

Edward nodded.

"And security guards?"

He tilted his head. "Are you thinking of breaking in? I don't bother with security guards. This is Maine."

"Right."

We ate in strained silence.

"Are you used to living somewhere with more security?"

I jerked out of my daydream at the question and waited for him to go on.

He waved his fork around as he spoke. Everything about him was cocky arrogance. I hated it.

"You don't seem like a woman used to living… like you do now."

"Are you calling me poor?" I tried to make my tone light. It didn't quite come off.

"Wealth can smell wealth. You've had money before. You've lived a different life before."

I turned away from his intrusive stare and focused on the trees at the end of the property.

A shadow moved.

I blinked at it. It looked like a man dressed in black. He was too far to make out properly.

Frowning, I leaned forward, causing Edward to turn and follow my gaze.

By the time he did, the figure was gone. "What is it?"

"I could swear I saw a man standing there, just on the edge of the woods."

"What was he doing?"

"Watching us."

Edward turned back around and chuckled. "If you think you can cut lunch short by imagining a sniper in the trees, it won't work. You should stop fighting me with all your might, Sophie. I already told you I'm a man who gets what he wants. I wanted to have lunch with you, and we are having lunch. If I want it to be a long lunch, it will be."

My annoyance at Edward expanded in my chest, and just like that, I was done.

Smiling politely, I wiped my mouth and pushed back my chair.

"In that case, I'm afraid I have to go."

Edward frowned at me. "Why?"

"Because I want to. Keep the portrait, have someone else finish it, I don't care."

"Sophie, now wait a minute."

Edward trailed after me as I retraced my route back through the house, grabbing my bag on the way. I left the wrapped painting on the hallway floor.

"No, I've waited long enough."

I pulled open the front door just as Edward reached an arm out to stop me. I gripped his wrist and twisted it into a lock before I could stop myself. He gave a bark of pain but couldn't move from the position.

"Don't touch me. I never gave you permission to touch me." I released his wrist and stormed down the steps. Damn it. My hotheaded temper had once again got the better of me, but I just couldn't stop myself. As soon as I was back on the street, my temper cooled, and I realized how dumb that had been. Hadn't Edward just reminded me yesterday that Leo was being treated in his wing of the hospital? It had been a veiled threat, clearly, and now I'd gone and pissed him off.

I'd have to make nice, but not today. Today, I needed to calm down.

I slowly walked back toward my car. The feeling of eyes on me returned. Was Edward watching me through his cameras?

As I got in the car, I stiffened, registering something that hadn't been there before.

A bouquet of white lilies lay on the dashboard. A black ribbon was tied around the stems.

Inside the car.

SOFIA

*a*fter a dinner of canned soup and crackers, I sat on the phone with Leo for a good half an hour. He had his own phone, so I could call him at the hospital after visiting hours. I had offered to sleep with him in the chair by the bed, but he'd been insistent that I sleep at home. He worried more about me than he should.

The bouquet of lilies played on my mind. First, who the hell would give me them? Second, and most worryingly, how had they gotten inside the car? My rational mind reassured me that there had to be an obvious explanation. Maybe I'd forgotten to lock the door, and Edward had had a member of staff run out there and put them by my car as a surprise, for when I left, since he was clearly bent on impressing me. That was the logical answer. Still, the thought of them stuck on the edges of my mind, like a burr.

Trying to stave off my paranoia and loneliness at being home alone on a Saturday night, I decided to work a little on my most private, personal paintings. The ones that I never took off my property.

Painting had always been a hobby, though as a student, I'd been more interested in the history of art. In another life, one where Antonio De Sanctis hadn't been my father, I'd have loved to work with old art, in restoration, or curation. Instead, even before he'd threatened the unborn child inside me, there had never been any chance that I'd have a job that I'd love. I'd marry who my father told me to, and that was it. The art degree he allowed me to get was just a way for him to keep me busy until my sell-off date. I took comfort in the fact that the shitshow that had been the last seven years had at least deprived Antonio of his virgin bride poker chip.

I headed outside and down the porch to the left side. Angelo had helped me covert the garage of the little house into a workspace. A studio of my own.

Inside the garage, I flipped the overhead lights on, the scent of turps and oil paint meeting my nose.

I approached a large canvas that was covered in a sheet. I knew what lay beneath it. It was something I painted often. A moonlit forest, with a starry sky, and the faint shadow of a boy with his head tilted back, looking up at the moon. Leo thought it was him, and it was in a lot of ways, but it was also his father.

I settled onto my stool and turned a light toward the canvas.

Reaching for my paintbrush, noticing a slightly scruffy-looking area of trees, I nearly knocked over the jar of fresh brushes I kept on the table beside my stool. As I bent to steady it, a hard knock sounded at the door to the garage.

I froze, my heart all but jumping straight to my mouth. After a moment, silence fell again. I felt unsettled, the memory of the flowers suddenly pushing back to the forefront of my mind. What if it wasn't nothing? I wouldn't be able to work until I checked it out.

Heading back through the main part of the garage, I neared the door.

This time, the knock thundered through the entire building. It was so loud, my hands flew up to protect my face, and I cringed to a stop. Heart pounding once more, I peeked at the door. It sounded like someone had thrown a rock against it.

My skin rippled with the feeling of being watched again. In a second, I was right back to earlier and that uncanny crawling sensation working over my skin.

"Hello?" I called, my voice sounding oddly loud in my ears.

I approached the door again and turned the handle. It opened easily. Stillness flooded through the crack, the kind that was particular to where we lived. The distant sound of waves crashing on the beach was not too far from us, and the hum of crickets living in the bushes filled the night with their music.

The soft murmur of far-off cars passing on the nearest road drifted to me. It wasn't that late, only ten, and everything sounded normal.

Everything was fine.

Then why are you so scared? The mocking voice in my head needed to take a hike. I had to get a grip. I drew myself up to my full height and put my shoulders back. I was Sofia

De Sanctis, I didn't cower. No one might know who I really was here, but I did.

Striding to the nearest tool bench, I pulled a long screwdriver from its slot in the table and tucked the hilt into my palm. The shape was comforting, similar to a *liccasapuni*, the *paranza corta* weapon of choice. I might know it's better to run, but if I had no choice, I could still fight. Even if it was just against the demons in my head.

Pushing the door open, I stepped out into the night. The streetlamps stopped a little way up the street and didn't reach my property. I had motion sensors set up, however, to bring a floodlight on when triggered. It was angled at my front lawn, and the side courtyard, right in front of the garage.

Right now, the light was on.

Something had triggered it. It was probably just an animal. That was what usually triggered the light.

I couldn't remember if I'd locked the front door. Maybe I'd forgotten, since Leo wasn't home. I was distracted and sloppy. I'd never be able to work if I didn't check.

Steeling myself, I started across the courtyard toward my porch. As I got closer to my stoop, my light came on, flooding the front step with light. I jerked to a stop as I saw my front door.

This time, a new lily bouquet sat at my door, tied with another pristine black ribbon.

Purity, innocence, rebirth, death. I'd looked up the meaning of lilies. It hadn't been comforting. They reminded me of my mother's funeral.

As I got closer, moving forward in shuffling steps, the screwdriver feeling like a hot poker in my palm, I saw that they weren't perfectly white. There were dark-red droplets sprayed across them, like paint against a fresh canvas. Blood against white petals. All beliefs that I was overreacting fell away.

Terror filled me, and I fumbled with my phone, even as I rushed up the stairs toward the door. I had to get inside. It felt like a hundred eyes were on me as I stood on the stoop. It was official. This wasn't just in my head. Someone was watching me, threatening me in some undefinable way. Trying to scare me, and it was fucking working.

I dropped the screwdriver as I dialed 911.

As I bent to grab it, my finger poised to call, a message came in, the sender unknown.

> Only the guilty cower from judgement, prom queen.

EVERY SINGLE OTHER thought fled my head as I stared at that sentence, ripped straight out of my darkest fantasies. It couldn't be real. It was impossible. Nikolai was in jail, and he thought I was dead. It *couldn't* be real. But, if it wasn't him, then someone had found me who knew all about me. Someone with a very personal grudge to bear.

My terror piqued, even as I spun around and looked out at the dark road. There were a hundred places to lurk and never be seen.

Nothing moved on the quiet street, and tears stung my eyes.

"Hello?" My voice echoed around the empty street. I felt stupid, scared, and poised to run if a shadow moved my way. "I've called the cops. They're on their way!"

My phone chimed again.

Liar.

I tore my eyes from the screen and looked into the darkness. I fancied I could feel eyes on me, but maybe I was just paranoid. No matter what my mental damage was, one thing was certain. Someone had set these flowers up and bled on them.

"Nikolai?"

I didn't know why I said it. My rational mind knew it was impossible, and yet his name filled my mind. Someone was fucking with me, and my first thought was that it could be him? It was probably kids. The little hellions who went to Hade Harbor High were just spoiled and sadistic enough to think harassing a teacher at night outside her home was a fun game. It was a nickname that kids could use. Why not? I'd even confessed once to a few students that I'd been a prom queen back in my heyday.

Spinning on my heel, I dismissed my partially completed 911 call. The cops wouldn't do anything about this, and I didn't like them sticking their noses into my life, if I could avoid it.

I unlocked the door and cast a last long look at the street, before stepping inside and slamming the door. The noise echoed around the empty living room, the dark woods lingering just outside the dark windows at the back, mocking me with their secrets.

I sank down into a rocking chair that stood just on the other side of the sliding glass doors that overlooked the back patio, and stared out at the night, my phone gripped in my hand. I couldn't go up to bed right now and sleep soundly. I was too unsettled.

I stared at the dark woods that ran across the end of the backyard, my skin creeping.

I could swear that the dark stared back.

SUNDAY WAS ROUGH. I'd barely slept the night before and was jumpy and on edge all day. I spent most of it at the hospital. I wrestled with whether to tell Chiara and Angelo but decided not to. They had already spent too much time fixing my problems. They were friends, not babysitters.

As time passed, I started to think I was overreacting. The kids who'd decided to mess with me would really enjoy how on edge they'd made me. The worst part was how thoughts of Nikolai had pushed into my head. I kept seeing him. Stolen glimpses around the hospital, walking the halls, a specter in black, ducking into a cab, disappearing around the bend in the stairwell. Like his memory was a ghost haunting me, or some kind of messed-up wishful thinking. I did a hundred double takes, only realizing I was wrong with closer inspection. It made me feel like I was going crazy.

After the hospital, I drove home by the grocery store and ran in, quickly locating the frozen meal section. I loaded up on a couple of dinners for while Leo was away from home. I cooked all his meals, usually. It was better for his health and compromised immune system. I didn't care about my health, only his.

There were only a few of the type I liked left, right at the bottom of the freezer, and I had to stick my head deep down inside the freezer section. When I straightened, I piled the frozen dinners haphazardly on top of the freezer and glanced up, hoping to snag a nearby basket.

That was when I saw him again.

Nikolai Chernov. In the flesh. This time it was more than a glimpse.

It was a memory. It had to be. This had happened to me before. When I'd first arrived in Hade Harbor, I'd seen him everywhere. I'd kept expecting him to show up. How could prison stop a force of nature like Nikolai Chernov? It was impossible.

Slowly, I'd realized that it wasn't him, and bit by bit, I'd learned to ignore it. Today, though, something was different. All the times I'd known Nikolai, he'd been wearing one of his past outfits, one from my memories. Ripped jeans and dark t-shirts, leather jacket and shit-kicking boots. Now, the vision of Nikolai wore black slacks, perfectly fitting his long, lean legs, and a black dress shirt, open at the neck. He leaned against the meat counter, watching me like a wolf watched a rabbit it was about to devour. He looked casually deadly in those clothes. No longer a volatile heir to a dangerous throne, but the king himself. His head was shaved severely, revealing new tattoos scrolling across his scalp. I'd never imagined that before.

He wasn't grinning. The twisted, mocking charm he'd always had was overlaid with seriousness. It wasn't like him at all.

My hand slipped on the boxes of frozen meals, and they cascaded to the floor.

I looked down at them, hurrying to crouch and pick them up, as people looked at me, stepping over the mess I'd made.

When I looked up, Nikolai was gone.

Maybe no one was messing with me at all. Maybe I was just going crazy.

THAT NIGHT, after checking the locks on my doors ten times, I dug out the old burner phone I had rarely used. It had one number in it.

Renato answered on the second ring.

"Sofia? What's wrong?"

His familiar voice made me feel things I didn't know how to process. When I'd lost Nikolai to prison, forced into a lie by my father, I'd lost my brother as well.

"Nothing, I mean, I'm not sure. Probably nothing. I just wanted to see what was going on. How's father?"

"Still alive, if that's what you're wondering."

A fucked-up pang of disappointment went through me at those words. What kind of monster wishes for their father to die? I could only be what he had made me.

Ren cleared his throat. "I'm glad you called. I was trying to figure out a way to reach you."

"Why? What is it?" I held my breath, my heart beating painfully. That damned shortness of breath that I always got before a panic attack. I forced my breathing to calm, counting in fours to slow down the creeping anxiety.

"He's out. Nikolai Chernov walked a few days ago."

Somehow, I'd known my brother was going to say those very words before they hit my ears. It might have felt impossible, but it was inevitable. Of course he'd find me. *Of course he would.*

"He's really free?"

"Yeah, he's really free. Fuck knows how, considering what he got up to inside. I have no idea, except that Ronan Black might be able to argue Lucifer himself back into Heaven. He's out there, Sofia. I thought you should know."

"Does Father know?" I gripped the phone tightly.

"He knows. He isn't happy about it."

"But he can't do anything. That wasn't the deal. He can't break it now. Nikolai Chernov is safe from the De Sanctis family," I reminded my brother. I knew I didn't have to. We were both aware of the terms I'd agreed to years ago, but I needed to hear the words to reassure myself.

"Frankly, I'd be more worried about the De Sanctis family being safe from him. He visited your grave. Security informed me. He burned down half the fucking chapel on the grounds. Not only that, but he's also targeting De Sanctis men. He's graduated from lunatic to serial killer in prison. You need to be careful."

A fist of agony and guilt clenched around my throat, choking my words. I nodded, a lone tear dropping down my cheek. When I thought of Nikolai, the tears were never far away.

"Anyway, I better go. These calls should be short. Don't forget your end of the deal, *piccolina*."

"I know. I know the bargain I sold my soul for. You don't need to remind me."

"If he finds you, call me right away. If he's a threat… call me right away."

"If he's a threat, then no one can save me from him. Calling you won't help me. No one will be able to help me." That simple fact was absolutely undeniable. My confession remained unspoken. *I think he's already found me.*

Ren was quiet for a long moment before sighing. "One day, this will all be over, and you can come home."

"Home? Casa Nera was never my home. It was only ever my cage."

And Nikolai Chernov was the man who had set me free, and I'd thanked him by betraying his trust.

It was a debt I could never, ever repay.

My greatest sin.

11

SOFIA

"When you're planning this painting, I want you to think about the negative space," I said to my class on Monday afternoon.

A hand shot up.

"Yes?"

"What's negative space?"

I fought a sigh of frustration. I'd just given a definition a second ago. "Can anyone answer that?"

The class was quiet for a long moment, and then a deep voice spoke. Cayden West.

"It's the space around the thing you're drawing. The darkness between things," he said.

I looked at him. His face was down, he was staring at his notepad, and he had his hood up, a pet hate of mine. He was a new student at Hade Harbor High, and I didn't know what to make of him. Within days, he'd joined the ice hockey team and was already their ace. He had instantly joined the group of hockey stars who ruled the school, nicknamed the Ice Gods. He was a foster kid, and Coach Williams had taken him in, no doubt, so they could use his skills to win nationals.

"It doesn't have to be dark," a voice objected.

Cayden finally brought his head up and swung it in the direction of the person who had dared to disagree with him.

Lillian Williams. The coach's daughter. She was one of my favorites and didn't fit the usual mold of girls at HHH, being more interested in microbiology than social media. She enjoyed art, however. It was her break from the courses she'd loaded up on in order to get into the highly competitive Hade Harbor University.

She and Cayden were now foster siblings, presumably, and cohabiting. The tension around them tainted the air. Cayden was staring at Lily. I wondered how Lily was taking having a stranger in her home. She was seventeen, nearly eighteen, and Cayden didn't have an innocent, easy-going bone in his body. He looked like a kid who had been through the wringer and out the other side. There was a hardness to him that made painful, jagged memories crowd my head.

Memories of another life. Of tragic men who smiled grimly in the face of danger.

Twisting the band on my finger absently, I watched Lily and Cayden argue without words.

"Sure, it could be, but darkness makes it better. Everyone loves a little darkness," he muttered.

I had a feeling his words were for Lily and her alone. His eyes never moved from her.

I could still remember what it felt like to be watched like that.

I should probably interrupt their fiery staring contest. "You're both right. It could be a background of any kind. It's really just the space that isn't supposed to be the focus," I said and paused when the bell rang loudly overhead. Thank god, three classes down, two to go. I hadn't slept well for three nights in a row, and I needed a break.

The students surged out of their seats, an explosion of chatter filling the air. It was just before lunchtime, and I decided to eat outside. The weather was so lovely. After a quick tidy, I grabbed my sandwich and headed out. Hade Harbor High had a beautiful setting, with dense woods to the back, and now I headed along the small trail that led to the entrance. The kids weren't supposed to come into the woods during school hours, but plenty did. There were a few picnic tables and benches dotted around within the first few minutes of walking. I headed for my favorite one, right next to a small bubbling stream.

Setting my sandwich down, I reached for my phone, looking for some mindless diversion.

My mind returned immediately to the subject that had plagued me since I'd spoken to my brother.

Nikolai Chernov was free.

Maybe he'd already found me. Ren's words were terrifying. Nikolai had been killing De Sanctis men. He'd burned part of a church down. It was extreme, even for him. Seven years had passed. Seven hard years for me, so I couldn't even imagine what they'd been like for him, locked up with other criminals, the worst that the East Coast offered. It sounded like he was even more dangerous now.

He was always dangerous. You just had a free pass.

After what I'd done, I was pretty sure that free pass would have expired. I didn't want to know what had happened to those on the receiving end of Nikolai's hate. I didn't think there were any around to tell the tale. His father certainly wasn't. My blood suitably chilled, I shivered in the cool breeze. The sun had gone behind a cloud, and the air in the woods took on a different feeling.

Then, I felt it.

The creeping sensation of being watched.

Twisting around, I stared at the trees around me. The woods were still bright enough, muted sunshine falling in slices of gold against the deep-green leaves and the warm brown of the well-traveled paths. It wasn't a creepy wood by any stretch of the imagination, so it was the first time it occurred to me how far I was from the school building.

It was the first time I realized how no one would hear me scream.

My shoulders edged up to my ears as I put my phone away and took a bite of my sandwich. It was probably nothing. I'd been tense before. I used to live in a state of constant tension, and with Leo away, it was probably just wearing on my nerves. I ate quickly, unwilling to run away, in case it was my imagination, or more likely, asshole students who thought it would be funny to spook a teacher in the wild. While they weren't allowed out here, I had no doubt that the Ice Gods came out to these woods whenever they felt like it. I'd seen Cayden dragging Lillian out here the other day. The only reason I hadn't gotten involved was that she'd assured me it was nothing to worry about.

I finished my lunch with a stubborn determination, barely tasting it, and got up. As I walked away from the woods, heading out of the tree line, I heard it. The snap of a twig under someone's foot. I stopped, all the hair on the back of my neck rising. I had a sudden, terrible paranoia that if I turned around right now, there'd be someone behind me. I took a step forward. A soft crunch echoed my footstep.

Terror and the urge to act flooded my mind. In the past, I'd been the girl who'd fight, the knife-wielding Mafia princess who practiced *paranza corta* and had taken a *liccas-apuni* blade to prom. Now? Now I was a mom, and a woman who had learned firsthand how her strength stacked up to a predator.

Now, I ran.

I burst forward with a surge of speed, running as fast as I could for the tree line. It mocked me, so far out of reach, as I pelted along the trail, my soft, slippery-soled ballet flats sliding on the pine needles of the forest floor. I heard something behind me, a swish of fabric, like someone was chasing, and then, worst of all, a soft chuckle. It was dark, crawling along my veins and sending fear crashing into me, pushing the last of my energy into my limbs. Just like many a damsel in distress before me, with the break in the trees just out of reach, I tripped. I went down hard, biting my tongue as I landed on my outstretched hands. My phone flew across the ground and disappeared under a bush.

I froze in the position, on my hands and knees. My palms were burning. I felt terrified and ridiculous at the same time.

What if it was really him?

Would I run from Nikolai when I was the guilty one this time?

No, I wouldn't. I didn't want to.

I twisted around before I could question the sanity of it.

My butt hit the floor, and my gaze searched the path behind me.

There was no one there.

I stared at the green-black shadows between the trees. Was someone there, watching me right now? Or was it just the ghost in my head, tormenting me? Nothing moved, and slowly, my heart rate dropped back to the range of normal.

When I finally found my phone, dusted myself off, and walked out into the woods, I smacked right into a hard chest, nearly falling.

Powerful arms gripped me and kept me upright.

"Miss Rossi? Are you okay?" voices asked me.

I spun around and got my bearings. The Ice Gods stood on the trail before the wood. They were looking down at me with a variety of confusion, some concern, and a little annoyance.

"I'm fine. I just thought there was someone in the woods."

Cayden West looked up at the dark tree line. "Who?"

"I don't know, I ran... he nearly caught up with me, though," I said, taking a deep breath. As much as I might feel uncomfortable about the Ice Gods, I felt safer now, standing with them. They might be assholes, but they were strong, and tough.

Cayden narrowed his eyes at me and then jerked his head to his teammate, Marcus. "Take Miss Rossi back to school, we'll have a look."

"No, it's okay," I found myself saying as three of the four headed into the trees.

"Don't worry about us, teach. Worry about the creep in the woods, if we find him," Beckett, the only Ice God with the same imposing stature as Cayden, called confidently to me, just before the two of them disappeared into the shadows along with Ice God number three, Ashton.

"Come on, Miss Rossi, let's get back to school grounds. You know we're not meant to come out here during lunch, right?" Marcus teased me.

I fell into step beside him.

"That's for students," I reminded him. Shouldn't I report what had just happened? I'd just let three eighteen-year-olds race after a possible assailant. I said as much to Marcus.

"Naw, don't worry about it. What would you even say? 'I think, but I'm not sure, that someone I didn't see was chasing me in the woods.' If you say anything, we'll just get in trouble for going off grounds at lunch, and with the big game coming up, we can't really afford detention right now."

"Like you'd get detention. You four can do anything you want, and you know it," I muttered, concentrating on getting to the gates.

He was right, however. The boys would get in trouble for being out, and the mystery figure would be long gone. If he'd even been there in the first place.

"Can I get that in writing, teach?" Marcus grinned at me.

"I'm ignoring that and going inside. Thanks for the escort."

"Anytime, Miss Rossi, and I mean that sincerely, from the bottom of my heart, any time you need a big strong protector, you call me," Marcus said and raised a rakish eyebrow at me.

If I didn't know better, I'd think this eighteen-year-old jock was flirting with me.

I left him at the gates and headed back upstairs to the art room and my office.

As soon as I stepped inside, I felt the shift in the air.

It felt like someone had been inside. I looked around. The papers on the surfaces were still as madly disorganized as ever. A real downside to growing up with maids was the lack of functioning cleaning skills. It made it particularly difficult to tell if someone had been through your things or not.

I approached my desk, the paranoia from the woods returning tenfold. Had that really just been my overactive imagination or something else? Someone else.

I sat at my desk, my gaze drifting over my things. It stuttered to a stop when I saw it. A print that hadn't been there earlier. I picked it up gingerly.

I recognized it a little, though it wasn't one I was overly familiar with. It was *Madonna of the Swallow*, by Carlo Crivelli.

In the print of the famous painting, a swallow perched over the Madonna's throne. Dropping the print, I pulled up the search bar on my phone and typed in the painting's name.

I scanned the results, and darkness tugged at the edges of my vision.

"The swallow depicted in the image represents resurrection."

I set my phone down and stared blindly at my desk. A swallow, representing resurrection?

My lastochka, I'll always find you, wherever you go, the past whispered in my ear.

Feeling my sandwich threaten to return on me, I put the print of the painting into a drawer and slammed it shut. I couldn't fall apart right now. I had work to get through, papers to grade, and a professional shiny smile to paste on for at least four more hours.

I could fall apart later, at home, with a bottle of wine, behind locked doors, like a normal person.

12

NIKOLAI

That night, I dressed in clothes that felt more like me than the ones I'd been given, courtesy of Ronan Black, when I got out of jail. Black jeans and a t-shirt, a leather jacket over the top, and steel-capped boots. I dressed slowly and methodically, with a sense of ceremony. It was a special occasion, after all. Tonight, I was done waiting. Tonight, I'd play with my prom queen again, finally. Her time was up.

We'd both been playing Sofia's game for seven years.

It was my turn. Tonight, I'd finally take it.

Her house was designed for men like me. Isolated, unsecure, and dark. I went in the back where she had no motion-activated lights to blind me. The sliding door to the back garden was locked but slid open easily under my magic touch. Seven years in prison, and I still had the knack, just like riding a bike or hogtying a hostage. Some tricks are never forgotten.

Her house smelled like the sea and the forest, and another hint of something I'd long ago given up hoping to smell.

Her. *Sofia.*

My shoes were silent as I made my way across the polished wooden floors of her open-plan sitting room. It was a modest house for a millionaire's daughter, prettily furnished in creams and blues. I made my way up the stairs, my ears straining for the sounds of someone awake.

I felt like I was walking through a dream. Really, hadn't I been dreaming since that day in the visiting room, when my brother had told me that the only woman I'd ever loved had died? I shouldn't forget Irina, of course, another woman I'd loved and failed to save.

At the top of the landing, there were several closed doors. I ignored them for the open one at the end of the hall. I could feel her in there. Like that string that had been tied between us when we'd only been kids in a brutal, uncaring world, it had never been severed. She'd carried her end into the afterlife and made me a walking dead man. A body without a heart, existing, but never living. But it had all been a lie. My little prom queen had gotten good at lying, it seemed. She needed to be reminded that we didn't lie to each other. She could lie to anyone she wanted, but not to me. Never to me.

I prowled down the hall silently, and when I reached the room, the scent of my dreams filled my head.

She was asleep, unmoving in a big white bed, her short dark hair spread out in strands against the pillow. I was at her side before I could stop myself, looking down at the woman who had haunted me nearly my entire life. She was sleeping soundly and showed no sign of waking when I reached out to touch her. I had to touch her to know she was real.

My fingers met the plush velvet of her cheek.

A shock went through me at the contact. A pulse of life, soul-deep. It struck against my bones. The storm inside me quieted for a moment.

I dragged a painful breath through aching lungs. I couldn't tear my eyes from her.

Sofia De Sanctis. My ghost. My love. My greatest triumph and biggest failure. Her skin was like cream under my fingers. I couldn't stop running my hand up and down her bare arm. It was dangerous. It might wake her. I didn't care. Let her wake up to a dead man, dressed in black, with empty eyes, looming over her bed.

She shifted in her sleep, rolling onto her back and throwing her arm over her head. I couldn't stop staring at her. My hand fell to her face, and then lower, circling her neck. All the times I'd held her right there, her precious pulse fluttering against my palm, flashed through my mind. Now, I needed it more than anything. I needed the visceral proof that this woman was real. Alive. I circled her neck. Her pulse pounded against my hand with reassuring regularity.

I found my hand pressing against that slender column, pinning her to the bed. Warmth crackled across my chest, white-hot, burning my frozen insides. I gasped out a shuddering breath. It felt like the emptiness inside me was on fire, melting my bones and boiling my blood. I pressed more firmly, and she let out a small breath. One of her hands fell to my hand. In her heavy sleep, she pulled ineffectively at my grip.

Her head turned from side to side, but she didn't wake. I could strangle her to death right now, and she wouldn't even fight me. Her life was in my hands. I could correct this bizarre twist of fate, and leave her body tucked up tightly in bed, and try to forget that in the end, she had betrayed me.

She hadn't died; she had only let me think she had. My little swallow had flown her cage after all. She had freed herself and never looked back. I hadn't realized that she wanted to leave me behind as well.

She gasped. Her hand scrabbled at my wrist, and I let go. She pulled a deep breath into her tortured lungs and turned on her side. She was really out of it. I assumed she hadn't been sleeping that well lately. Our games were keeping her up at night.

She barely moved as I bound her. When she woke from a pinch to her nipple minutes later, it was already too late. She jerked from sleeping to awake and stilled as soon as she sensed the constriction around her wrists and ankles.

Her eyes searched wildly, but she couldn't move enough to turn her head. The tight connecting rope between her wrists and ankles stopped her. I kneeled on the bed behind her, out of her eyeline, and straddled her hips, reaching around her face from behind, a ball gag at the ready.

Assessing the situation, she made a moan of outrage and wiggled. I could have watched her rounded ass jiggle temptingly on the sheets all night, but we didn't have time for that.

I tutted loudly when her struggle continued for more than a minute, growing more and more agitated.

"That's enough, Sofia. You don't want to tire yourself out. You're going to need your energy, prom queen."

She stilled at the sound of my voice. I climbed off her and moved slowly behind her, pacing where she couldn't quite see.

"Tonight, my little swallow, we start our game."

I circled around in front of her and crouched. Her face was finally in view. Her mouth looked sumptuous, propped open by the thick ball. Finally, for the first time in seven years, our eyes met.

It was like touching a live wire with my bare hand. Her dark eyes widened, panic washing through her, surprise. I was gratified to see guilt in there, too.

A long line of tears dashed from one of her eyes. My gaze traced the movement, transfixed.

I reached out and wiped away the tear. When my finger touched Sofia's cheek, she closed her eyes. I could swear she pressed her face closer to my hand. I jerked back like she'd bitten me.

"Don't cry, prom queen. You'll hurt my feelings. I'm happy to see you. It's the best fucking day of my life."

Another line of tears escaped Sofia, and her mouth moved like a sob was trying to work out around the gag.

I stroked her hair. Just touching her in some capacity thrilled me.

"Don't act so surprised. You knew I was coming for you, deep down. You knew I was close, didn't you?"

Her eyes confirmed my words.

"Did it scare you, or thrill you?"

She swallowed hard, her slender throat moving with effort, given the way her head was pulled back. She was utterly beautiful, bound and helpless, with tears falling down her smooth cheeks.

"Now, let's talk about the game, shall we? I didn't realize that you'd already been playing with me all this time. Sleeping lions, was it? Well done. You got me. I can admit it. But your turn is over. It's mine now, and I want to play another schoolyard classic. Truth or dare. Are you game?"

A torrent of protests sounded around the gag. I grabbed her chin and used it to nod her head, up and down, in agreement.

"Excellent. You're going first, and I choose dare. I know that's not how you play it here in this country, but this is the way I know. Your way is too easy. I choose, and you do it. You can choose next time for me. Okay?"

I nodded her head again, gripping her chin firmly as more tears escaped her.

"Stop crying, prom queen, or I'll give you something to cry about." I pushed her hair back off her forehead, where it was sticking to her tears.

She was staring up at me like *I* was the ghost and not her.

"Shh, it's okay. Everything is going to be okay." My voice was low and deep, hiding the chaos swirling inside me. "Now, you're going to play with me, aren't you?"

I smoothed her short hair down, wiping her tears with my thumbs.

"Did you miss playing with me at all? I missed playing with you."

She sniffed and seemed to gather herself. She straightened.

"Are you ready to play?"

She shook her head, her eyes beseeching me. She wanted the gag off. She wanted to poison my mind with her lies again. I couldn't let that happen. Not yet. The screaming inside me was too loud to hear her gentle words over anyway.

Blood demanded blood, and Sofia had let me mourn her for seven years.

Now it was her turn to cry.

"Good girl. Now, it's my turn first, remember? Don't worry, it's a fun one. I dare you to live."

Her eyes widened, locked on me, earnest in a way that tugged at my ragged mind. I pulled the chloroform-soaked rag I'd brought with me from my pocket and clamped it over her mouth. She sagged into my arms a minute later. I smoothed her hair back, allowing myself one second of weakness before we started the game.

I let myself feel relief, there, alone in the dark with her unknowing body, before I mastered my wild emotions and hefted her over my shoulder.

The game was waiting, and there was a box in the woods with her name on it.

13

SOFIA

I rose slowly from a thick swamp of dizzying lethargy. It felt like when I used to dose myself with tablets to get some sleep in Casa Nera. I hadn't used them in years. Being the only adult alone at home nowadays, with Leo to look after, I couldn't afford to take anything, and sleep too deeply.

Now, I dragged myself to consciousness. It was painful. I wanted to close my eyes and sink back into comforting sleep, but something prickled at me, screaming at the edges of my mind for me to wake up.

I opened my eyes. The light was dim, and the air felt close. It didn't seem like my room, or smell like it either. There was a damp, earthy smell that I associated with the woods, and a harsh, fresh pine scent that rubbed along my senses harshly.

I sat up and smacked my head off a low ceiling. Falling back, I felt the same hard wood beneath my head as I'd just slammed my forehead against. I also realized at the same time that my hands were tied together in front of me.

Panic erupted in my chest, and my lungs cramped down on my breathing, making me hyperventilate. Last night came rushing to me. Waking up bound and gagged. Nikolai looming over me in the dark, as real and terrifying as ever.

No, not really, not even close. He was much, much worse. All the softness, as little as there had been to him, had melted away, and cold, calculating menace, with a side of insanity, had taken its place.

I forced a deep breath. I had to keep calm. I could freak out about being in the crosshairs of a psychopath later. First, I had to get the hell out of wherever he'd put me.

I wriggled my hands, grateful to feel give in the rope. A moment or two of twisting this way and that freed them.

Maybe he wasn't as unhinged as he'd seemed. He didn't even bind my wrists that tightly.

I ran my hands up over the ceiling that I had hit my head on, moving to the side to see how far it went. My feet hit the bottom at the same time as my hands met the close sides.

I was encased completely in a wooden box.

A coffin.

Panic descended again, blinding me. It was dark, the air thick, and I was inside a coffin. A coffin! Of course I was. I was crazy for thinking that Nikolai wasn't cruel and insane. He really was worse than ever. I'd let him think I was dead, and he'd put me in a coffin. He might even have buried me, for all I knew. My panic made my breath short and my pulse pound. I felt dizzy. My fingers scrabbled against the wood, despite knowing that it wouldn't make a difference. I felt like a trapped animal. I opened my mouth and screamed, the noise deafening in the small space. I kicked the bottom and smacked my forehead off the roof of the casket again.

Get a grip, Sofia, I told myself sternly, letting my body go limp and concentrating on getting my breath back first. Nikolai said it was a game. Even if I was just his unwilling partner in a sadistic game, he wouldn't just kill me like this. Then the game would be over too quickly. If he'd wanted to do that, he could have done it last night in my room.

No, there had to be a way out. He wanted to scare me, and he'd really fucking succeeded, but the game wouldn't be fun to him if there wasn't a way for me to escape.

I had to keep calm. My hands rose back to the walls of the small box around me. I felt around slowly, this time making sure I was covering every inch, which wasn't easy in the dark. Level to my hip, I felt it. A metal lock. I slid my fingers around it, trying to figure out the shape. It was smooth, except for a small slot, too thin to get my fingers into. I tried to wiggle my nail inside, but it was too short.

Still, it was a start.

Next, I dropped my hands to the floor of the box and felt about. I was sweating. My thin cami and shorts were sticking to my overheated skin. A desperate cry left me when my hands came up empty.

Has he really left me in here to suffocate to death?

My fingers brushed against something metal just as I started to truly panic.

I stilled, grasping for the metal shape, working it out from under me.

A knife, the regular kitchen drawer type.

Holding it in my hand like it was my only lifeline, I brought the blade to the lock. I was shaking too badly to get it in on the first try. I had to use both hands to steady them enough to work it into the lock. It fit perfectly. A soft click sounded, and a slither of light appeared around one edge of the box lid.

I heaved at the heavy wooden top over me, and cool air rushed in as a gap appeared. Light flooded over me, blinding me, as I heaved with all my might and shifted the heavy top to the side. Fresh air and the sounds of the ocean filled my head and I blinked in the sunlight.

I was morning. I looked around the woods. They were as beautiful and peaceful as ever. Still drawing harsh breaths of fresh air, I pushed myself out of the slim space I'd made sliding the top open and fell to the pine-needled floor of the woods. The smell of fresh dirt filled my nose, and I'd never been more grateful for anything.

My harsh, hysterical breaths were the only sound in the silence around me. I stared at the shadows between the trees. Was he watching me? I pushed myself to unsteady feet.

I dare you to live.

I took a staggering step away from the box. Just the sight of it made me shudder. I turned and took another step and screamed as I fell backward, just in time. A deep hole had been dug close to the casket. A grave.

A twig snapped in the woods to the left side of me, and I lost it.

I turned and ran. My bare feet slapped against the worn trails as I raced through the trees. I knew where I was. I ran this trail often. If I could keep up my pace, I'd be home in minutes.

I sprinted as fast as I could, considering I couldn't catch my breath.

Ahead, my back garden appeared, and my house, looking quiet and sleepy in the early morning light. It showed no signs of the horrors that had happened there just last night.

I made it to the garden, sure that Nikolai was right behind me the entire way.

I bounded up the back porch steps and through the gaping back door. The sliding glass door had been left open.

As soon as I got inside, I whirled around and pulled the glass door shut, just as I steeled myself to look outside and see if he was really behind me.

There was no one there.

The backyard was undisturbed. The woods looked innocent and green at the edge of the yard.

I headed straight to the kitchen and grabbed a long, thin knife from the drawer and then ran to the front door and checked that it was locked.

I got the chain on before my strength left me. I slid down the door, my back pressed against the wood. The knife was gripped in both hands, like a prayer.

Hysterical laughter bubbled up in my throat.

Like any prayer could save me from Nikolai Chernov. Like any lock could keep him out.

"Are you laughing or crying, prom queen?"

14

SOFIA

I scrambled to my feet, knife clutched in my hands. Nikolai lounged against the wall opposite me. He must have been sitting in the kitchen. I hadn't even thought that he might still be inside.

"Don't come near me," I warned, pointing the knife at him. The end was shaking. I didn't want to look scared, but the adrenaline of the coffin wake-up call was still surging in my veins.

"I find it interesting that you grabbed a knife instead of the phone."

He lobbed something toward me, and my phone clattered off the seat beside the front door.

"When an intruder enters your house, don't you know it's best to call for help instead of trying to defend yourself with a weapon that could be turned against you?"

His gaze stayed on me. He looked like he was having the time of his life. His mocking eyes swept down me, taking in my rumpled silk shorts and thin cami top. The hunger in his look made it hard to breathe.

"Come on, Sofia. Call the cops. I won't stop you. Send me back to prison. It would be so easy. I'll even confess to harassing you."

What the hell? It wasn't enough for Nikolai to fuck with my safety and body, but he had to mindfuck me, too. He was still the man who had crawled so far inside my head, I'd never been able to get him out.

He pushed himself off the wall and approached.

"Don't come closer." My warning was muted at best.

He tilted his head to the side. He had a predatory grace that was stronger than ever. "I don't see you calling the cops, *lastochka*. Are you sure that's smart?"

"Maybe I just want to finish you myself and put you in that box you left so handily in the woods."

Nikolai laughed. There was something jagged in that sound. It wasn't quite right. He stopped in front of me and spread his arms open. "Go ahead then. You won the game. You got out of my little box. Hurt me back."

My throat was so dry it ached. My arm hurt from holding it out before me for so long. Nikolai advanced until the point of the knife pressed into his chest, just above his heart.

"Can you still remember how it feels when the blade slides in? If I'm going to die, it's only right that you should do it. You sliced up my face when we were kids, then you cut out my heart and left me to bleed to death for seven years. It's only right that you should finish the job."

His words struck me hard. Tears gathered at the corners of my eyes.

"Take your shot or stop pretending that you can." His words were too hard for the look in his eyes.

His hand slowly closed around the knife, and he tugged it out of my hand. He was right, after all. I couldn't hurt him. I deserved his wrath. Every single second. The guilt that had plagued me clung on to his hurt. He tossed the knife away and moved closer, his gaze dropped over me again.

His hand came to my chin, and he tilted my head back, so my eyes never left his, then dropped his grip to my neck. He circled my throat, pressing lightly at the sides. His gaze slid lower, to my chest, scouring across my breasts.

"Your nipples are hard. Are you that cold?" His finger rose to one of the tight peaks, pressing through the thin silk of my top.

I flushed, embarrassed by the evidence of how my body reacted to this man, even when he was threatening my life.

His finger traced a circle around my nipple, and I shivered.

"I can feel your heart beating," he muttered, his fingers against my pulse.

He stepped closer to me, resting his forehead against mine. His fingers closed on my nipple now, pinching. The touch rode the line between pleasure and pain. His breath was hot on my forehead, and my eyes closed for a second, enjoying his volatile touch. I didn't know what the hell he was going to do next. I should be more scared than I was. I'd clearly lost my goddamn mind. Maybe Chiara was right, it was dangerous to go too long without sex. The hormones had messed with my survival instincts.

His hand closed over my entire breast, squeezing it just the right amount to make my knees weak. Thoughts of this man had kept me company in my cold bed for so long, that now, his touch was all my fantasies come true.

He kept one hand on my breast, and the other hand landed on my stomach, pressing lightly against me and sliding down the way. How could I have gone from terrified and furious to wet and desperate so quickly? I really was as crazy as him. He tugged at the elastic waist of my shorts, snapping it against my skin.

"Last chance to call the cops on me, prom queen. Take it or leave it."

His hot breath burned my cheek. My face tilted up without my consent. It wasn't Nikolai doing it, but my own desire.

I felt his smirk against my skin as his hand dropped lower, sliding between my legs.

I was embarrassingly wet and had no panties on to hide behind. He pulled the shorts down by the gusset, and they went easily, pooling in a silk puddle around my ankles. His hand delved between my legs, long fingers finding my clit before stroking down my slit. Then he thrust two fingers inside me. The sudden stretch hurt, but not in the way that made me want to stop him. It felt good to be ruthlessly touched like this. Any touch of his felt good.

My head fell to his shoulder, and he jammed me against the wall to keep me up. His thumb rubbed my clit relentlessly, and his fingers worked inside me, so thick and long, my pussy drooled over them, trying to suck them deeper.

His hand picked up speed, finger-fucking me fast now, and only the wall and his hard body kept me from falling. I was holding his shoulders, my legs awkwardly splayed as I was chased toward coming. I could feel it, the first twinges of a hard orgasm rushing within reach. Just as my pussy clenched, he pulled his fingers abruptly from me. I cried out. It was disappointment, not pain. My eyes snapped open, and I glared up at him. He leaned a hand on the wall, and the other the one that had been inside me, he brought to his lips and cleaned with his mouth.

"Do you think you deserve to come, Sofia?" His deep murmur made me shake.

Embarrassment scorched me, and my hand was flying for his cheek before I could rethink the wisdom of such a moment. He caught my hand before it could land, and only more embarrassment filled me. I pushed at his chest, trying to get some space between us. I felt like I couldn't breathe. As I twisted madly, my bare foot slipped on the polished wood floor, and I fell.

I never met the floor, however. Nikolai somehow managed to cushion my faceplant, getting his knees under me just in time. I twisted away from him, kicking at him with my legs. He was laughing. The bastard. Whatever I'd hoped to come off as, if we ever met again, it wasn't a desperate housewife who exploded at the first touch of a man. My pride had gone out the window. My dignity was lying at the bottom of that half-dug grave.

"Come on, prom queen, you know better than to think you can get away from me that easily." He added a tut at the end of his mocking words, only infuriating me more.

A lucky kick landed on him, and his breath whooshed out. I managed to wiggle away at a crawl. His hand landed on my hip after a second and flipped me over. This time, I landed harder, my back flat against the floor. Nikolai knelt at my feet, his hands wrapped around my ankles like manacles I'd never be able to break. He yanked me closer, pushing my knees apart so I was splayed wide open before him. More heat flooded my face, and the rest of me, a liquid drip inside that hungered for his rough touch.

Our eyes met as his hand went to my pussy.

"What are you doing?" My voice sounded throaty. I had no idea if it was worry or want in my tone. It felt like both.

"Reminding you who this cunt belongs to. Stop me and call the cops… or shut the fuck up and be a good girl for me, for once in your life."

I stared at him, pulse pounding in my ears. It wasn't a choice really. I was never going to call the cops on Nikolai. I would never send him back to jail, and somehow, despite all that had happened between us, we both knew it.

A wicked, satisfied smile stretched across his face, and then he was moving.

He pushed my thighs to the floor, loomed over my exposed pussy, and spit downwards, before swooping in to lick me. His hot tongue worked right up my center, from ass to clit and back.

"Fuck, you taste good," he muttered against my skin, before pushing his long tongue as far inside me as it could go. I rose on my elbows and watched him. I couldn't take my eyes away. This was real. He was here, pinning me to the floor and eating me out like he hadn't decided whether to spare me or devour me.

Those fingers from before sank inside me, and he added a third. An involuntary cry left me.

"Are you fucking kidding me with this cunt?" he growled, almost sounding angry. "So tight, and so goddamn pretty."

I fell back and gazed at the ceiling, bursts of pleasure moving across my skin as he latched his lips around my clit and laved it, biting down on it, sucking it into his mouth. His fingers pumped in and out of me, curled just right to press the spongy spot on the front wall. I felt like I might pee myself. It had been so long, and after pregnancy and everything, maybe I'd lost all control down there. I gripped his head, trying to shift his insistent tongue, nearly scared of what would happen when I came.

"Try and move me again, and lose a finger," he warned and dove right back into driving me crazy.

I came with a strangled cry, his name spilling from my lips. I couldn't control my words. I was begging him, pleading with him, thanking him. I was a mess. He hummed approval against me as my thighs tightened around his head, locking his clever mouth in place. I soaked his face. Maybe even the floor below. The full feeling burst like an overfilled balloon, and I was locked in pleasure so long, I lost track of time. I couldn't see or hear. I could only feel. When I'd floated back down toward earth, little by little, I found Nikolai's gaze on me. His expression was unreadable. I was a mess. Wet, and splayed out on the floor. His face was wet, too, with my juices. I wanted to curl up and die on the spot. He ran his thumb over his lips and popped it in his mouth. I couldn't look away. His hand was bloody from where he'd gripped the blade of the knife.

"You're bleeding," I said quietly.

"I've been bleeding for seven years. Don't pretend to care. We've always made each other bleed, haven't we?"

He stroked my hair back from my sticky forehead, his tender touch at odds with his cold words.

"It's been my turn for seven years. Now, it's yours."

I WAS LATE FOR SCHOOL. I was lucky I had made it at all. After the fastest shower in the world, trying to scrub dirt and blood from my feet, I'd gotten dressed, looking over my shoulder the entire time. Now, pulling into the parking lot of Hade Harbor High, I saw I was too late to miss the student rush. I had also forgotten what day it was.

The lot was packed with demons, ghouls, and sexy vampires.

Halloween. It made a sick kind of sense, considering the nightmare my life had turned into overnight. Today students were free to dress up for school, and tomorrow night was the Halloween-themed dance.

Inching forward, I cursed my luck as the parking lot flooded with kids drifting purposelessly away from their cars. There was no way of getting to the staff lot without leaning on my horn, and it probably wouldn't do any good. These entitled little assholes at Hade Harbor High would move when they pleased. Something I'd learned about Maine in the last seven years was the pace was just different. It had been a steep learning curve for someone who'd gone to school in New York.

I took a deep breath, tried to halt my tapping foot, and waited.

Ahead of me, a girl drifted across the parking lot. The crowd was thinning out now, and she was daydreaming, lost in a biology book, by the looks of it. Lillian Williams. She had headphones dangling from a cord in one ear and was oblivious to the world around her.

A towering figure reached her and leaned over her shoulder, tugging the earbud free. She stopped and looked for who had stolen her music. She looked up, and then up some more. Cayden stared down at Lily like he couldn't tear his eyes away.

A horn blared behind me, and Cayden looked up. He fixed me with a look, clearly thinking I was the one who had beeped him, then he strode off.

I became dimly aware of the sound of the bell ringing through the cracked window.

Crap. I was late.

I hurried through my first class, feeling distracted and paranoid. When I had a free period, I sat at my desk and held my phone in my hand. I should call Angelo and tell him everything. At least someone would know what had happened when I went missing.

I couldn't overcome my reluctance. What if Nikolai hurt him? There didn't seem to be any lines he wouldn't cross now. I couldn't risk it.

Leo. The thought of my secret hung heavily over my head. Was Nikolai too far gone to be safe around anyone? What about his own son? I gnawed on my nails, a habit I thought I'd kicked a long time ago, but here it was.

As I stared at the phone, it chimed in my hand. A message from an unknown number.

> Happy Halloween, prom queen. Did you enjoy our game?

I DROPPED the phone like it had bitten me. I looked around the room. There wasn't anywhere to hide in here. He couldn't be here. He was just fucking with me. With shaking fingers, I picked up the cell.

> You're a fucking lunatic. Maybe I'll go to the police after all.

IT WAS ONLY a moment before he replied.

> No, you won't, and we both know it. Now, let's get down to it. What do you pick for me? Truth or dare?

I SWALLOWED HARD. He was right. I wouldn't go to the police. I couldn't even tell my brother, unless I wanted my father to find out, and then Leo's life would be in danger.

> Truth.

> Predictable, but fine. What do you want to know?

> Are you going to kill me?

THE QUESTION FLEW from my fingers before I could stop myself. He was typing for a while before his answer came.

> No, lastochka. I'll never kill you, you have my word.

MY CHEST LOOSENED at that revelation. How fucked up it was that I'd even had to ask that to the father of my child, and the only man I'd ever loved, I didn't want to think about. I was just setting my phone down when the last message came in.

> After all, a swift death is a great mercy.

15

NIKOLAI

I waited for Sofia in the back of her shitty car, in the parking lot of the high school. Lying on my back and staring at the cloudy sky, with cut-out blue patches, I waited contentedly for my prey to finish work. It was quiet, with only the faraway sounds of students running outside on the track to break the stillness. Lying there, comfortable, warm and free, knowing that soon, Sofia would be near me, I felt the closest to content I'd felt in seven years. When the bell rang, she arrived quickly. She was fidgety, searching over her shoulder as she hurried toward her car. She knew I was near, she could feel it, she just didn't know where.

She got in and locked the door without glancing in the back seat. Once the doors were locked, she looked out the window. I could see the line of tension in her shoulders.

"Looking for me?"

My voice sent a yelp from her, and she spun around just as I easily eased my body between the seats and into the passenger side.

She stared at me, her eyes round, mouth open with surprise. Her hand went for the door, just as I reached across her. This close, the scent of her light perfume and the addictive scent of her skin threatened to undo any kind of self-control I had around her.

"I wouldn't do that, if I were you. Buckle up, safety first."

"What are you doing? You're just stalking me now?"

"Stalking is a pedestrian word for what I'm planning for you." I put my own belt on and reached into my pocket to withdraw the butterfly knife that I'd picked up today.

Sofia stilled. "Are you threatening me?"

I tutted. "No. I'm reminding you that getting out of the car right now, calling for help, involving anyone else, won't end well for them, so I wouldn't risk it, if I were you."

I flicked the knife open, moving it between my fingers with ease. Sofia's gaze was riveted to the blade.

I smirked at her. "I'll let you play with it later. I know you like your knives."

She scowled at me and then turned her attention to her keys. She slid the key into the ignition and turned it. Nothing happened. A chuckle left me.

"This car is a real piece of shit, you know that? Antonio De Sanctis doesn't care about his only daughter riding around in this death trap."

"My father has nothing to do with my life."

"Clearly."

On the third attempt, her engine turned over, and she pulled out. The lot was packed, but no one looked in the car as she drove slowly through the crowd.

"Have you seen Kirill? I wonder what he'd think of what you're doing." She took a shot, and I appreciated the effort, but she clearly had no idea how my brother had wooed his wife.

"Not yet. He has children, you know. Two of them. I haven't met them. I can't be trusted around kids, or his wife, apparently."

"Why?" She seemed to turn even paler.

"I wasn't a good boy in jail. Chances are that Kirill thinks I'm too unhinged. Too violent."

"Is he right?"

I bared my teeth at her. It could have been a smile, but it wasn't. "What do you think?"

She tore her gaze from me and focused on the road. Her hands were clenched tightly on the wheel. "So, where are we going? I'm not taking you to my house."

"How rude. Your hostess skills really need work, prom queen. Turn right up here."

She shot me a look that was half worried, half pissed off, but followed my command. We drove through the little town she had settled in. The ring on her finger caught my attention, winking in the late afternoon sun.

"Are you married?" No one had come home to save her from me last night, so I thought it unlikely.

"No."

"Have you ever been?"

"No."

"You better not be lying, prom queen. I'll find out if you are. It would be easier for us both if you told the truth and gave me his name. Save me the trouble of hunting him down myself. I'll only be angrier then, and he won't go peacefully to the afterlife."

"You're crazy."

"Yes. I am," I stated flatly. "You wanted to speak last night… now's your chance. Tell me your excuses."

She hesitated. She was thinking so hard, I could practically hear it. It drove me crazy that she was full of secrets and I had no way to pry them out of her. If I couldn't threaten them out, or scare them out; I had no idea how to find out what had really happened in the past. Had her father threatened her? Had she just decided to make a clean break from all the devilish men in her life, and my name was on the list? Had she stopped loving me? Had she ever really loved me in the first place?

She was silent so long, I knew I wouldn't get my answers right now.

"You've nothing to say? Last night you seemed desperate to speak… changed your mind after that little game in the woods?"

She stayed mulishly silent. If I knew Sofia at all, and I did, I knew she could be stubborn as fuck. It used to be endearing. Now I wanted to strangle her.

"Pull over here," I instructed.

She did, turning on her blinker. We stopped just off the road.

I stared straight ahead, flipping my butterfly knife around in my hand, playing with it. She watched me, her body rigid with tension.

"Now's your chance. I won't stop you." I nodded to the squat, one-story building across the street.

Cop cars were parked outside the precinct, and a few boys in blue were hanging out on the front steps, talking.

Sofia followed my gaze. She stared at the police station, wetting her lips.

"I don't see you moving," I pointed out after a moment.

"Why are you doing this? Is it a test?" She turned to look at me. My clever little swallow always knew me better than anyone. "You want to see if I could really turn you in?"

"Maybe. Maybe I want to realize what it means if you don't get out of the car right now and walk in there and tell the first officer you see that a man held you at knifepoint in your car, and he's still outside."

Sofia turned to me. Her insightful eyes latched on to mine. In the afternoon light, they looked lighter than usual, flecked with dark green. "You really trust me not to, don't you?"

"Trust is a strong word, after what you've done. Really, I just don't care. Jail, free… they've all become much the same."

Her eyes looked sad. "You buried me in a coffin in the woods the other night."

"I'm aware. You deserved it. You're supposed to be dead. Waking up in a box is the least you could do. You want to tell me why yet? You got the sob story worked out?"

For a second, I thought she was about to share. Maybe she'd cry and explain. Maybe she'd lie again or be brutally honest.

Instead, she simply raised her chin and held her tongue. She was a locked box of secrets, and I could torture the truth out, but that wouldn't be any fun.

"You never know, prom queen. Maybe I'll forgive you."

"You're not exactly known for your mercy."

If Sofia was really planning on turning me in for stalking her, I might as well find out now, seeing as there was no way I was stopping. If I couldn't have her, I might as well be in jail.

"Tell me your sorry excuses for abandoning me, or walk into that station and make sure I can't haunt you forever, because those are your only options."

Her gaze never broke mine. Her hands were curled in tight little fists. I could feel her secrets, hidden behind high walls that I was no longer permitted to see behind. I was on the outside, and no amount of attacking the gates was going to get me in. Frustration mounted inside me, making that bloodthirsty beast of madness gnash its teeth. I wasn't a patient man, and Sofia was testing every single ounce of it I had. I wanted her story, as sorry and inadequate as it would be. I needed it, and for some reason, she didn't want to tell me. That could only mean the truth was the worst possible reason. The one we couldn't come back from.

That she didn't love me, like I loved her, and she never had. My fury clouded my gaze, making my body hard and the urge to do violence simmer below my skin.

"Fine. If you don't want to use that beautiful, lying mouth to talk, use it for something else."

Her eyes widened. "Meaning?"

"So, now she talks? Meaning… I gave you the chance to call the cops. I gave you the chance to hurt me, and I've given you the chance to plead your case… if you don't want to do any of them, then you can at least clean up the mess you made this morning."

She blushed hard. It was a startling thing to see that she could still be so achingly sweet at times. I lowered a hand to my belt and undid it, losing the seat belt and shifting my hips forward so I had a modicum of space.

"I can still taste your cunt from this morning and the way you came all over my face. My days of jerking off are behind me, and you've left me with a cock so hard, it could put someone's eye out. Fair's fair, isn't it? Your turn, then my turn. Will you keep playing with me? Or will you walk into that station and never have to see me again?"

It was a powerful bluff. She could easily call me on it. What she didn't understand was how little I had to lose. I wanted to see how far I could push her. I wanted to see if she really feared for her life in my hands, or if somehow, just like I trusted her, a part of her still knew that I'd put her life over my own, every single time. It was just the way I was wired. I knew no other way.

I slid a hand into my jeans. Fuck, I was so hard it hurt. I wanted her touch like I'd never wanted anything. I wanted her to fight herself and lose. I wanted her to understand that I wasn't the only fucked-up one.

I pulled my cock out. It was leaking from the top, desperate for her touch. The cool air in the car blew over my skin. That chaos in my chest stilled again when Sofia looked down, her gaze landing right on my dick. She wet her lips. An involuntary movement, and utterly soul-destroying.

"Hurry up, before one of those cops come and check out why we're stopped here."

A look of panic chased across her face, closely followed by determination. There she was, my stubborn girl. Slowly, she reached out a hand toward me.

"Take me all the way out, *lastochka*." My voice had dropped to a gravel tone. My throat was dry, awaiting her touch.

Her hand made contact with my cock, and it jerked sensitively under her touch. She seemed fascinated by the response. After a second, she moved again, this time more purposefully, taking me firmly in her fist and pulling me out of my tight jeans. It was difficult. I was so hard, it was unwieldy. She muttered a curse, and I watched her, turned on and amused at the same time.

When I was fully free, all nine inches jutting proudly up, she wrapped her hand around as far as she could and slowly pumped. It felt indescribable.

"Make it nice and wet." My voice was a hoarse grunt.

She leaned over me, and in a move that I'd never forget, dribbled a long line of spit over her fist and the head of me. It was hot as hell.

"Fuck. Are you trying to kill me?" I growled, grabbing her chin as her hand spread her spit around, heightening the sensation of her lazy pumps.

I tilted her face toward me as her hand continued its motion. She looked so beautiful. Her pupils were blown, like she was the one lost in lust, not me. Her lips were slightly parted, and I slid my thumb between them. I ran my other hand through the silky chopped ends of her hair.

"I like this. It makes you look so innocent. Not like someone who could gut a man and walk away without a glance."

She turned her face into my palm as I freed her mouth, her hand tugging on my dick the entire time. Fuck, maybe I could come just like this, her face filling my vision, her hand on me.

"You're running out of time, before we get a boy in blue knocking on the window."

My reminder sent pink to her flushed cheeks. She turned to look down at my cock and leaned forward. She licked the tip, toying with me, just as I gathered her short hair into a handful that I could tug.

"Let me remind you how it's done. Open up wide." I guided her mouth down on me.

I was big, and thick. I knew it was a lot to handle, but Sofia tried like a champ. My cock met the back of her throat, and she gagged softly. I brought both hands to her head and moved her up and down, a few careful bobs to make sure she was as stretched out and ready to take me as she could be. Then I tightened my hand on her hair and held her head in place. My hips rose, and I pushed right to the back of her throat, then out. She moaned around my cock as I set a rhythm of fucking her mouth, holding her pinned in place.

I lost track of time, but it couldn't have been long, since my body was so on edge. Her hot breath against my skin and her clever tongue swirling around my tip was too damn much. I pulled her down as far as she could go and spilled down her throat. Jet after jet of cum left me. It felt like my soul was disappearing down her perfect throat as she swallowed around me.

I smoothed her hair back when the pulsing finally ebbed and let her up. She pulled back, gasping for breath, her face red and eyes wet. I swiped the cum from the edge of her mouth, rubbing it over her lips like gloss.

"How can such beauty hide such cruelty?" I wondered aloud and then laughed softly. "Someone once said that about me, too."

I could still remember that guy, a priest nonetheless. The good father had been using his position in the church to start a little indecent video company, using the unpaid talents of the drugged-up kids who came to Sunday school. He'd also owed the bratva a hefty sum from gambling debts. I'd been told to get the money out of him; instead, I'd cut off all his fingers and toes, and then his tongue, before sending him to Hell. Viktor had been displeased.

"You're the cruel one. What are you going to do to me?" Her voice was still strong.

"Whatever I want. That's something you have to accept, if you don't get out the car right now and go into the station."

She blinked at me hard, and a tear escaped her already wet, sooty eyes. "You're so sure I won't. Why?"

She swallowed hard. I wondered if her throat hurt.

"Because, I know you. Despite the time apart, I still know how your brain works." It was the very reason why it was hard to square away her fake death and her stubborn silence. It didn't feel like Sofia. It was half the picture, and she wasn't telling me the rest.

"Haven't you thought that maybe you don't know me anymore? It's been years."

"Years, decades, lifetimes… between you and me, it doesn't matter. Time has no meaning. I'll always know you."

She dashed away that stray tear, the one sign that this cost her as much as me. "You're wrong," she said simply, and just like that, opened the door and got out.

I watched her cross the street and walk right into the police station.

16

SOFIA

I stared at the early morning sun tracking across the ceiling of the motel room I'd stayed in last night. Yesterday, things between me and Nikolai had threatened to spin out of control. So, I'd done the only thing I could think of. Called his bluff. I'd gone into the station and went to visit a friend who worked in records. After endless small talk, I'd left out of the back exit and made my way in a taxi to Chiara and Angelo's house, before changing my mind and going to a motel.

I had battled with myself all night whether to tell them what was going on. In the end, I couldn't risk it. Nikolai was unpredictable and dangerous. I couldn't put them in danger for me. I felt like I was going crazy. He wanted the truth. He thought he was prepared for it. Neither of us were. His words from the night before played in my head on an endless loop.

"Kirill has children, you know. Two of them. I haven't met them. I can't be trusted around kids, or his wife, apparently." And that was his own brother. What would he do when he knew

what I'd hidden? How would he react? I was fairly sure he wouldn't actually kill me, but then again, I'd never seen him so provoked. Fear had made me hold my tongue. It was the truth that I was too scared to share. The killing blow.

I got up, feeling exhausted, and checked out, heading to school in the same clothes as yesterday.

School felt endless. I was jumpy. Every creak in a quiet room or footstep echoing in an empty hall had me spinning around, ready to run. Finally, it was over. I called Chiara before visiting hours at the hospital.

I'd drawn the short straw and was chaperoning at the dance tonight. The setup was intricate. Hade Harbor High took their seasonal events seriously, and I was already late, but I had to check who was hanging out with Leo tonight. Thankfully, both Angelo and Chiara were going over to St. Mary's for the entirety of the visiting hours, so I could do my duty at the dance. Luckily, I had my costume for the dance already hanging in my classroom.

"Seriously, it's cool. I'm looking forward to hanging out with my little lion." Chiara voice was comforting. "I have a present for him anyway."

I groaned. "He doesn't need anything. You spoil him."

"Well, he's my godson. Who else am I going to spend all my money on? I'd like to spoil you, too, but you won't let me," Chiara complained.

"I'm an adult. I don't need spoiling."

"That is precisely where you're wrong. Everyone needs spoiling sometimes. Anyway, I have to go inside. I'll talk to you later!"

The thought of not seeing Leo for even one night made my heart ache, but with Nikolai breathing down my neck, it was only a matter of time until he found out about him. The very idea terrified me. I had longed for it for such a long time, to be free of the guilt I carried. But the truth remained that my father was determined to destroy us, even if Nikolai could forgive me for hiding Leo from him. It felt like I was stuck in a rat's maze, scuttling this way and that, only to find every exit blocked off before I could reach the end. Now, the idea made me want to grab Leo and escape at night on a bus heading across the country. I had my fake documents that Renato had given me. We could just run.

Even as I thought it, I knew it wouldn't work. Now that he knew I was alive, Nikolai would only find me, and I'd be somewhere new and alone. He'd never stop. Not only that, but finding a donor for Leo meant staying, no matter what.

A few hours later, the school was bustling. The music from the gym blared out of open windows as I wandered around, keeping an eye on the students as they danced. The entire school had been festooned with spooky decorations, and the lights were low. I passed a display of severed heads on an altar. It was genuinely creepy. Maybe it was less the decorations and the fact that there was a homicidal maniac stalking me that had my nerves on high alert.

Students were everywhere. Their costumes ranged from the truly gruesome to the absolutely scandalous. My own outfit was lame at best, considering I hadn't thought about it until a couple of days ago and grabbed the first thing I could find. A party dress, my old prom queen sash, and a little red food coloring dripping from my mouth, with a pair of glow-in-the-dark vampire teeth I'd found in Leo's toy box.

The atmosphere in the gym was relaxed now, and the initial awkwardness of the beginning of the dance had passed. Plenty of students were dancing with abandon and having the time of their lives. The last dance I'd been to like this had been prom. Just the thought brought Nikolai to my mind.

"Miss Rossi, a dance?" Marcus appeared in front of me.

The Ice Gods didn't usually go for school dances, and they were drawing plenty of longing stares. They had made about as much effort as I expected of them. They were dressed in their hockey uniforms and blood-flecked goalie masks, Jason Voorhees-style.

"We both know the answer to that."

"Worth a shot. Here, some guy gave me this to give to you."

Marcus held out a note. My blood turned cold in my veins.

"Who gave it to you?"

"Some guy with a sick mask on. Why?" Marcus looked over his shoulder toward the gym's entrance. "Is he a weirdo or something?"

Or something.

"It's fine. Enjoy the dance."

With shaking fingers, I opened the note.

For tonight's game, hide-and-seek. Your dare, prom queen, is to find who I'm hiding, before she's never seen again. Hurry up, Cici's waiting.

CICI? *Chiara.* Nikolai had Chiara hidden somewhere. Would he hurt her? I couldn't wait around to find out. I headed out of the gym, urgency building in my chest as I groped for my phone and shakily pulled up Chiara's number. I clamped the phone to my ear as her line rang and rang. I headed away from the busiest area around the gym. Where would he take her? Somewhere quiet, where she wouldn't be found.

My art room? It was worth a try. The sound of my heels echoed through the corridors. As I went, the number of stragglers from the party reduced, until I was striding up dark corridors alone. Chiara still wasn't picking up.

I switched to Angelo. His phone went straight to voicemail.

I shoved my hand in my mouth to muffle a cry of frustration. I couldn't afford to be noisy. Obviously, Nikolai was expecting me, but I didn't need to make it easy for him.

I slipped my heels off and left them by a locker. Reaching back into my bag, I closed my hand around my *liccasapuni*, my *paranza corta* knife. I'd barely thought about the blade in years, and had found it stashed in the glove box of my car. Now, it felt like my only lifeline.

I made it to the bottom of the stairs to the next floor. Glancing over my shoulder, I froze. A figure stood at the other end of the corridor. He was dressed in black and wore a mask that was vaguely reminiscent of a skull, but black and neon, with Xs for eyes.

Nikolai?

I put a foot on the first step, and the man started toward me. He didn't move like Nikolai.

I ran up the stairs. Once I reached the upper floor, I spun in the direction of the art classrooms. So much for being quiet. He was already following me.

I sprinted on silent feet along the hall, not daring to look back. The realization that I was running around my place of work wielding a knife registered dimly, but I couldn't care about that right now, not when Chiara was in danger. I approached the art room and slowed, peeking through the circular glass window at the top of the door.

It wasn't that dark inside. The desk light was on, and a figure dressed in black sat at my desk. The same neon mask sat over his face.

How had Nikolai beat me here?

I couldn't see Chiara anywhere in the room. This couldn't be where he was keeping her. I was still stretching up to peek in the window when my phone rang in my hand. I got such a fright, I nearly dropped it.

I answered, raising it to my ear with trepidation.

"You called?"

"Chiara?" I croaked.

"Yes, bitch, who else did you think you called ten times? My ringer's off. We're at the hospital, remember?"

"You are?"

"We are. You want to speak to the little lion?"

Her question came just as the figure at the desk inside my classroom turned its terrifying mask my way. I felt the moment his eyes connected with mine.

I backed away from the door. He'd just been trying to get me isolated, and like a fucking idiot, I'd fallen for it.

My back came up against something hard. I froze as hands closed on my hips. It was a person, standing flush against me.

"Boo."

I whirled around, my knife rising as I registered that the person standing in the neon mask in the hall behind me couldn't be the same person sitting at my desk inside my class.

My hand holding the knife made contact with the mask, turning the man's head sharply to the side as the metal glanced off the hard plastic.

I didn't wait around to see if it was Nikolai or not. All reason had left my head at this point, and I was in survival mode. In this case, survival meant getting back to a highly populated area. I was running before masked man number one recovered.

I sprinted to the end of the art wing corridor and nearly fell down the stairs that led to the science wing. The sound of footsteps in hot pursuit pounded through the stillness.

I got to the bottom of the stairs. There, the corridor split in two directions. One was the science classes, and eventually, the way back to the gym and safety. The other way was toward the shop classes, an area I didn't know well. I knew it was the opposite direction from the gym, however, with a side door that led toward the woods. I took two steps toward the direction of the gym, people and safety, just as a figure strolled into view at the end of the hall.

It was one of the men; which one, I had no idea. He ambled toward me, his black-gloved hand trailing over the lockers. He was whistling a tune. *Run rabbit, run rabbit, run, run, run.*

The sound of the pursuing footsteps had stopped. I turned slowly, looking up the stairs. On the top one, only thirty feet away, the other man was sitting in an easy crouch, his mask tilted to the side.

I backed away. I had no options left. I turned on my bare heel and made for the shop classes, and that door to the woods.

I made it as far as the last classroom, when the small side door at the end of the corridor was nearly within reach, before someone caught up with me. His hand went around my mouth at the same time as his hard arm clamped across my stomach. Then, we were moving backward.

It was Nikolai, I could tell. It was the way his strong hands held me effortlessly but didn't hurt. It was the scent of him. Like coming home after being lost for years. Was there a twisted sense of relief in that? Yes, as fucked up as it was, I'd prefer the devil I knew. Who the hell was working with him to terrorize me, I had no idea, and didn't want to know. Having one psychopath in my life was already too many.

"Shh, prom queen. Stop squirming so much, it's making me want to chase you down again."

I stilled, trying to drag air into my lungs from behind his glove.

The door to the classroom closed behind us, as I struggled against him. He allowed me to twist in his arms before backing me into the edge of hard table. I hated his mask. It was even scarier when I couldn't see anything familiar about him.

"Did you find your friend?"

His mocking tone sent anger through my panic. He was reducing me to an animal, mindless in my fear, while he was just playing with me.

He released my mouth.

"You're absolutely mad. How did they ever let you out? Does your brother know how unhinged you are? You're a menace to society," I spit at him, a rapid torrent of anger and fear escaping me with my first free breath.

He simply chuckled. "And yet you only pretended to turn me in yesterday, didn't you? I suppose a saner man would just kill you, and Angelo and Chiara, and be done with it. In my world, a betrayal like yours demands an answer. What answer would you like?"

Something inside me snapped. I couldn't keep quiet while he leveled that kind of charge at me, when losing him had cost me everything.

"I didn't betray you. I didn't want to," I started and stilled quickly. Nikolai had pressed a gloved finger against my lips, shushing me.

"Wait, I've heard this one before. Let me guess? Did Daddy threaten you if you didn't pretend to be dead? Or wait, maybe he threatened me in prison... am I warm?"

I didn't know what to say to that. The truth was a lot more damning. I'd lied to protect Leo. I didn't know how Nikolai would react to knowing he had a son, and I'd hidden him.

Those freaky X eyes stared into my soul. "Did he threaten me, and you thought it would be safer to play dead than anger daddy dearest?"

He wasn't completely wrong. He just didn't know about Leo. I couldn't tell him. He was too frightening right now. Still, I could be honest about one thing.

"Was it a crime to not want you to die? Was it a betrayal to care that you lived, even without me?"

Nikolai was still. Tension rose between us. I wanted to see his eyes. I reached for his mask, and he tutted, shaking his head. He wasn't holding my arms, his hands were just braced on either side of the desk behind us, bending me back, making me arch my spine into him. His hips had pinned me in place, and I could feel the weight of him against my center.

I shivered. I could feel his belt buckle and something else. Was he hard? The thought-twisted as it was right now, considering how he'd just chased me through the school-made me feel hot all over. It had been so long, and the only touch I'd ever known was this man's. My body was trained to respond to the smell of him.

"The crime, Sofia, was believing in your father's empty threats, over me. You chose him and let him dictate both our lives. You didn't choose me. You didn't believe in me. That's your betrayal, *lastochka*."

"He meant it—"

"I don't care!"

Nikolai's sudden roar stole my voice. I'd never heard him so angry. It wasn't just anger. It was hurt and that was much, much worse. That piece of me that had been breaking since he'd found me cracked again. It was my resolve to hold out against him. His threats couldn't break it. His terrifying games couldn't dent it. But his vulnerability? His hurt, shown so plainly? That nearly made me lose my head completely.

He leaned his forehead against mine. The mask felt hard and wrong. I wanted to feel the heat of his skin.

"I don't care what excuses you let yourself believe to assuage your conscience. The truth is that once your little cage was blown open... you couldn't wait to leave me behind. Say it."

I shook my head, sudden tears building behind my eyes. He really thought that? It was heartbreaking. In his eyes, I was a real villain.

"You're wrong."

"You never cared about me, you just pretended to... you were playing the long game, and I was the fool who never even suspected it. Isn't that the truth?"

I shook my head. "No."

He wasn't listening. "I lost everything when I found out you were gone. Since that moment, I've not known a moment of peace…" He shuddered slightly and pulled back. "And now, neither will you. It's only fair."

He stepped back, the moment of quiet between us slipping away. He looked down at my knife, clutched uselessly in my hand. It was the hand with my tattoo. My bird in the cage. He seemed to still and then slowly reached for it, holding my wrist for his inspection. In all our tussles so far, between darkness, long sleeves, and his distracted mind, he hadn't noticed it until now.

He rubbed a finger across it, back and forth, his masked head tilting slightly to the side as he considered it. All the things we hadn't said to each other seemed to build at that second, and I wanted to confess it all in a long rush. About Antonio, and Leo, and how I'd missed him. About the guilt I felt, and how seeing him again felt right in a way I had given up hoping for, even if he was scaring me. I deserved his punishment. Maybe it could heal the pain and guilt of hiding Leo for so long. Maybe it was the only thing that could. Before I could speak and spill my guts to him, he shook his head, a subtle shake, like he was pushing away the soft, vulnerable moment that seeing the tattoo etched on my wrist had triggered.

"Enough sharing circle time. New game. Tag. I'm it. If you get caught, you get fucked." He stepped back, giving me space to move around him.

Fear and heat shot through me, making my blood pound even harder than before.

"If catch you, I won't be gentle. I've been in jail for seven years, *lastochka*. I've forgotten everything I ever knew about being gentle." He jerked his head toward the door. "Run fast, unless you want that."

I still couldn't move. Words I didn't know how to say crowded my head, until Nikolai lunged toward me.

"Go!"

Finally, my brain snapped back to reality, and I listened.

I went.

17

NIKOLAI

I used her head start to try to drag some sanity back into my mind. The dark possession that filled me when I was within arm's reach of Sofia fogged my thoughts. I wanted to hold her. I wanted to strangle her. I wanted to eat her alive. Most of all, I wanted to bury myself so deep inside her, fill her up with my cum so full, she'd never get me out.

Yesterday had given me the answer I was so desperate for. Sofia might fight me and lie to me. She might keep her secrets from me. But she wouldn't run from me and she wouldn't send me back to jail.

That meant, in my world, she wanted to play. I'd oblige her.

I prowled the classroom, holding myself back just long enough. I was a fair sportsman after all. I hadn't been exaggerating. Once I found her, I was going to fuck her until she screamed. If she really thought she could evade me, it would only make it more delicious when I caught her.

I gave her a good sixty seconds before I started after her.

I'd already dismissed Bran. He'd hit it off with some teacher and wanted to go and flirt with her some more. He was useful for herding Sofia in the right direction, and of course, terrifying her, but now I needed him gone. No one would get to see Sofia bare and begging except me.

The back of the school opened out into dense woods. They were the ones I'd already chased her through a few days ago, when she'd run right into the arms of the ice hockey players who had been sneaking off school grounds. One of them had been overly interested in my little *lastochka*. He might need to play a little one on one, with his head as the puck, to understand. No one touched Sofia, Ms. Rossi, or whatever it was she was called here. No one except me.

I entered the woods. It was quiet, but there was a slight rustle straight ahead.

Sticking to the path, prom queen? It was like she wanted to get caught.

The smell of the woods filled my head, comforting and new at the same time. It wasn't the same scent as the woods of my childhood. The underlying salt of the nearby ocean and the different plants and even the soil all made things a little different. I caught a glimpse of her in her shiny, pale-pink dress. I discarded my mask, sick of the way it fogged up my breath. I wanted to feel the forest air on my skin.

Sofia was different, too. The woman running ahead of me wasn't the same one who'd run from me seven long years ago. The first time she'd run through the woods from me, my little insurance policy, trying to get away and be a good girl for her daddy, I had only felt want for her, not anger.

Sure, she'd allowed her father to enter into talks of an arranged marriage with my brother, but we'd both known there was no chance of it happening. That was the only thing I could possibly have been angry at her for. I wasn't angry at her for scarring my face when we were both younger, or for running away when she was supposed to be my insurance. I wasn't even mad at her for slipping that fateful message to the trucker who had brought the De Sanctis family down on us, and started my long incarceration in Casa Nera, and then, as fate would have it, prison.

None of that mattered now. None of it compared to the white-hot anger her betrayal had bred. She'd broken not only my heart but my mind.

She zigzagged through the trees ahead of me on the trail. I could catch her easily, but it seemed wise to run off a little of my energy, and hers. I wanted her panting and spent when I finally ran her down. I wanted her to tremble.

The truths were too hard to swallow, but seeing her alive, unharmed, smiling with her students, driving to work, living her little life, had forced them down my throat.

She rounded a bend and disappeared. I charged after her. Once around the bend, I slid to a stop. The trail before me was empty, when it shouldn't be. She'd veered off the path.

"Sofia? *Lastochka*, I told you to run, not hide, you had better odds that way," I called to the dark woods around us. It was too damn dark to follow her trail.

Instead, I closed my eyes and focused on the sounds of the forest and the smell of Sofia. I could make out her perfume in the air, faint as it was. It was a scent I'd dreamed about every single night for seven years. I'd never forget it. She hadn't changed it, I was relieved to find out. Breathing deeply, pulling her scent into my lungs, I listened.

There was a faint rustling to the left, something small and uncaring about human presence. An animal of some kind. In the other direction, there was a slower, more careful sound, like someone trying very hard not to be heard.

I lunged to the right, startling Sofia into crying out. My body slammed into hers just as she attempted to stand, and we both tipped to the pine-needled ground.

"Got you, little swallow," I breathed against her temple as I wrestled her writhing body onto her back.

She arched her chest forward as I grabbed her hands and pulled them above her head. Straddling her thighs, I felt alive in a way I hadn't in years. Maybe it was the chase, maybe it was just her, but my blood was pounding in my veins, and that odd sense of unreality felt better here. Everything felt more real again, just touching the woman pinned beneath me.

Like always, when it came to Sofia, she was the poison and the cure.

"Niko," she breathed, just as one of my hands fell to her neck, so prettily framed by her new hair.

I surrounded it with my palm, pressing firmly in, restricting her breathing a little, so her eyes grew wide. Those dark-brown orbs never left me. I released her hands just long enough to pull a tie from my pocket.

I bound her hands before she could realize my intention.

"Why are you doing this? If you want to hurt me, just hurt me, don't play all these games."

"If you knew how I felt inside, you wouldn't say that," I warned her.

She swallowed hard. She wasn't fighting me. Why wasn't she fighting me?

"I'm already holding back," I muttered. The dizzying fun house inside me came screeching to a halt when she spoke.

"Stop then. Don't hold back."

Her soft murmur crept under my skin. The silence inside me was deafening. She had surprised me. I wouldn't have thought that was possible anymore, given the level of fucked up my head was at these days, but she had.

"Do what you want. I won't fight you."

I looked down at her, my perfect, precious little swallow. She should be scared. She should be beaten. She wasn't, though. Even lying on the forest floor, her fine dress rumpled, her hair wild, hands bound over her head, she wasn't. She met my eyes with unflinching strength.

"Do your worst. That's what you've always done. I can take it." She wet her lips, and the movement nearly undid me. "I deserve it, after all."

A bitter chuckle left me as I reached for her knife, which she'd carelessly dropped next to her on the dirt.

"If you think that hint of self-awareness will get you mercy..." I started.

"I don't. I don't want mercy from you. We've always been honest with each other, haven't we? I broke that promise. Punish me."

She continued to stare at me, uncowed by my threats. The silence inside me continued. For the first time in seven years, the chaos was quiet. Because of her.

"You'll regret asking for that, prom queen. I'm not the man you knew."

"I already regret so much, what's one more thing?" She arched her back, and her tits threatened to pop out of the satin neckline of her gown.

I lowered my hand to her chest, sliding it down in that valley. She still had perfect tits.

My hands moved to her ribs, and I tugged her bra down with one swift pull. She arched her back into me again as my hands brushed over her tits.

I pinched her nipples softly, and she gave a soft moan.

"Don't." My warning was like a whip. Her eyes flew to mine.

"Don't, or I'll gag you." I couldn't take the sound of her sweet pleasure.

I knew my control was ragged at best. It had been seven years of nothing but my hand and memories of this woman. The blow job the other day had only further loosened my self-control, which was already a tattered thing. One more rip, and it would fall to pieces.

I moved her knife to the edge of her dress, and her eyes widened. The moonlight caught on the blade as I cut. The thin material parted under the sharp edge of the knife as well. She was still as I cut the top of her dress, barely daring to breathe, it seemed. The sash I worked down to her waist. I had no idea she still owned that damn thing. I'd never forget the first time I'd seen her in it. It felt like it had all happened in another life.

I spread open the sides of her dress and let my eyes feast on her chest. Her skin looked darker in the dim light and from her coastal lifestyle. I wondered if she went to the beach often. I wondered if she went with other men. Men like Edward Sloane. I'd nearly jumped the fence when they'd had lunch together the other day and slit his throat right there at the table. I had managed not to, but that didn't mean I was going to let him live. He coveted what was mine. His days were numbered.

Dark possession filled my chest as I lowered the knife to her sternum. She was so still, I imagined I could hear her heart pounding. I could certainly hear my own.

"Are you scared, *lastochka*? Between us, you're still the only one who's ever cut me in anger." I trailed the knife down her chest, between her glorious breasts, and slid it beneath the lacey fastening of her bra. It opened in the front. How fun.

The knife cut hard through the fastening, until the bra sagged apart. Her dark eyes glittered up at me. Running the blade across one perfect slope, I reached her nipple. I could feel her fear. It was delicious. Still, she didn't try to push me away or beg me to stop. She was resigned to her fate. Maybe I was simply living up to her expectations of me. I didn't care. I was too far gone to care.

"Are you scared I'm going to cut you? Or touch you?" I wondered aloud, undecided as to which. "Maybe my touch was always abhorrent to you, even more than a cut, but you needed me to get away from your father." The thought had plagued me since I'd found out she was alive.

She frowned, a delicate line running between her elegant eyebrows. She shook her head, her eyes fixed on me. Disagreement. It stirred something in me.

"You're still the only man I've ever been with. The only man I've ever wanted to be with."

Her soft words felt like claws, sinking into unprotected skin. I stared at her. That damn storm that lived in my chest only calmed further at her words. The beast was satisfied with its possession of this woman. The only one I'd ever wanted.

I set the knife aside and leaned forward, unable to wait one more second to taste her.

My mouth closed around her hard nipple, already proudly sitting upright like a little rosebud in the cool night air. I sucked it between my teeth and rolled it against my hot, wet tongue. She shivered; her skin prickled beneath my hands. I gripped her other tit with my fist, hefting it, squeezing it, thumbing the nipple, while I feasted with my mouth. Moving higher, I sucked a dark bruising love kiss against her collarbone, and then another, a chain of them.

"Have fun covering these up for school, let those fuckers with hard-ons and lingering eyes know… your owner has returned," I murmured against her skin, dragging my stubbled mouth back and forth, then landing on her other tit.

She moaned, a sweet sound, and I clamped a hand over her lips.

I moved my hands to my jeans and pulled myself free, my cock angry with pent-up desire. It nearly hurt when I pumped my palm up and down, the dry friction burning. I didn't mind the pain. I welcomed it. My life had given me nothing but pain, and it had become my most faithful companion.

It had never deserted me, unlike the stunning woman moaning beneath me.

I pulled one of her nipples between my teeth and lightly bit down. She gasped, her hips desperately bumping upward to meet mine. Sofia wanted to be fucked like this, tied up and gagged on the forest floor… by me.

I didn't know how that made me feel, only that this was supposed to be the start of her punishment, not fun.

I bit harder around her nipple, nipping the sensitive skin, and moved my hand faster on my cock. Releasing her tit with a pop, I let my other hand fall away and leaned back. She made a beautiful sight, lying on the ground, hands bound, her bare chest red and well-sucked, nipples puffy and desperate for more. Leaning up on my knees, I pushed her dress up until her black lace panties were on full display. Reaching out a finger, I stroked it down her middle.

She was soaking wet.

"You're sodden for me, prom queen? You want me that badly?"

She stared at me, unabashed. Then she nodded.

"You want the man who contemplated burying you alive last night?"

She took a shuddering breath. "I'm just being honest."

"How novel for you."

I reached for her panties, using the knife again.

I felt my release barreling down on me, just at the very sight of her eyes on my cock. She didn't look nearly scared enough. Something about the want in her eyes undid me. I shouldn't have seen it. I should have blindfolded her, too, but as it was, I couldn't avoid it.

I tore off her panties and cast them aside. Prowling across her, it hurt how much I needed to be inside her. I pressed her legs apart, pushing roughly between the cradle of her thighs. My cock brushed against her wet heat. I slipped my hands beneath her hips, raising her just enough to press inside. I wasn't gentle. I gave her no escape. Maybe my roughness would make her push me away. Or maybe she would change her mind about wanting me.

She did neither. My deceitful little prom queen opened her arms and pulled me closer. Her surrender threatened the remaining shred of my sanity. She clung to me, brought her hips up to meet my ruthless thrusts, matching my desire at every turn. Her hands pulled at me, her lips pressed against my neck and up my throat, scattering kisses along my jaw. If she was trying to undo me, it was working.

I was going to come, I couldn't last. Not when she was kissing me so sweetly, apologizing in tiny, silent ways with every move. She was still my little swallow, and now, she sat in the palm of my hand, waiting for me to crush her, if I wanted.

I didn't want to. I never had. I could only ever love her. I didn't know how to do anything else.

The pace increased between us, and the wet slap of our bodies meeting sounded obscene in the night air. There was something primal about fucking her there on the forest floor, against the dried leaves and pine needles. There, in the woods, where I'd always found comfort, I found her again. My *lastochka*, welcoming me with open arms, no matter the pieces we'd torn from each other.

She cried out first, her pussy clamping tightly around my cock, her entire body clenching. I kissed her roughly through it, swallowing the sounds of her pleasure. I wanted it all for myself. I needed it. She came endlessly, tightening with pulses and flutters so strong, it sent me over the edge. Following her, I came with a silent growl, stuffing my cock as deep as I could inside her, streaking her insides with my cum, filling her right up. She brought a hand to my cheek, pressing a sweet kiss to my forehead. A flash on her finger forced my brain back to life. She never had explained it.

"Whose fucking ring are you wearing while your tight, needy pussy sucks up my cum?" My voice was harsh. I was surprised I could speak through the orgasm I'd just had. After seven years of denying myself, I was surprised I could do anything at all.

Her cheeks flushed. "I don't want to be hit on."

"It's just a disguise, then?" My cum was welling out of her hole. I watched it, fascinated. It felt wrong to see it seeping out. My dick was still hard. It would probably take a year of fucking her to take the edge off and make up for lost time. I had no problem with that, but Sofia might. Too bad she didn't have a choice. "You still think I can't tell when you're lying, prom queen?" I pushed myself back inside her, my hard cock gliding through the cum inside her cunt.

She gasped. Her pussy was still twitching inside.

"I'm not lying."

I pulled out after a few thrusts and slid to the side. A little rearrangement, and I had my wet dick poised at her mouth.

"There was a time I would have believed that." I rubbed the dripping tip of myself against her lips until they were shiny with both our juices. "Now, I can't trust this mouth more than this. Lick me clean."

I gripped her chin with firm fingers. She held my eyes with hers as she slowly opened her lips and licked the head of me, before taking me inside the hot cavern of her mouth. Fuck. It felt unbelievable to be touched by her. A woman who had been my obsession since the first night we'd met, when she was a sheltered Mafia princess, all of seventeen. As she polished my dick with her tongue, I realized I could come again. I leaned forward, trapping her head and forcing my cock further inside. She welcomed me in, her eyes on me, widening her jaw as far as could to take me. Skull-fucking her into the forest floor hadn't been the plan, but she was sucking me off so well, I couldn't hold back. I fucked her face, my tip hitting the back of her throat. She had nowhere to go. The sound of her soft gagging nearly undid me.

I pressed deep and let her work me with her tongue. She quickly tipped me over the edge with her eager sucking. I pulled out, wanting to see visible evidence of my possession of her. Kneeling over her prone body, I came hard, long ribbons of cum striping her bare tits, all the way up her neck. One particularly urgent jet hit her chin, dripping across her parted lips. I came for a long time, the pulsing of my balls feeling endless as I marked her with my cum.

If the sight of her before had been hot, the image of her covered in my cum, her tits shiny with my possession, seared itself permanently in my brain.

I stood on legs that were none too steady and tucked my half-spent cock away. I stepped away from her and collected myself. The knife was still on the ground beside her, and I kicked it closer to her now. I crouched beside her. She was watching me with an unreadable look.

I couldn't stop myself from smoothing the backs of my fingers down her smooth cheek.

"You didn't go to the cops. It was your last chance."

She nodded. "I know."

"I guess, in the end, we're still made for each other, *lastochka*. Be a good girl. I'm watching. From now on, just assume I'm watching."

I reached for her hands, bringing the left one to my lips and enveloping her ring finger in my mouth before she could pull away. I closed my teeth around her wedding band and slid it off slowly. I took it from my mouth and tucked it into my pocket. Finding the knife again, I pressed it into her bound hands.

Her eyes were stuck on me, like she was scared that if she looked away, I'd disappear. I could understand that fear. I had the same one.

Tearing my eyes from the perfect sight of her, I turned and walked away.

NIKOLAI

"That's the only bad side of Hade Harbor," Bran complained as he frowned at the menu written on a chalkboard, sitting out on the boardwalk. "Who the fuck wants a fruitarian brunch? We need to get back to New York for the food alone."

We kept walking until a familiar-looking chain came into sight. It was safer to stick to the familiar with Bran. The man had an insatiable appetite, and I couldn't take his complaining when he didn't like the meal. Prison had been torture enough.

"You go. I'm not leaving," I told him as we grabbed a seat on an outdoor patio.

A table full of girls dressed like they were on a fall-themed photo shoot watched us sit, grinning like the Cheshire cats.

"Excuse me, but are you guys actors?" One of them leaned over and smiled coyly at us.

Bran took her in, from her October-chic outfit to her gym bunny body and blonde hair. He grinned at her, resting his arms along the back of his chair.

"Why, I should be asking you that, gorgeous," he said.

"Oh my god, does he have an accent?" moaned another girl at their table moaned.

"Only when it suits him," I muttered, my gaze moving to the menu sitting on the driftwood-style table.

"You have one, too, and yours is even sexier," the original woman said, leaning toward me.

I ignored her.

"Why don't we all eat together?" a bright voice suggested.

Bran raised an eyebrow at me and then laughed as he took in my bored expression. "I'd love to, ladies, but my friend here wouldn't. I'm afraid we'll have to pass."

"Why? Is he taken?" The first girl pouted.

"Married, actually," I tossed at her.

I could feel the disappointment radiating off the table as they finally turned back to their bottomless margaritas.

"Married? Does the bride know?" Bran asked.

"She will soon." I smirked at him. "Is it just me, or are the women more reckless here? Can't they smell trouble when it's right in front of them?" I tossed the menu aside.

Bran shrugged. "It's a college town. An ice-hockey town at that. They're probably used to guys who look hard as nails but are just regular jocks underneath. They can't tell the difference."

165

"Well, if someone tries to give me fruit leather instead of bacon, they'll get a chance to see firsthand."

Bran watched me with narrowed eyes. "You seem different today. Did you have fun with Sofia De Sanctis after chasing her around the school last night?"

I couldn't stop my smirk when I thought about the night before. "What do you think?"

"Christ, man, you really can't stay away."

"It's not your problem. It's hers."

"What if she goes to the cops?"

"She won't."

"How can you be sure?"

"She had her chance, and besides, it's not in her nature. She's a De Sanctis. She doesn't trust the cops. She doesn't trust anyone." *Except me, apparently.* Her blind trust in me during our forest chase had kept me awake all night. How could she just give herself over to me to do my worst with? Didn't she know what I'd become?

"To the world, Sofia De Sanctis is dead. That means I can do whatever the fuck I want to her, without repercussions. She's mine to fuck with. If you don't like that, you should go home. I'm sure your sister is looking for you."

"Don't be touchy. I won't get in your way. She's good for you."

"In what way?"

Bran studied me. "Don't knife me, but you seem... satisfied. I take it your dry spell has broken?" His smirk was absolutely filthy.

"A choice isn't a dry spell. Anyway, I need to know more about what's going on in Sofia's life. Who is that Sloane fucker to her? Why is she always at the hospital? What about Angelo and Chiara? Do they have a kid?"

"That is a lot of questions. I can see there's going to be homework for this trip," Bran muttered. "I have one for you. Whose ring is it your girl wears?"

"No one's. Well, not anymore anyway." I reached into my pocket and pulled out the band that nestled there. I laid it between us on the table.

Bran whistled. "You stole her ring?" He picked it up and turned it around in his grip before setting it down.

A little pink Post-it landed on our table just as our food came. The girl from before stood beside me. I glanced at the girlish writing and cell number for a second before picking it up. I flicked it over the patio, toward the ocean, as the girl standing beside me spluttered in disbelief.

"So rude!"

"As are you. I told you I'm married. Which part didn't you hear?" I ground out and tossed my head toward the exit, my attention never leaving my plate. "Now get out of here before you put me in a bad mood."

"You don't have a ring on," she pointed out, getting on my last nerve.

I pushed back from the table, threw my napkin down, and stood up to face her. She didn't cower, I'd give her that. I towered over her, my annoyance radiating off me in waves.

"I don't need a ring to remember that I'm not interested. Get the fuck away from me before I stop being nice."

She blinked at me, once, twice, and then turned and hurried toward her waiting friends.

Sinking back into my chair, I picked up my fork.

Bran was quiet for a long moment before clearing his throat pointedly. "So, you wanna find out about Mr. Bigshot around town, Edward Sloane, or should I?"

"I will. You take Angelo. I don't want him knowing I'm here yet."

"You think Sofia won't tell him?"

I shook my head. "She won't risk it. She doesn't want him hurt."

Bran sighed and put his arms behind his head, looking at the blue fall sky. "That's some fucked-up relationship you guys have there. Poor woman. She never really had a chance."

To be free of me? No, she never did.

AFTER BREAKFAST WITH BRAN, I checked out Edward Sloane. The man was predictable as hell, and considering how rich he was for the small town he lived in, he didn't seem to exercise much caution. Given how he made his money, that was stupid, but then most rich men were. They seemed to think their money made them untouchable, while, in reality, it just made them a target.

He had a fancy little office in downtown Hade Harbor, but it didn't take much digging around to see that it was a front. Sure, Sloane had invested his ill-gotten gains in plenty of legitimate ways from property to other small businesses. The guy clearly thought of himself as some kind of savior in the area, holding meetings where struggling business owners came to prostrate themselves for aid. It was sleazy as hell, and that was before you added in where his actual money came from.

I didn't have any concrete evidence yet, but I would bet my life that Edward Sloane was part of the chain who transported drugs, arms, and people up and down the East Coast, and cut a pretty profit from it.

LATER THAT NIGHT, I let myself into Sofia's house when the sun had already set. Downstairs was painfully clean. I'd had a key made so I didn't have to break in every time I wanted to visit my little runaway. I headed to the kitchen first. At breakfast time, it had been clear that Sofia's fridge was running woefully low. I set the bags I'd brought on the table and the takeout on the counter. It had taken me a while after getting out of prison, but I was finally able to stomach a more varied diet. Tonight, I'd eat with Sofia, whether she liked it or not. I left the takeout under a towel to keep it warm and headed upstairs.

When I got to the top of the stairs, the shower was running. What lucky timing. I tried the handle of the bathroom. It turned easily under my hand.

The air was foggy and perfumed with lavender. Sofia's body was clearly visible behind the misted glass. I shut the door behind me and leaned against it, waiting for the water to go off. When it finally did, I grabbed a towel from the rack, just before Sofia's hand appeared from behind the screen door to reach for it. Her gasp told me she'd finally opened her eyes and seen me, lurking in her white bathroom like a creep.

"What are you doing here?" She groped for the next nearest towel.

"You never put the chain on the door."

"Like that would have stopped you," she ground out.

She had a spark to her words tonight, and I enjoyed the sound.

"You think locking the front door is going to keep me from you? You think you can hide from me in a motel? You should know better. Come out here and let me see you."

"What? No!"

"Come out, or I'll come get you."

After a moment where I could feel her battling with herself, she stepped out around the partition. She was holding the towel against her bare front. Just the sight of her bare legs, still dripping wet, turned me on. It had been so long. Endlessly long, really. Now, just the sight of Sofia's bare shoulder, dotted with glistening water droplets, made me hard as nails. Ambling toward her, I reached out and took her towel. She held on to it for a moment, then released it. She was naked. I stared. I couldn't tear my eyes from her. I might have forgotten to blink. It was dim in the bathroom, and I wanted to turn all the lights on and inspect every inch of her, but she was uncomfortable. I didn't like to see it.

"What are you doing?" She was flushed. Her arm had covered her breasts, and another was slung around her middle.

"Looking at you. I want to see how my memories match up to the reality."

I drew closer to her. She was stunning. Even more so than she'd been in her youth. Her body had developed a ripe, lush fullness she'd never had when she was younger and living on her father's meal plan. Seven years, and her life alone had made her a woman.

"Have you let anyone else touch you?" My mind jumped from topic to topic. My tone was light, but the dark possession inside me was far from it.

"I told you I hadn't been with anyone but you."

"I'm not asking about fucking, I'm talking about all of it… kissing, touching, fucking handholding," I clarified, that possessive demon inside me breaking free.

"Are you asking me about my dating life? You really think I'd tell you?"

I wandered behind her, reaching a hand toward her bare ass. Christ, it jiggled enticingly when she shifted her weight from one hip to another, tapping her foot.

"No, I don't, I suppose. You're too smart for that, and no one likes attending too many funerals. They're always on a weekday, and who has the time?"

I couldn't stop myself from gripping her ass. The bare cheeks were just too tempting. I took one in each hand and spread them apart. Her breath hitched, and she stepped forward, trying to get away from my touch. I tutted and pulled her back. My fingers wandered between her cheeks.

"I found a place you didn't dry yet. Let me."

I stroked my fingers up and down her cleft, past her tight asshole and down to her pussy. She was wet, enticingly so. I wrapped one arm around her neck from behind, her head landing in the crook of my arm. I carefully tightened it, until she was leaning back into my hand, with her back arched.

She swallowed against my forearm.

"Why are you here? You're going to bury me without the box this time?"

"Don't give me ideas. I came to have dinner with you."

She froze. I'd surprised her, clearly.

"What dinner?"

"Don't worry, I brought it."

"I've eaten," she snapped at me, and her entire body shuddered as I slid just my fingertip inside her.

Christ, she was as tight as ever. Had she really not let anyone else be inside her while I was gone? I didn't know what to make of that. It made me feel things I wasn't ready for.

"Liar. Let's go. I'm hungry." I pulled my fingers from her with effort and slapped her ass before leaving her to get dressed. "Don't bother with panties, unless you want them ripped."

IN THE KITCHEN, I opened up the takeout boxes and waited for her. She came downstairs cautiously, poised to run. I took in her clothes. A sweater dress in a relentless black.

"What's with the outfit? Going to a funeral?"

"I'm in mourning for my life," she muttered and dropped into the chair besides me.

"Are you really not going to eat?"

Her eyes fixed on the pad thai longingly. I pushed the carton toward her.

"Keep your strength up. You're going to need it."

She scowled at me but reached for the chopsticks in the bag. We ate in silence for a moment.

"People miss a lot of things in jail. For me, it was real food… and you."

She stilled, her eyes darting to mine. I ate steadily. It was fun to shock her with glimpses of who I used to be. It wasn't a lie either. The parts of me that had remained human, in any way at all, were all her.

"What was the food like?" Her voice was quiet.

"You can't even imagine. It's food you wouldn't feed animals. That's all they are, really, locked inside little cages, clawing and biting at each other, waiting for their chance to be free so they can burn the world."

"And you?"

I nodded. "Me, too."

She swallowed, her throat convulsing. It was beautiful.

I pushed my plate away as soon as I'd finished. The entire meal had taken five minutes. Another legacy of prison.

I tapped the table in front of me. "Sit. I want my dessert."

"Nikolai," she started and then trailed off when I touched her lips.

"Tell me the truth and make me believe it. There'll be no mercy for you until you do. Sit here in front of me right now, I want to eat your lying cunt."

"I told you last night-" she started, trailing off when I shook my head.

"I want to hear why you tried to leave me behind. I want to hear why you believed in your father more than me." She had never loved me like I'd loved her. It was the only truth I could accept, as my damaged, fucked up heart already believed it so firmly, anything else would sound like a lie. I needed to hear that dark and most painful truth. I wanted to hear her say it. "Now, sit."

Her breath stalling, she stood and gracefully sat on top of the table. Her knees stayed together.

"Don't fuck around, Sofia."

I pushed her knees wide. She wasn't wearing panties, like instructed. It gave me a jolt of satisfaction to see how she obeyed me, even while fighting me. I could tangle with her the rest of my days and never get bored.

"Hold your knees and keep your legs open, or I'll tie you down."

I couldn't wait to taste her again. After being deprived of her for so long, it was like a dam had burst. While I'd been denying my needs, punishing my body for my failure to protect her, and feeling guilty for sullying her memory by jerking off with her sweet perfection in my mind, she'd been alive and well, and lying to me. The taste I'd had so far had been over far too quickly. I needed weeks, maybe months, of licking her cunt, sinking inside her-no matter what she was doing-before the urgent need for her faded. It might never fade. Time would tell.

I leaned in and inhaled, filling my lungs with her sweet musky scent. "You're still wet here. You need to learn how to dry yourself off better after your shower," I mocked. "Should I teach you?"

She was leaning on her elbows, her neck bent sharply to watch me as I bit hard kisses and nips up her thighs. I wanted to bruise her. I wanted my love to leave a mark on her, like she'd marked me. I licked a long, wet stripe up her center.

"You need to dry inside and out," I muttered against her skin before sticking my tongue inside her, a deep, no-holds-barred plunge that brought my nose to rub her clit. I tongue-fucked her like that, enjoying the flavor of her utter surrender and desire. She could try to lie to me, but I could taste her arousal. She still wanted me as much as I wanted her. Maybe she was a little unhinged, too, these days.

I moved lower, dragging my tongue to her ass. "Don't forget to dry here, too. Everything needs to be nice and clean."

I pressed my tongue against that soft pucker, and her hips jumped off the table. I put a hand on her belly and held it in place as I explored her with my tongue. There wasn't any part of her I didn't want to own. I wanted to rub my cum into every crevice, press my fingerprints into every inch, and make sure she never forgot who she belonged to again.

Just like my body could never forget hers.

I returned to her clit, just as I reached to the side and picked up one of the fancy knives I'd brought to the table. This one was spare. Her eyes widened when she saw it. It was her *liccasapuni*. The *paranza corta* knife with the long thin blade and wide, round handle. The first and only weapon she'd ever successfully cut me with.

"Open your mouth." My voice was deep. My order undeniable.

Her chest was rising and falling faster and faster, but despite her fear, or maybe because of it, she complied. I trailed the blade up her body, turning it in my hand so I held the sharp end, and brushed the handle past her lips and into her mouth.

It filled it perfectly.

"Get it nice and wet for me, prom queen." I fucked her mouth with the hilt for a few seconds, until her spit was dripping down the blade, too, then pulled it free.

She watched with rapt attention when I put it at her pussy.

It slipped easily inside. Gripping the blade tightly, I carefully pumped the hilt in and out of her. It was long, long enough to keep her perfect pussy far away from any sharp edges. Leaning in, I fastened my lips around her clit and laved it. She cried out, her hips bumping against my face.

She rose quickly. A woman on the edge. If she was being honest, my little swallow hadn't been with anyone in a long time. Now, she'd never have the chance to be with anyone else again, other than me.

She burst in my mouth, a flood of pleasure. Her juices were sweet, like nectar. I fucked her with the knife hilt the entire time, until she was spent and sweating on the table.

Pulling the knife from her gently, I closed her legs and brought the hilt to her lips. Her eyes widened, and I thought for a second she might refuse. Then she opened her mouth, and I slid the handle inside.

"Clean up your things."

Her cheeks flushed pink, but she complied, her eyes burning into mine.

"Good girl."

Setting the knife aside, I clenched my fist. Warmth blossomed in my palm. I ignored it. What was a little cut compared to the thrill of touching this woman? There was no comparison. I undid my jeans and pushed them half down, unable to wait one more second to be inside her. Pulling her hips to the edge of the table, leaving a bloody handprint on her legs as I did, I pushed inside her. She groaned, biting her lip. The expression of her pleasure was addictive. I curled my bleeding hand around the back of her neck and pulled her face to mine, kissing her while pounding my hips against hers. The table scraped across the floor, loud and annoying, the glasses shaking with our efforts. I fucked her hard, and she met my every thrust with raised hips, bucking against me, panting and sweating. Looking simply glorious. She came first, pulling me close, her tight pussy clamping down on me harder than ever and milking my length.

I pulled out to come on her mound. Enjoying the sight of my release striping her thighs and pussy. Moving a hand to the cum on her cunt, I wet my fingers in it and then massaged it into her inner thighs and belly. She watched me without speaking. I wanted her to smell like me, and now she did.

. . .

AFTER, I followed her upstairs to her room. She kept nervously glancing back at me, her teeth worrying her full bottom lip. Inside her room, she stood awkwardly, while I stripped off my clothes. Her gaze on my body was a turn-on.

"Still like looking at me, prom queen? You always did like to look." I dropped my jeans and boxers and stepped out of them, tossing them onto a chair and turning to face her.

Her eyes dropped to my half-spent cock before she could catch herself. Cheeks turning pink, she turned away, folding her arms over her chest.

"What now?"

"Now, we go to bed. Isn't that what happens at bedtime?

She glanced curiously at me over her shoulder. "Together?"

"Yes, together. Just assume that your days of sleeping alone are a luxury you're no longer afforded."

"Is that supposed to be a threat?" She tossed those intriguing words at me as I rounded behind her. Putting a hand to her lower back, I pushed her toward the bed gently.

"I suppose that depends on how lonely you were, Sofia, doesn't it?"

She reached the mattress and climbed on. I followed, snapping the light off on the way. The smell of her sheets rose around us, that particular scent unique to Sofia. My head spun. She moved to the other side of the bed to get away from me, and I tutted, dragging her back to the middle.

"You don't sleep over there. You sleep right here," I told her, arranging her on her back in the middle of the bed and lowering myself between her legs, dipping my hips to line my drooling cock up with her entrance again.

She was still wet from coming on the table. My dick was already getting hard again. Another legacy of my abstinence seemed to be recovering my youth, in terms of having an unstoppable hard-on around this woman. I wasn't complaining. I slipped inside her like a hot knife through butter, her slick muscles parting beautifully for me.

She gripped my shoulders, a breathy moan leaving her. When I was deep inside, I relaxed my weight to the side and pulled her with me, hitching one of her legs over my hip. We were face to face, heads sharing the same pillow, and I was still sunk balls-deep in her perfect little cunt.

"Every single night, you're going to fall asleep just like this, on my cock. I want to know where you are every night. I'll know if you move. I'll know if you so much as sneeze. I can't have you running off again on me." *Not when I just found you.*

I thrust in and out of her a few times, and she groaned, arching her hips. I grinned at her reluctant enthusiasm. It was too dark to make out her face, but her body's reactions told me everything I needed to know. She was turned on, desperate to be fucked. Well, too bad for her, I wouldn't be obliging her anytime soon. I would wait until she was asleep and wake her up fucking her. Then I'd do it again, and again, until morning.

19

SOFIA

My classes the next day were sleepy and quiet. No doubt the kids were tired or hungover after the dance. It took a special kind of mean to hold an event on a weeknight with an early start the next day. Lillian and Cayden were both absent, which made my bullshit meter hum, but I just hoped she was okay.

Cayden had Nikolai potential, from what I'd seen of him, and Lily was too young to deal with that. Normal people wouldn't be able to deal with that.

I wasn't remotely normal.

I'd slept better than I had in years. Washing the smell of Nikolai off in the shower this morning, I allowed my mind to drift over my encounters with him since he'd found me. Maybe I was dangerously sex-starved, like Chiara constantly accused me of, but they were the hottest things that had ever happened to me.

I wanted more to happen. I wanted more of him. I wanted it all.

Even more than the physical relief of being fucked by a man who took no prisoners and whose body fit mine like it was designed for it, was how light I felt this morning.

I'd been carrying so much guilt. Endless pounds of it were a constant weight on my shoulders. Last night I'd come close to telling Nikolai everything and letting the chips fall where they may. Maybe he didn't know about Leo yet, but taking his punishment for lying about being dead made me feel better. All my childhood years of going to church and learning about the healing power of doing penance for my sins must have stuck somewhere inside. The day flew by, and I checked my phone more often than I could admit.

When the last classes ended, I hurried to get ready to leave. I was going to the hospital, and I couldn't wait to see Leo. Yesterday, not seeing his little face all day had been torture.

I made it to the door of the classroom before a knock sounded.

Fighting irritation, I plastered on a school-friendly smile and opened the door.

It fell abruptly as I took in who was standing there.

Edward Sloane, and he'd brought flowers.

"Sophie, I came to apologize."

He pressed the bouquet into my hands and walked around me, simply letting himself into my classroom, forcing me to stay.

"It's not necessary. I'm busy, I have to run."

"It is necessary. I was rude the other day, forcing you into lunch and imposing my schedule on you. I apologize."

I watched him warily, waiting for the catch.

"I'd like you to finish the portrait. No one can do it as well as you can."

"I don't think it's a good idea."

"I'll double your pay, how's that?"

Narrowing my eyes at him, I leaned against the doorframe. "Why would you do that? You were already paying me too much."

"I disagree. When I looked at other artists in the area who could complete the piece, it was impossible to find someone. You undervalue your talent. Please. This painting is important to me. Name your price."

I studied him. I needed the money, and he seemed genuine enough. "Fine. I'm almost done anyway. I'll work on it tonight. Did you bring it?"

"I forgot. I've been in back-to-back meetings all day. I'll have it dropped off."

"Fine." I checked my watch and straightened up. "Now, I really have to go."

"On your way to the hospital?"

"Yes, Leo's been admitted."

"I hope it all works out well for him. He deserves it." Edward left the room without having to be asked.

"Thank you."

I locked my classroom behind him, gave him a swift smile, and left.

St. Mary's was busy when I arrived, and I had to circle the parking lot for a good ten minutes before I found a space. Once I snagged one, I hurried inside.

"Mom!"

Leo jumped up when I reached the children's ward and wrapped his little arms around me as far as they would go, which wasn't that far. I pressed my face into the top of his silky head and breathed in. Ah, there it was. The good stuff.

"How are you doing in here?"

"Good! Yesterday *zio* and *zia* brought me a gamepad!"

My eyes narrowed in on the shiny new tech on the bed. "Did they really?"

Leo nodded enthusiastically. "Can I keep it?"

I smoothed his hair back. "Sure you can, just don't play it all the time, okay? How are you feeling?"

"Fine, normal." He climbed back into bed and peered at the bag in my hand. "What did you bring me to eat?"

"Spaghetti and meatballs."

He pumped the air. "Yes! Can we share it with Charlie?"

Leo jerked his head over to the little boy in the bed next to him. He had his head shaved and the shadowed eyes of a cancer patient.

"Sure we can, if his nurse says it's okay and he likes it."

"He'll love it, you're the best cook in the world," Leo said with perfect sincerity.

I settled myself in the chair next to him. I couldn't keep the grin off my face. I should be more anxious about Nikolai showing up and finding out the truth, but I just couldn't find it in me. Maybe I was too burned out on stress. I wasn't capable of fear in the way other people would be anymore.

Or, maybe, despite everything, you still trust him.

If that was true, I didn't know what it said about me.

I STAYED AS LONG as I could at the hospital and only left when Leo was ready to sleep and the nurses were giving me looks. I drove home, my mind on the donor issue. The doctor had updated me that the tests were looking good so far but the most important results would come in a few days.

I pulled up at my house and stopped the car. It was dark already, but when I opened the door, I could hear the sounds of the ocean. Inside, I flipped on the lights and got rid of my coat and boots. I left my handbag on the counter and grabbed my phone. I checked the doors before heading upstairs. The back porch door gave me pause. Had it really only been a few nights ago when I'd run through there and locked it, expecting Nikolai to be advancing on me like a bloodthirsty demon from Hell? It had been. Renato's words about him had done a number on me. He was right, though. I should be careful. Nikolai had told me time and again that he wasn't the man I'd known. Considering how dangerous the man I'd known had been, it was a sobering thought.

I headed upstairs. While drifting down the hall, Leo's door was ajar. I usually closed all the doors in the house, since the slightest draft seemed to make everything slam.

I went to close it and realized that the light was on inside.

I pushed it open slowly, my heart all but jumping to my mouth.

The bedside light was on, casting shadows around the walls.

Nikolai said in the rocking chair beside the bed, one of Leo's stuffies in his hands. This one was a wolf.

He pinned me with his silver eyes as I stepped into the room.

"Have something to tell me, prom queen?"

20

SOFIA

*N*ikolai sat deathly still. One tattooed hand stroked the toy's head. It was a deceptively calming movement. I could feel his menace and wariness from across the room.

While part of me, that part that had been terrified of my father my entire life, contracted with fear, the other part, the one that had fallen in love with this terrible, complicated man, eased. It was over. The lies were done. The chips would have to fall where they may. I had no control over that anymore.

"Come in, let's talk." His words were a quiet command.

I felt like I was falling from a great height as I walked into the room. His eyes were locked on mine, and I couldn't tear myself away.

"So, talk," he said after a moment, while I stared dumbly at him.

"It's not Angelo and Chiara's kid in the hospital," he said. His prompt loosened my tongue.

"No, it's not."

"It's yours. He's yours. You didn't think to mention it?"

"When? When you gagged me, or locked me in a coffin, or hunted me through the woods?"

My challenging tone sent one of Nikolai's eyebrows up in a mocking expression.

"I guess I shouldn't put too much stock in your assurances of honesty. Still telling lies, *lastochka*? How disappointing."

His soft tut sent my color high.

"I was scared of my father."

Nikolai sighed. "So what else is new?"

A bitter laugh left me. "Not like this. I've never been scared of Antonio like this." I turned around and reached for a picture frame on the dresser. There weren't many of them. Framing pictures was just another one of those domestic things I never seemed to get around to.

Now, I clutched the frame hard between my fingers and closed the distance between us.

Nikolai tilted his head back to keep me in sight as I loomed over him, my legs brushing his knees.

Just like in the past, when trusting this unpredictable, dangerous man had felt like jumping off a high cliff, with no certainty that I would reach the water, I hesitated on the edge. His gray eyes stared into mine. Steady. Just like his son's. In that moment, my mind was made up.

I was done carrying this burden alone.

I was done.

I handed Nikolai the frame.

He turned his attention to it slowly. My heart was pounding so loudly, I could barely hear anything else. His head tilted down, and his eyes locked on the photo.

In it, I held Leo on my knee. We were both laughing. I was looking at the little boy who had changed my life, and Leo was looking at the camera. His eyes looked silver in the light of that sunny afternoon.

Nikolai jerked, an involuntary response, like how you might fold over after a sucker punch. He stared at the photo, and I stared at him. His long, tattooed hand fell to the glass, and he traced a long finger over the image of Leo.

It felt wrong to be standing over him. I needed to be closer. I sank to my knees in front of him so I was able to look up into his face.

His expression was blank. Only the tic of a muscle in his jaw betrayed that he was even alive.

"If Antonio had only threatened you, I would have told him to go to hell. Who could take out the devil himself? I would have written you, visited you. No one could have stopped me."

I took a deep breath. I was crying, I realized with a shock. Tears were running freely down my cheeks. My biggest sin, and my most awful regret, were being dragged out into the light, and I couldn't control my pent-up emotions.

"But Antonio didn't only threaten you. He threatened him, and I couldn't take any chances with"—I took a deep breath, saying the words for the very first time—"our son."

Nikolai flinched again. His eyes still hadn't moved from the picture. He wiped beneath one eye, slowly and deliberately. A tear fell on the glass of the photo. It wasn't mine, but the sight of it only sent more of my own down my cheeks.

I'd been so alone. So terribly lonely and so afraid for so long. A sob wrenched itself from my chest, sounding wretched and ugly in the silence between us.

Nikolai's hand landed softly on my cheek. His finger wiped the dripping tears away, though only more fell. I was really crying now.

"Don't cry, Sofia. Tears can't change the past." His voice was rough. "Nothing can."

He shifted, placing the photo on the bed with a soft reverence I'd never seen before. Then his hands went to my face. He stroked his thumbs across my cheeks, washing away my tears. I blinked at him, my eyes swimming and unfocused.

"Get up, prom queen," he softly urged.

I clung to his arms as he stood from the chair and took me with him. My legs felt uncertain as I held on to his arms. His voice was low as he pulled me into the warmth of his chest.

"You don't kneel. Not for anyone, and not for me."

My head jerked up, and I stared at him in surprise. That gentle reverence was in his voice, too. My eyes finally cleared enough to be able to see his.

He wasn't angry. He wasn't vengeful. He wasn't manic with that terrifying energy that had sent me running into the woods the other night.

He was calm. His eyes were resolute. For the first time since he'd come back into my life, he looked like Nikolai from the basement of Casa Nera. He looked like the man who had held my hand and stopped me from falling over a rusty broken railing, even though it meant he'd get caught.

He was still there, deep down inside the damage that jail and lies had caused. My heart squeezed hard.

"What do you mean?" I managed to force out.

"You, Sofia De Sanctis, kneel for no one."

His arms went around my legs, and he picked me up before I could really process what he meant. He held me tightly to his chest, bridal-style, and left the room that smelled of Leo. I reached out when we got to the door and switched the light off. Nikolai turned slightly to take us both through the narrow doorway. In that moment of darkness, he looked up at the neon glow that suffused the room in the sudden darkness.

Stars.

A multitude of night stars.

The night sky that had always connected us.

His hands tightened on me to the point of hurting. I didn't care. Sometimes, some things should hurt. This was one of them. I'd been hurting for so long, it barely registered. He pulled away from the night sky I'd built for our son and walked us down the dark hall. I stared at the underside of his jaw and the tattoo that licked up his neck.

Moonlight passed over us as we walked past windows. I couldn't resist bringing my hand up to touch his jaw. He was real. He was here. It still felt like an impossible dream. The thought of Antonio finding out, which had once terrified me, didn't seem to matter anymore. Nikolai was free. I wasn't alone anymore.

I'd never be alone, with the weight of the world on my shoulders, again. I knew it without asking. The thing between us, born in darkness, forged with pain and fear, had never died. Not in all this time.

We reached my room, and Nikolai closed the door with his foot before advancing to the bed. He placed me gently on it and stepped back, reaching out to turn a light on beside the bed, and chased away the shadows between us. There was no more hiding parts of ourselves in the darkness.

I was in the middle of the mattress and rose on my elbows to watch him. His face was unreadable in the dimness of the light. I could see his hands, though, and I watched every single second of him undressing. He tugged his leather jacket off and let it slide down his arms like a snake shedding its skin. His T-shirt followed, baring his beautiful, tattooed torso to me. He was so broad now. He barely looked like the young man he'd been all those years ago, locked in the basement. Now, he was all grown up. His shoulders were wide and thick with bunched muscle. His torso was flat and tight with packed strength. His body looked like a lethal weapon. Only his tattoos remained unchanged, though there were a lot more of them now. Crude, prison-style tattoos. One caught my attention. On his chest, right over his heart.

A swallow mid-flight. The wings were outstretched.

A free bird. A *lastochka*.

He continued to strip, his jeans and boxers going next, kicked into a corner with his boots. He straightened up, naked before me. His cock was hard, lying in a long, thick line up his belly, straining desperately forward. He stood there and let me look at him. His eyes were on me the entire time. He stared at me like I was something he'd never seen before. A person he'd never truly met.

My body heated and my heart pounded at his look.

There was a world in his eyes that took away my breath.

Then he moved, prowling toward me and reaching for my shoes first. There was a solemn kind of ceremony to his slow unfastening of my shoes and the way he rolled my socks off. He pulled my jeans down in the same way, and then my panties. I sat up when he reached for my sweater. My face came near his, and I could smell the scent of his skin, and bodywash. That pine-and-leather musk that had always been unique to him. The smell that made my body sing. My bra followed my T-shirt, pushed out of the way and forgotten. We were both naked. My skin prickled all over at his careful inspection. He stroked a hand down my damp cheek. I was sure my face had to be blotchy and red after that cathartic crying jag. It certainly stung like it was. He was positioned over me, his weight held on his corded arms. I wished he'd lower himself to me. I wanted to feel his weight pressing me into the mattress, owning me. I wanted it more than anything.

Instead, his hand wandered down my neck and along my collarbones. His mouth followed. His kisses were hot and dragging. His stubble prickled my flesh and I shivered, while his teeth nipped and bit.

He reached my breasts. Again, he stared at them, thumbing the nipples.

I jerked when he spoke.

"You fed our son with these breasts?"

The question was so unexpected, I couldn't do more than nod. His hand closed over one, squeezing it lightly, and then his mouth enveloped my nipple. His tongue was shockingly hot after the cold air of the room. He stroked my nipple with his tongue, sucking and lathing it, tugging it between his teeth. I could have felt embarrassed. My body wasn't what it had been seven years ago. There were the places I'd hidden from him last night with my strategically placed arms. Areas on my body that our moonlit chases hadn't illuminated. My breasts sagged, and I had stretch marks, not to mention the lines on my tummy or the slight puckering around the C-section scar. It had been a difficult birth.

"I hadn't known it was possible for the girl I knew to become more beautiful…" He trailed off when both breasts were well sucked, pink and aching. "But here we are."

He moved down. I was so wet now, I could feel my want working down my thighs, dripping onto the bed. Soaked didn't cover it. He worked his way down my body and paused at my belly. I bent my legs, sucking in my stomach instinctively. It was my go-to whenever that particularly vulnerable area of my body was exposed to other people's eyes, which only happened at the beach nowadays.

"Don't hide from me, *lastochka*. Don't you dare. This body is still mine. My prize. Never forget that." His lips found the scar. He paused over it, tracing his lips back and forth.

I felt compelled to explain somehow.

"It was a difficult labor. He was breech," I started. The medical talk sounded totally wrong in the intimate atmosphere between us.

"Were you alone?" Nikolai's question caught me off guard.

"I don't remember the C-section. I was so tired," I admitted.

The entire birth had been a rush of pain and fear, and the memories were hazy now. It had happened suddenly, and by the time Chiara and Angelo had heard, it was all over. The only thing that stuck in my memory, brighter than any star in the sky, was the moment when the nurse put Leo into my arms. The fog had cleared, the tiredness had lifted, and everything else had failed to matter.

"Yes, I was alone, until I wasn't..." I mumbled, senseless words, lost in pleasure.

His lips slid along the scar, pressing kisses as he went.

"My brave, strong *lastochka*. You aren't alone anymore, and you never will be again."

With those words, he pushed my knees wide and licked up my center. Growling low in his throat, he rested his entire face against my pussy, his tongue pressing deep inside, lapping at me, like he wanted to drink me up.

"Whose ring were you wearing?" he pulled back to ask now. "Don't tell me it was just for show again."

I searched for his face with my hips, needing more of that delicious pressure. He started to lick me again, and I sank my fingers into his hair.

"You didn't look too closely at it, did you? Figure it out yourself."

He bit down on my inner thigh. I groaned.

"No more secrets." He nipped me again, making me laugh.

"It's yours. Didn't you see? I've always been yours." The words left me in a rush, and I blushed. Thankfully, it was too dark for Nikolai to tell.

His grin against my thigh told me he knew anyway.

"And you didn't think to tell me when I first found you? Hmmm?"

"You weren't very approachable." His tongue was right back on my clit, laving it in rough circles. "I was scared. Scared you'd never forgive me."

He hummed against me. "You should have realized by now... I'd forgive you anything. Scar my face, get stabby with your *liccasapuni,* turn me in to the police... I'll always forgive you. I'll never let you fall, remember?"

Tears sprang to my eyes. "It's been so long, I didn't know if you'd still feel that way."

He worked his way up my body, and before I knew it, he was pressing inside me.

"I have no other way of being, prom queen. Loving you is in my bones."

21

SOFIA

*R*inging pulled me from a dreamless sleep.

I fumbled for my phone on the nightstand, and my hand hit the bed. I never slept in the middle. I cracked my eyes open and blinked at the empty mattress beside me, my phone flashing furiously from the bedside table. I shuffled to it, my muscles aching in all kids of places.

"Hello?"

"Good morning! Dinner today? I thought I could meet you at St. Mary's, and once visiting hours are done, we can go out. Just the girls."

I took a deep breath, trying to force my brain to work. Last night felt like a dream.

"Okay, sure. Let's do it."

"What's wrong? You sound weird."

Chiara knew me far too well.

"Nothing. I'll catch you up later. Girls' night sounds good."

"Okay, great. Now I can't wait. I can just tell it's something juicy."

"You sound way too excited about that."

"Girl, I've been waiting for something juicy from you for years. I'm due."

I hung up and put my phone back. As I did, I noticed a shine on my hand. My ring had returned to its place on my finger.

Nikolai had to have put it back on.

Where the hell was he? I glanced around the room. There was no trace of him. Had I imagined it all? No, the ache between my legs proved that he'd been very real.

I laid back and stared at the ceiling. I had to get up and get to work. I had to shower. I must smell like him. I had to get it together. I would, for sure. I just needed five more minutes to linger on the memories of last night.

SCHOOL HAD DRAGGED by as I tried to reassure myself that I wasn't waiting to hear my phone ring. It hadn't rung, in any case, not for a call or a message. Not that I was fixated on the fact that I had bared my entire soul last night to Nikolai, and he'd disappeared immediately after, and not called or texted. Nope. I didn't care.

When the last bell of the day rang, I'd never been so ready to leave. I headed out early. I just wanted to get to the hospital and see Leo.

Kids spilled out across the parking lot, and I powered through in the direction of the staff lot.

A black Jeep pulled up in front of me, stopping me in my tracks.

The door opened, and a tall man got out. He was broad and tattooed, like a blond-haired, green-eyed Nikolai, except this one managed a smile that didn't look murderous. Students scattered and stared. Of course they did.

It was the Irish guy from the coffee shop. I narrowed my eyes at him as he leaned against his Jeep and looked me over. Bran. His name was Bran.

"Taxi service." Bran smirked. "In you get."

He opened the passenger-side door for me, ignoring the curious looks of passers-by. Several girls had their phones out, snapping discreet pics of the bad boy.

"Excuse me, do I know you?"

"Ouch, I thought our coffee shop encounter was very memorable."

I studied him. "If I was going to remember you for anything, I think it would be for chasing me through the school in a mask the other night. That was you, right?"

"A gentleman never tells."

"Do you know Nikolai Chernov or not?"

"Only as well as a brother."

"I guess you also gave him my number to terrorize me with?"

"You look fine to me. His terrorizing must have gotten lighter since prison. The *Palach* is losing his touch."

"The *Palach*? What does that mean?"

Bran shrugged with perfect nonchalance. "I don't speak Russian, love, I have no idea."

"Sure you don't. Why are you here?"

"I told you. I'm your taxi service. Point me in a direction, and I'll go."

"I have a car here, you know."

"Yeah, I'm familiar with that piece of shit. You won't be driving it again. Let it rust in the lot or get towed for all I care."

"Excuse me?"

"Nikolai doesn't want you driving that death trap. He wants me to drive you."

"Babysit me, you mean? Where is he anyway?"

Bran lounged with indolent grace. "Why, you missing him already? He'll like hearing that."

"I'm not—" I bit off my words. What was the point in denying it? "I can drive myself."

"But I'm not going to let you, so just do us both a favor and let me take you to see your son."

"And my car? I can't just leave it here."

"Have it towed, like I said. Or I'll get it taken to your house, whatever you want."

I sighed, checking my watch. I really needed to get going to the hospital. "Whatever. Just this once, and only because I'm going out for dinner with Chiara after, and she's driving." I got into the car. It was quietly expensive inside. The kind of luxury I hadn't experienced since I'd left the De Sanctis lifestyle.

Bran settled into the driver's seat. "Chiara, is that the little firecracker from the coffee shop? The one who was talking about her husband, spitting, and daddy in the same sentence?"

"You shouldn't hit on her if you value your life."

"Hit on her? I was thinking I could hit on both of them. Their bedroom sounds like an interesting place."

"Fair enough. So, where is Nikolai, and why has he sent you here?"

Bran handled the car expertly through the crowd. "Niko's in New York. He had some business to see to. And the reason why he sent me here is obvious, love. The man's obsessed with you and always has been."

That probably shouldn't warm my heart like it did.

I traced a circle on my knee. "So, you mentioned prison."

Bran grinned at me. "If you want to grill me, go ahead, love, I'm an open book."

I hesitated. It seemed wrong somehow to go behind Nikolai's back and try to find out what the last seven years had been like for him.

Bran nudged me with his elbow. "We never slept together. We were roommates, not bunkmates, if that's what you're wondering."

My cheeks flushed with the vivid image that jumped into my head at Bran's words.

"Well, that's not my business, I guess."

"That's where you're wrong. That man lived like a monk in your memory. I'd say that was your business. You need to make up for that lost time. Wear him out, he needs that. I've never seen him as relaxed as he was this morning."

"You saw him this morning?"

Bran chuckled. "Jealous again? Don't worry, I told you, you're the one he loves. He never stopped, you know, not even for a second. Not even when he nearly lost his damn mind inside."

The hospital came into sight ahead. My mind was swimming with Bran's insights, and I couldn't lie to myself that it wasn't exciting to hear anything about Nikolai at all. After a day of waiting to hear from him, Bran's overprotective taxi service soothed my ragged nerves.

"I'll see you tomorrow morning to take you to work."

"It's really not necessary," I said, stepping out of the car.

"Yes, it is, because your car is at school, Miss Rossi, if you've forgotten."

"Right. Okay, fine."

"Your enthusiasm is infectious." He grinned at me.

Man, I'd bet many a lady had fallen for that grin.

I took a step toward the hospital before pausing. "Is Nikolai going to be gone long?"

Bran's knowing smirk made me roll my eyes.

"I just want to know what to expect."

"With the youngest Chernov, it's best to expect the unexpected at all times. He'll be back very soon, don't you worry."

22

NIKOLAI

I left for New York at first light. Leaving Sofia sleeping, smelling like me, unguarded, her head on my shoulder, had been nearly too difficult, but I'd had gotten a message I couldn't ignore.

Overnight, my world had changed. I had to be ready for it. For so long, I was the man whose mother's love was measured by the sound of the rope swaying and Irina's lifeless feet hanging above me. Last night, I had learned of another kind of motherly love, one so different, I'd never even imagined it was possible.

Sofia De Sanctis had turned her back on her rich, privileged life, and everyone and everything she knew, to protect our son. My son. She had let me torture her, bury her alive, and chase her down in the woods like a demon, to protect our son. She was no longer just the woman I loved and my obsession. She was something else entirely. Something so high above me, I could only worship at her feet, and I would do that, but first, I had to make sure I could protect my family.

I met old Artur in a Russian *banya* in Brighton Beach. The timing couldn't have been better, as I needed a favor from him. It was time to see if his prowess with explosives was all he made it out to be.

"I didn't know you lived in New York," I said to the older man.

"Here, there, everywhere is home for the *vory v zakone*. I came to visit my brother's widow and heard you got out. A happy coincidence."

"You heard from who?" My frown deepened as Artur waved his hand vaguely.

"You think you can get out and not make waves. In this city, there is only one Nikolai Chernov. You are known, Niko. You should be more careful. You're the kind of name that lesser men would love to test their mettle against."

"They're welcome to try."

Artur let out a bark of laughter, slapping my bare shoulder. "Spoken like a man with nothing to lose."

His words hit me in the gut. Was I still a man with nothing to lose? No. As soon as I'd known she might be alive, I'd had something to lose. Now, I had everything.

"Well, I don't plan on hanging out in the Russian community, or New York even. I'm sure I'll be fine."

"You won't dabble in bratva business with your brother? You're just here for a visit?"

I considered my answer as we stripped off for the sauna. I picked up a small towel and wrapped it around my hips. Heading through the swinging double doors into the steamy, balsam-scented air, I breathed deeply, enjoying the heat.

"I don't plan on staying."

"Are you going traveling or looking for someone? The one who got away?"

Artur's knowing tone sent me turning toward him. Unease rippled through me. I didn't want anyone knowing that I'd found Sofia. Fuck, I didn't want anyone knowing about Sofia, period. She was mine to do what I wanted with, when I wanted. I wouldn't allow anyone to stand in my way.

Artur chuckled and dropped the subject, moving toward a wide wooden bench along the wall. He patted the space beside him. "Sit, Niko, don't worry, I'm not going to ask you to tell me your secrets. I want you to meet some people."

Settling beside Artur, I peered into the steam. Meet some people? Here? I hadn't imagined that the meeting I'd been waiting for would happen while I was naked in a sauna.

Shapes gradually shifted into view. There were three other men in the banya. Every single one a powerful-looking Russian, judging by the tattoos. I took stock of the ink, assessing the position of each man as I went. Stars on the shoulders and knees denoted rank, as did the epaulets of a general on each shoulder.

They were high up in the *vory v zakone*. This was my official introduction.

"Nikolai Viktorovich," the one who sat in the middle said, his deep voice sinking through my bones.

I nodded toward them, knowing there was a very real possibility that I wouldn't walk out of this room alive.

"Artur, this is the man you think should be *vor*?" The same man spoke again.

Artur nodded beside me. "He is worthy of keeping the code. A man of honor, who understands our way of life. He would be a strong *vor*."

"And what do you have to say about it, Nikolai Viktorovich?"

"I've never asked to be *vor*," I started.

The man to the right tutted. "It is not something to be asked for, it is something to be bestowed. Knights are chosen by the kings. The question now is, are you worthy, like Artur Ivanovich believes you to be?"

"We've watched you, we are happy with your judgment. You conducted yourself with dignity in prison and upheld the code. Getting out early was your brother's doing, and I wouldn't say he cooperated with law enforcement, as much as corrupted it. For me, you deserve the marks of *vor*."

The third man, silent until now, finally spoke. "Do you know the code of the *vor*?"

"I do." The principles of the *vory v zakone* came naturally to me.

The three men exchanged glances, and the middle one slapped a hand to his bare knee.

"Very well, Nikolai Viktorovich. Your past speaks for itself, your conduct is worthy, and you aren't eager for the title to be bestowed upon you, refusing to lie or barter for the honor. That is the mark of a man who can carry the title of *vor* with honor."

Artur slapped a hand to my shoulder, grinning at me. "Welcome to the *vory v zakone*, Nikolai Viktorovich."

The third man, the quiet one, uncovered a long black box that had been sitting on the bench beside him, and opened it, while another picked up a bottle of vodka from the floor.

"Kneel, Nikolai," Artur urged.

I stood, forcing myself to walk to the middle of the steamy room and kneel. The three men who had passed judgment on me stood over me. One gripped the vodka, the other a crude, rudimentary ink gun.

"Do you plan to stay in New York?"

"No. I will leave to find my own place."

The men were quiet, considering my words.

"Vasily will do the honors of your tattoos. It's his specialty," the leader said. "I'm Sasha, this is Dima."

I lowered my head as Dima raised the vodka bottle over the back of my neck, splashing the liquid on my skin, and then moved to my hands. Sterilizing the flesh for the needle.

"I'm honored," I said grimly as Vasily brought the tattoo gun to my skin, the buzz filling my ear.

The familiar scratch of the needle filled my head as the other men relaxed their formal air and passed the bottle of vodka around. Artur sounded positively giddy. The old fuck had started to think of me as the son he'd never had in prison, and he seemed satisfied that he'd done his best for me. Being *vory v zakone* was a huge honor. It should provide me, and the entire Chernov bratva, with a heightened sense of security. Kirill would be pleased to have a *vor* for a brother. Personally? It meant the power to take over Edward Sloane's business with ease, and whatever else that involved Russians in the area. It was what I needed to do to protect Sofia and Leo.

The tattoo gun droned, and vodka swam in my blood. The sauna air was making me dizzy, but I gritted my teeth and kept my position. I lost track of time as they inked their exclusive marks onto my skin.

"Your nickname in prison was the *palach*. It shall be your *vor* name as well. Welcome to the brotherhood, Nikolai Viktorovich Chernov: *palach*."

THE TOWER WAS the same as I remembered it from the outside. The inside was a different story. A towering monolith in Manhattan, one of the hottest property zip codes in the city. Kirill met me at his front door, once I'd been through several rounds of security.

"Nice to see you've beefed up the security here. Before, just anyone could wander through," I quipped. Of course, I was one of the worst offenders to abusing the former security at The Tower, as I'd killed many guards when I kidnapped Mallory seven years ago.

Kirill's impassive face cracked a smile at that.

He pulled me close into a brotherly hug. It was an unprecedented move from him.

"What's this? A show of affection? Don't tell me having kids has made you soft."

"You'll see one day," Kirill said, pulling back.

My eyes jerked to his, but he showed no sign that he was implying anything about Leo.

Inside, I noticed the changes to the penthouse. For starters, it was a lot bigger. Now, Kirill and Molly had taken up residence on the top two floors of the building, and a massive staircase connected them. When Kirill had lived here alone, it had been a soulless, sterile place. Now, I saw evidence of Molly everywhere, from the warm-colored curtains, to the soft chairs and art on the walls. Of course, there were bookcases in just about every room, and toys. Fucking toys everywhere.

"Kids! Come and meet your uncle Nikolai," Molly shouted through the cavernous house. She hugged me under Kirill's warning stare.

"Uncle? Aren't you teaching them Russian?"

"Kirill is." She grinned.

I looked at my brother and chuckled. "So no one is. I see *dyadya* has his work cut out for him." While we were half brothers, with the happily deceased, powerful *pakhan* Viktor Chernov as our father, Kirill had never grown up in Russia.

I turned to see two small humans entering the room. I was curious about Kirill and Molly's life, and my niece and nephew. My brother and I had made peace. Funnily enough, we got on better than ever with one of us incarcerated. Most of all, we had broken Viktor's legacy, and every day we didn't try to kill each other, we defied him.

"Are you our uncle?" the bigger one said. The girl, Kira.

I smiled at her. I knew what I looked like these days, with my wild eyes, shaved head, and even more tattoos than ever. I was also hardened in a way I hadn't been before prison. Seven years had only made me more unstoppable, and the aura of danger that surrounded me couldn't be mistaken.

Despite that, Kira approached and stuck out a little hand. Her tiny nails had glittery pink polish on them. I swore I'd never seen anything as small and perfectly formed.

"*Rad vstreche, Dyadya,*" she said, her accent passable.

"*A ty,*" I responded. "If you ever want to practice speaking Russian with someone, I'm your man," I told her.

She nodded, shaking my hand with a serious expression.

She jerked her head toward her little brother. "This is Ruslan. He's shy."

"Is he? That's all right, it's okay to be shy sometimes," I said quietly.

Crouched there on the floor, I watched the little boy peek out from behind his big sister. Then he emerged, one timid step after another. I marveled at how normal the children were. Untouched by the violence that had destroyed my life, and Kirill's. Somehow, despite their father being *pakhan* of a powerful bratva, they still smiled with perfect innocence. That kind of innocence had to be preserved. As Ruslan approached, and solemnly put his hand in mine, shaking it with intense concentration, I vowed to myself that I'd help preserve it, any way I could. I'd make sure Leo also had the same kind of innocence. I could tell Sofia had fought hard to protect it, and so would I.

"Okay, now, I'm going to give your uncle some tea. Why don't you two go and play," Molly said.

"Can't *Dyadya* Nikolai come with us to the playroom?" Kira challenged her mother. "I thought he was here to meet us, not you."

"Miss Chernova, stop being such a handful and give me a minute. You'll get him all to yourself soon," Molly said, a stern look on her face, though her lips were twitching.

She and Kirill headed in the direction of the kitchen.

I got up to follow them, heading toward the distant clank of dishes. "Don't tell me Olga is still the housekeeper here."

Molly snorted, an elegant sound. "Just try and take away the best nanny I've ever had. She's housekeeper supreme these days, and in charge of every single person, myself and Kirill included most days."

"Nikolai Viktorovich," a voice called to me as I entered the kitchen. Olga hadn't changed much since I'd last seen her. She was standing at the kitchen island, her hands white with flour.

"*Proshlo mnogo vremeni*," I said.

She smirked at me. "*Dobryy den.*"

"And for the idiots in the audience who can't learn Russian no matter how hard they try?" Molly perched at the island and looked expectantly at me.

"She's missed me," I translated wrongly.

Olga huffed. "I'm glad to see prison hasn't made you any more bearable."

I looked at the pastries she was arranging on the baking tray. "Don't tell me you're making *pelmeni?*"

Olga shrugged and avoided my eyes.

I couldn't stop my grin. "So, you did miss me, then."

"You caused Kirill Viktorovich and Mallory so much worry. Of course, I'm glad you're out, so they can stop thinking about you all the time."

"Right, whatever you say," I murmured and winked at her.

She huffed and bustled off.

Molly was laughing at the back and forth.

Kirill was standing on the balcony outside, and I went to join him, the wind instantly buffeting me. I peered over the high railing down at the city below. Central Park was a huge green square, outlined in gray city blocks.

"I was surprised by your call," Kirill said, studying me.

"I was surprised that you answered."

Kirill shrugged. "I'm glad you're out."

"I'm surprised you trust me around the kids. I got the impression that you didn't."

"Well, *palach*, your reputation in jail isn't a secret. Once I heard you got your *vor* marks, however, I knew."

"Knew what?"

Kirill's face split into a rare smile. "You've decided to live."

I laughed. I couldn't help it. My brother had never minced his words, and it seemed he wasn't about to start.

"You're still in business with the De Sanctis family?"

"Reluctantly. After everything that went down, I wanted to end all deals, but once I start going back on my word, it isn't worth shit, as you know."

I nodded in agreement. He was right, of course. In our world, where there was no law greater than ourselves, a man's word was more important than anything.

"Well, get ready to renegotiate your terms. They'll be having a change of leadership soon."

"Is that right?" Kirill raised an eyebrow at me. "Just make sure that killing Antonio doesn't bring Renato down on my neck. I don't want another bloodbath on my hands in my city."

"Believe me, if anyone hates the fucker more than us, it might be him."

A beat of silence, and then Kirill looked out at the city. His kingdom. "If you need me, I'm there. You know that. He's taken too much from you to stand by. I want to bury him, I've just been waiting for you, and the right time."

"Aw, that might be the nicest thing you've ever said to me," I mocked gently.

He gave me the finger.

"Very mature."

"Will you stay in the city? A *vor* in the bratva would be a great strength." Kirill changed the subject, knowing how our squabbles could devolve quickly.

"No. I can't. I'm heading north, but I'll be sure to visit."

"Hmm, I know that look. Have you found someone to obsess over? I thought that was reserved for… her."

I grinned at my brother. "*Bratan*, do I have a story to tell you. Grab a drink, pull up a chair. This one has a twist you'll never see coming."

23

NIKOLAI

When I set off from New York, after claiming one of the bulletproof SUVs from Kirill, I couldn't wait to get back to Maine. The city was loud, stinking, and chaotic. Somehow, in the quiet woods and crashing ocean of Hade Harbor, a slither of calm had lodged in my chest. I couldn't wait to get back.

I couldn't wait to get back. Back to them. My family.

I expected there to be traffic. I expected there to be delays. What I didn't expect was to be forced off the road on the side of the highway just outside New York.

Four cars boxed me in and drove me onto the hard shoulder. I tapped a quick message with my location to Artur and checked my gun.

Men got out of the cars around me, waiting for their boss. A low, simmering anger sparked in my blood when I recognized the figure who stepped carefully down from one of the cars.

Antonio De Sanctis.

He headed into the woods beside the rest area. I got out of my car and was instantly surrounded. He couldn't kill me right here, not with the deals he had going on with Kirill. I followed him into the woods.

He stopped just inside where the roar of passing cars was muted. He stood with his back to me, while his men arranged themselves in a circle around us.

"Tony, what a nice surprise. A little dramatic, but that's your style, I get it. Always overcompensating, aren't you, old man."

Antonio turned slowly. He had aged a lot in the last seven years. I could only be grateful that he was still alive. I'd been looking forward to killing him for so long, I'd never get over the disappointment if he died before I had the chance.

"Still cracking jokes in the face of death, boy? I take it prison didn't knock any sense into you."

"Everybody dies one day. Your day is coming soon."

Antonio glowered at me. "Are you really threatening me? Can't you see who's in control here?"

"All I see is a sad, wasted old man who couldn't even keep his own family safe."

Antonio smirked. There it was. He didn't know that I knew Sofia was alive. He took pleasure in denying me that knowledge. Knowing that he was the man who had threatened Sofia's safety, Leo's safety, made me want to kill him right here and now. Sadly, he was right. It wasn't the right time. I was too outnumbered, and Antonio deserved far worse than being shot, clean and simple, by the highway. His death should take days. No, years, actually.

"Ah, yes, you're referring to my whore of a daughter. At least with her death she stopped embarrassing me. Honestly, it was a relief."

I was on him before I could stop myself. My first, explosive movement caught everyone off guard. I was able to get in close to him, and my first punch landed well in his gut. A second later, hands were dragging me back. I laughed as his bodyguards got in a few hits.

Antonio staggered over to me only when my hands were held too tightly to move.

"You stupid piece of shit. If it wasn't for your brother, you'd be dead, shot down like a dog at the side of the road."

"Too bad you can't do anything, clearly. All you can do is tickle me? Come on, guys, put your back into it."

"You are totally mad. Prison sent you off the deep end."

"Oh, Tony, you have no idea."

Antonio stared at me for a long time before straightening up and smoothing his suit.

"I wanted to see you, to remind you what messing with my family had done to you. I can see it broke your weak mind."

"Sticks and stones, De Sanctis. Let's just be honest. You wanted to see me to dig the knife in. You wanted to remind me about her and see the hole it tore, when she died, right? Cut to the chase, I don't have all day to stand around measuring dicks with you."

Antonio laughed, shaking his head slightly. "I see I was wrong. I thought you cared about Sofia. You were the only man in her life, did you know that? Except for her cousin, of course."

"Don't speak his name in front of me." The threat left me before I could hold it back. Damn.

Antonio's eyes lightened. "Is Silvio a sore spot? Is that because his murder sent you to jail for so long? Or is it because he kept trying to fuck Sofia, like an unfixed dog?"

Antonio leaned in, getting in my face. "You know, I don't think I ever told your brother. Sofia was pregnant when she died. I never was sure if it was yours or Silvio's." His small eyes burned with malice.

His casual words undid my self-control, and I was on him again. This time, the bodyguards got more involved. I revised my plans of killing him right here and now after all. The fucker just needed to be gone from the world.

The butt of a pistol to the forehead sent my vision blurring. I fell to my knees as Antonio staggered into his men's support. He was holding his chest.

"Too exciting for you, Tony? I forgot you had a bad ticker. I could probably kill you just by pissing you off. It comes naturally to me, so be careful." Blood dripped from my eyebrow, down my face and across my lips. I wiped it away.

"You're not worth the hospital stay," Antonio muttered and nodded to his men. He'd only come to gloat, clearly. His hands were tied.

They left me there on the floor of the woods. I stared at the blue sky framed by the trees above.

My mind strayed to Sofia and Leo. I wanted to be back there already, not here arguing with her father, a man who was soon to be dead. A twig snapping to the left of me sent me sitting up.

"Changed your mind and decided to finish the job?"

I twisted around to see who had found me now.

A man stepped out of the trees. He seemed to be alone. He was tall and broad, wearing an Italian designer suit like he was born for the job. He didn't have his sister's smile, but he did have her dark eyes.

He towered over me as I sat on the ground and peered up at him.

"Renato De Sanctis. Two De Sanctises in one day. Lucky me. To what do I owe the pleasure?"

Renato's jaw was clenched tightly. He looked in the direction his father had gone.

"Nikolai Chernov. We need to talk."

"About?"

"Sofia."

WE WENT to a diner off the highway somewhere. Renato looked out of place. He was as effortlessly classy as his sister. He was the kind who could blend seamlessly into high-profile events. He could probably sneak up on a senator in plain sight and cap him in the bathroom, something I'd never be able to do. The air of violence that clung to my shoulders was too strong, not to mention my dead eyes and tattoos. In prison, I had turned my body into a lethal weapon, and everyone with half a brain stayed back. Apparently, that rule didn't apply to the De Sanctis family.

Renato ordered an expresso and watched in shock as I ordered pancakes.

"You're seriously going to eat pancakes right now?" His deep, dry voice made me grin.

"You ordered a double expresso in a highway diner, and I'm the crazy one?"

Renato watched me, and I watched him right back.

"What are you thinking about?" he asked after a moment.

"You remind me of her. You're very similar."

"I don't look as good in a dress," Renato said.

"True. Your sister looks good in everything she wears," I chuckled.

"You meant *looked* good, right?" Renato said.

"Did I?"

He tilted his head to the side, studying me. "You've already found her, haven't you?"

"What do you think? There's nowhere Sofia can hide from me. If I didn't find her in the afterlife, I'd come right back to this world and look. It was pointless to try to and conceal her. All it did was piss me off."

"Have you hurt her? Know that if you have, this conversation is about to go downhill."

I smirked at him. "You get points for that. I've spent seven years deciding if you should die for failing her, and then weeks deciding if leaving her alone, and allowing your father to threaten her makes you worthy of dying… your stock just went up a minuscule amount."

"I take that to mean that you haven't hurt her."

"You can take it to mean that I will kill any man who does, including myself," I stated flatly.

Renato stared at me for a long moment. It was the stare of a brother sizing up his future brother-in-law.

He nodded at length. "I never wanted her to disappear. I never wanted to lie, but my father holds a lot of power in the family. It wasn't time yet to take over from him. I honestly thought he had a year at most. He was so ill after his first heart attack. But somehow, he's managed seven years. Sometimes I think he's never going to die."

"Oh, he's going to die, and soon. I promise you."

The waitress put down my pancakes and Renato's expresso. He took a sip and grimaced, while I cut into my first buttery, sweet mouthful. Since finding Sofia, even food tasted better. It was like I was slowly coming back to life.

"So, you're going to kill him?" he asked.

"Why, you want me to? Don't tell me you're going to be the kind of man who waits around for someone else to do the dirty work? A boss like that won't be respected."

"Don't teach me rules about a family you have no knowledge about. We aren't like you. In my family, respect to the one who has gone before is the most important thing. With age comes wisdom, and it's the mark of a strong capo.

Antonio is old and still has supporters. Alone, it would be difficult to unseat him."

He let out a deep, pained breath, his fingers tapping the table in a tattoo.

"I can't kill him. It'll risk my position as the next boss. But you could. With inside help, to get him alone, vulnerable… you could do it."

I finished my last mouthful, making Sofia's brother wait. Finally, once I finished chewing, I put down my fork leisurely and smiled at him.

"Now you're speaking my language, Renato De Sanctis."

He smiled at me. "Call me Ren."

"Ren. I think we're going to get along just fine."

24

SOFIA

*L*eo held his homework in his little hands and frowned at one of his assignments. He'd been keeping up with his homework well. The kid was a good student. I was pretty sure he was better than either of his parents had been. He was a natural.

Now, I was waiting around for the doctor before visiting hours were over. The night with Nikolai had been a few days ago. I hadn't called him. I didn't know what to think. Nowadays, I was good at putting things out of my head and continuing on, even if I was in turmoil inside.

"Ms. Rossi?" Dr. Evans materialized out of nowhere, as if my thoughts had summoned her. "Let's talk in my office."

I left Chiara to finish Leo's homework with him and followed the doctor.

She shut the door and sat. Her expression was solemn, and my heart immediately clenched at the sight.

"What's wrong? Is it something with Leo?"

"No. He's perfectly healthy, no infections, clear results from all major indicators. He is ready for the operation."

"But?"

The doctor sighed, looking regretful.

"It's the donor, isn't it? They've changed their minds, haven't they?"

She nodded slowly. "Apparently, a close call playing football got them thinking they should keep all their organs, just in case they need a back-up one day. I'm sorry."

"Don't be. You did everything you could. That's just life, isn't it." I dashed an errant tear away. "When can he come home, then?"

"Since he's here, let's finish up his dialysis. There are a couple of tests left. I think we should do them. You never know. Maybe we'll find someone else tomorrow."

I took a deep breath. Nikolai's face filled my mind. I nodded slowly. "Okay, let's prepare, since we've come so far."

"I know this isn't the result you were looking for, and I'm sorry."

I ARRANGED with the hospital to pick Leo up in the morning. I stumbled out of the waiting room and into a long corridor. My head was spinning. Hard hands closed around my shoulders. I realized that someone was speaking to me. I blinked up at the voice.

"Sophie, are you all right?" Edward Sloane bent over me, looking concerned.

"I'm fine. Why would you think I wasn't?" My voice felt like it came from very far away.

"You're crying."

I brought a hand to my cheek and wiped the wetness away. Oh, so I was.

"Let me take you home."

"No, it's okay," I started. My thoughts felt jumbled. The thought of the donor played again and again in my head. He'd changed his mind and ruined a life. He'd changed his mind.

Edward put a firm hand around my shoulders and started to lead me toward the elevators.

I couldn't hear what he was saying. There was a crushing weight of disappointment on my chest too heavy to shift. It felt like the world was ending.

We got into the elevator. His arm fell from my shoulders, leaving me hunched alone in my misery. I'd had this feeling before, of course, like the world was crashing down around me, and there was no way to save myself. Every single time it happened, it felt like it could never be worse. Then life proved me wrong.

Before I knew it, I was sitting in Edward's shiny, tinted-glass Jeep in the underground car park.

"Here, drink something. You look white as a ghost," he muttered, turning the bottle cap and handing it to me.

I took it with numb fingers. Everything was numb. He pulled out of his space.

"Come on, I'll take you home."

We pulled up the ramp and drove past the outside lot. I caught a glimpse of Bran's car. Shit, was he waiting for me? I should tell him.

I knew it, but the disappointment felt too strong to move, like it had locked me in place with invisible manacles.

We drove through town and then went right instead of left.

Home was left.

"Where are we going?" I wondered. My voice was hoarse, as if I'd been silently screaming for hours.

"I thought, since I have you, I should grab your painting, and we can drop it off at home together."

I stared mutely out the window, sipping the water to try to and bring a trickle of moisture over my aching throat. It hurt because of all the tears I was holding inside. The raging and screaming were all pushing up from my chest, and I wanted to let them all out.

We reached Edward's mansion by the ocean. The gates slowly opened. Inside, soft lights were dotted around the grounds, showing the property to its best advantage.

Edward stopped the car and got out. I stayed inside.

He opened my door.

"I thought you were just grabbing the painting?"

"I'm not sure how to wrap it. Can you give me a hand?"

My senses were tingling, the same ones that had always warned me of danger. I left the water in the car. I shouldn't have drunk any. I was rusty at protecting myself, but I seemed to be moving on autopilot.

I followed him reluctantly into the house.

"So, what's going on? You look upset. Bed news with Leo?"

I followed him down the hall toward a huge, sunken sitting room. "How did you know?"

"What else could rattle a mother so badly, at the hospital, no less."

Right, that made sense. "Yes, there's a problem with the donor. It might not happen."

The painting was propped against the wall. I knelt in front of it. His mother's half-finished eyes seemed to stare into my soul.

"I'm sorry to hear that. Have you eaten?" he asked after a pause.

I shrugged. My stomach chose that moment to let out a growl.

Edward nodded toward the couch. "Sit, and let me get you something. Please, it's the least I can do."

I shrugged, hardly having the energy to argue. I felt exhausted. All my hopes, everything we'd been working toward, gone on a whim. I pulled my phone out of my pocket when Edward disappeared. Pulling up Bran's cell number, I sent him a message.

> Went home myself, sorry for keeping you waiting.

I'll add it to Nikolai's bill. Anyway, I'm officially off duty from now on.

What does that mean? Is he back?

I TUCKED AWAY my phone when Edward called to me. Inside the kitchen, he had a few leftover containers out. He held up his hands when I came in.

"Okay, I admit it. I can't cook, and this is what my meals usually look like. But, I am great at reheating things."

He pulled out a chair, and I sat.

"What would you like?"

"I don't mind. You really didn't have to share your leftovers with me."

"It's fine. The alternative is sitting alone, watching TV and eating by myself. I work too much to date a lot."

I took a bit of reheated pasta. "And yet you certainly get around, or so I've heard."

My despair was making me blunt as hell. I couldn't bring myself to care.

Edward laughed. "Well, that's one way to put it. Casual sex has nothing to do with dating. I haven't met someone who I wanted to have a relationship with, until now."

Unease prickled along my nerves. "I do hope you're not talking about me. This conversation is old when it comes to us."

"Ouch. I beg to differ, and like I said, I'm a man who gets his own way." He sat back and studied me with an appraising look. "Does that piss you off to hear?"

I shrugged. "Not really, I've known a lot of men like that."

"Have you really?"

I nodded. "The funny thing is that most of them had to eat those words at some point, before the end."

Edward raised an eyebrow. "Before the end?"

I took a gulp of water. The food was salty. I looked pointedly at his plate. "You're not eating."

Edward shook his head. "I can't."

A gentle warmth was spreading through my body, like I'd had too much wine. It had been a while since I'd felt it, but I remembered the feeling. Motherfucker.

"Why's that?" I managed, holding on to the edge of the table.

Edward set down his fork and smirked at me. "I can't remember which dish I put most of the sedative in. I guess it was the pasta."

The world spun, and I slumped back into the chair. Edward's mocking smile fixed on me from across the table.

"You know, you really should listen when people talk, especially men like me. You seem to have known so many of them, and yet you don't learn."

"All the men I've known like you are dead," I mumbled.

"Is that right? Too bad for you, I'm perfectly healthy."

He stood and rounded the table toward me. I couldn't do anything but watch as he scooped me up. His arms felt wrong against me. I wanted to fight and scream, but I had no energy to do it. I turned my head from his hot face as he lowered it to mine, holding me against his body. I had to think of something. I had to do something. Why hadn't I told Bran where I was going? Why had I walked out of the hospital in a dream?

Edward walked along the hall of his beautiful house. I watched the lights of Hade Harbor in the distance, nestled just along the shore.

"Believe it or not, this isn't how I wanted this to go. I gave you plenty of chances to accept my advances. I'd have wined and dined you. I'd have taken care of your son for you. I still can."

"You think I'll trust you after this?"

"People have recovered from worse than this, and besides, from what I hear, you have dated far worse than me."

I blinked up at him.

He grinned. "Isn't that right, Sofia De Sanctis?"

The shock was like cold water to the face.

He chuckled. "I admit I had no idea who you were, until some Russians who work for me in the area told me. Apparently, you're pretty infamous in bratva circles, not that they're bratva anymore. Exiled from all respectable families, they come in useful. The Russians will do all kinds of things that others won't. They told me about your terrible taste in men."

We'd reached his bedroom. It was dark inside, and he didn't bother turning on the light.

Fear and disgust rolled through me. This was really happening.

Edward paused on the threshold, stilling suddenly.

There was a loaded silence, and the awareness of being watched by unseen eyes rippled over me. I knew that feeling. I knew those eyes. Relief hit me, and I stopped trying to force energy into my drugged muscles and went slack.

"Eddie, my ears are burning. Hasn't anyone ever taught you it's not nice to talk about people behind their backs?" Nikolai's voice was full of mocking and malice.

Edward's hands tightened on me. "Who are you?"

A dark chuckle came from the darkness.

Edward glanced down at me. "Who is he?"

Your worst nightmare. I tried to make my lips cooperate. "He's... the end of you."

Another chuckle from the dark. "She's right, my clever little *lastochka*. You should have listened to her when she told you to get fucked, Eddie boy. Now, things aren't looking great for you."

A light clicked on. Nikolai was sitting on a chair beside the bed. The bedside lamp spread just enough light over him to make him look utterly lethal. He had a gun clutched casually in his hand, but it was overkill really, given the general sense of menace he was giving off.

He had black gloves on. Edward's grip slipped. He was going to drop me and run off. Nikolai clearly had the same thought, as he levelled the gun at us and tutted.

"Put her on the bed, nice and gently. Not even a hair on that woman's head should be harmed, or you'll regret it."

Edward walked stiffly to the bed and put me down. I sank into the soft mattress. I was on my side, and I could see Nikolai and Edward perfectly.

"Are you okay, prom queen? Apart from having to suffer this guy's company for an hour?"

I nodded, my head moving only slightly against the covers.

"Good. Now, you relax. Eddie and I are going to play a game, then I'm going to take you home."

"What kind of game? My security will have seen you break in here. They'll be on their way."

Nikolai chuckled. "I don't think they will. I think your simple little system will show a nice loop all night. Your network was child's play for a professional to break into."

"And you're a professional?"

Nikolai tutted. "No, but my friend is. I had your system hijacked days ago. You see, I was always planning on paying you a visit."

"For what? Money?"

"Oh, Eddie. It's cute that you think you have enough money to impress me." Nikolai pushed himself to his feet and approached Edward, keeping the gun trained on him. "I do like your operation, though, it has potential. I like your house, too. Too bad it's mortgaged to the hilt and you have no heirs. I'm going to get it for a steal at auction."

"What the fuck are you talking about?" Edward's voice was shaking.

Nikolai leaned down to keep his eyes on his. The smaller man shifted uncomfortably, his fists clenching and unclenching.

"I'm talking about the fact that this, right here, is your last day on earth. I hope you enjoyed it."

Edward backed away, his face paling. "Are you serious? You're going to kill me? The police will get you."

"They can try."

"All because of some bitch?"

A flash of terrifying fury moved through Nikolai's steel eyes. "Eddie, *bratan*. You just had to run your mouth, didn't you. I was going to walk you off the cliff at the back, a quick, merciful death. But you just landed yourself even deeper in it."

"Who is she to you?"

"Words can't capture all the things she is to me, but I'll try to dumb it down for you. She's the mother of my son and soon-to-be wife."

Edward blanched, realizing that he wasn't going to be able to bluff his way out. "I apologize. I shouldn't have touched her. I didn't know." He had moved to the bargaining stage of grief for his life.

"It's too late for that. This isn't a game show. No second chances." Nikolai pressed the barrel of the gun into

Edward Sloane's forehead. "The only thing to decide now is how much it's going to hurt."

Was he going to shoot him right in front of me? My head was swimming, and the drug was really kicking in now that I didn't have the frantic energy needed to stay alert. Now that I wasn't alone here. Now that Nikolai was here to save me.

My vision turned blurry, the edges darkening, before sleep washed over me.

IN MY DREAM, I was surrounded by burning skin. Strong hands held me, turned me, spread me wide. Liquid heat pooled between my legs, and I squirmed closer and closer to the feeling.

I woke suddenly when a thick finger breached me.

I jerked against the head between my thighs. A smooth scalp met my touch.

Nikolai.

His tongue was laving my clit, and his finger was pumping into me. I was so wet, I knew he hadn't just started.

"Awake, finally, prom queen?"

I opened my mouth to speak, and a groan left it. I writhed against the sheets, bringing my hips up to chase his smirking mouth. He pushed another finger inside me, stretching me, rubbing against my G-spot, so the pressure inside felt like it would burst.

"Do you have any idea how many times you've already come in my mouth?"

I shook my head, unable to talk.

Last night threatened to return to my consciousness, and I pushed it back down. I'd think about it later. After. First, I was going to come hard on the face of the man who had protected me once again.

I was rising, lingering right on the edge. I could feel my orgasm heading toward me like a steam train. Just as my muscles twitched, Nikolai stopped.

"Hey!" I protested.

He chuckled as he flopped onto his back, grabbing my hips as he went. I struggled upright, finding myself straddling his upper chest.

"Ride my face, Sofia, if you want to come."

I looked down at him. If felt far too early in the morning to be so filthy.

"Come on, *lastochka*, suffocate me with that pussy, flood my face."

I considered his words for a moment. His gray eyes were staring up at me, and his lips were wet, already smeared with my juices.

I twisted around and changed position on his chest before I questioned if I could really handle my wicked idea.

Now I faced his feet and blushed as Nikolai whistled. My bare ass was right before his eyes.

"What a view, I could stare at it all day, but back up so I can eat you. Do it now while I'm asking nicely."

"So bossy," I grunted as I complied.

Moving my knees back, I yelped as Nikolai's arms came around my thighs, and I lost my balance, and landed, pussy-first, on his face.

He slapped my ass, just as his tongue landed back on my clit.

Well, two could play that game. He was naked. His cock was drooling on his belly, right up his hard-packed abs. I leaned down and slid the head of his dick in my mouth, making him grunt. His hands landed on my ass, gripping big, juicy handfuls that he used to move me back and forth. His tongue licked me mercilessly. I groaned around his cock. Every time I slipped forward, his cock worked further down my throat, gagging me. He flexed his hips, pushing deeper inside, so I was powerless to move. I couldn't free my mouth or my hips. I could only be devoured by him.

I came embarrassingly fast. It had to have been all the times he'd already made me come, while I was still asleep. When I reached the peak, my hips shamelessly humped his face, my pussy dripping into his mouth. My moans vibrated around his cock, and he got harder, right before he spilled in my mouth. He came in long spurts down my throat.

"Don't waste a drop," Nikolai commanded, snaking a hand down my body to hold the back of my head.

I struggled to swallow the musky load. He came for so long, I started to worry I might pass out on his cock.

"Fill your belly with my cum, before I fill your cunt."

I pulled back, the twitching finished, as Nikolai lifted me effortlessly. He turned me in his arms and kissed me deeply. Our tongues tangled, the mixed taste of both of our releases turning me on.

"Hmm, you taste and smell like me. I like that."

"What happened last night?" I stared up at him. "Where have you been?"

"New York, didn't Bran tell you?"

"I didn't need a babysitter."

"Clearly. If last night showed us anything, it was that there's no babysitter but me who can handle you."

"What happened to Edward?" I had to know. I watched Nikolai's eyes.

There was no remorse there as he shrugged.

"He got what he deserved."

"You killed him. Are the police going to look for him? What if you go back to jail?" It was one of my greatest fears.

"Don't worry. I won't. No one will find him, no one will miss him. In his line of work, there's a high mortality rate. Don't worry."

"His line of work? I thought he was a businessman?"

"Let's just say, his hands weren't as clean as he liked people to think. Don't waste another minute thinking about him. He's fish food."

It should have scared me, the way he casually dismissed the fact that he'd killed someone last night. It didn't. I'd grown up in the same world Nikolai had. Nothing shocked me. In fact, I was glad. There was the dark, brutal truth.

"Get dressed. We need to get going now, or I'll keep you here all day."

I leaned up on my elbow, admiring Nikolai's body as he stood and stretched. I reached out and grabbed his hand. A new tattoo sat across the back. It was eye-catching. The Cyrillic script was foreign to me. I touched it gently. It was still healing.

"What does it say?"

"It says, the *palach*."

"What does it mean?"

"It's a title. A mark of respect in certain circles. It'll help keep you safe."

"You didn't answer the question."

He smirked at me, pulling a black T-shirt over his head. "It means the executioner."

I stared at him for a moment, unsure how exactly to respond to that terrifying truth.

"Come on, let's go. The hospital's waiting."

I WAS WALKING into the hospital with Nikolai Chernov at my side. It felt totally unreal.

"What is it?" He shot me a faint smirk. "Not that I don't like your eyes on me, but you have an expression on your face like you've seen the Devil himself."

Seeing Nikolai in the warm, bright sunlight of Hade Harbor was odd.

"Sorry, it just looks wrong seeing you here like this. It's too normal."

"Well, contrary to popular opinion, I'm not actually a demon in disguise." He laced his fingers through mine.

"Right, like a demon would ever choose you for a disguise. It would be a terrible one. A real demon would choose some small, scrawny guy who fainted at the sight of blood. If they wanted to hide, that is."

He let out a bark of laughter. "Fuck, I missed you, prom queen." He pressed a kiss to the back of my hand.

We went up in the elevator.

His grinning eyes met mine in the mirror inside the doors. "You're nervous."

"No, I'm not. How do you know that?

"You ramble when you're nervous."

"And you make jokes," I pointed out.

He chuckled and pressed a kiss to our joined hands. "We make a good pair. Before we go to the ward, let's go and see your Dr. Evans, alright?"

I raised an eyebrow at him.

"I do my homework."

"We don't need to see her. I'm just taking him home today. It's not going to happen right now."

"We'll see. Let's go and see the doctor and find out about those tests."

I pulled him to a stop in the hallway. "You mean you're going to get tested?"

"The best candidates for donation are blood relatives. Adult males in the family. I know you know that, so the real question is… why aren't you asking me to get tested?"

"I-I don't know. I guess it still doesn't feel like you're real. You'd really give Leo your kidney? You haven't even met him yet."

"He's my son. He's our son." He stopped closer to me and ran a finger down my cheek. "I'll do whatever I have to, to get our son what he needs. You should have already asked me, but that's a topic for another day. I'll make sure Leo gets what he needs, even if I have to kill and cut out a hundred potential matches myself. Now, hurry up, the good doctor's waiting."

25

NIKOLAI

*D*r. Evans was a calm, capable-looking woman. Whatever she might have thought about having a six-foot-three man covered in tattoos enter her office and demand to be tested for kidney donation, she kept to herself. Of course, the fact that Sofia had told everyone she was a widow didn't help the matter. The doctor rolled with it like a pro and went through the details with me. I was going to stay and be tested as soon as possible, since Leo was all good to go.

An urgent sense of anxiety went through me that I'd never felt before. What if my kidney wasn't a match? What if I couldn't give my son what he needed? I had a son. A son. It still hadn't sunk in, but I had a feeling it was about to, as Sofia was leading me to the children's ward where Leo was.

The brightly colored curtains in the windows and cartoon-character covers were at odds with everything I'd known in my childhood.

I stopped outside the door, my feet frozen to the spot.

That horrible, swirling chaos was roaring in my chest. I couldn't handle normal human emotions anymore, clearly. Sofia watched me, seeing right into my ugly soul, just like always.

"How should I introduce you?" Her soft voice wound around my heart.

"However you want. You know him, I don't."

"Okay. Let's go in then."

She tugged at my hand, always so brave. She had always been brave. She'd been defiant in the face of the threat I'd first posed to her, as a young woman on the cusp of life. She'd lived with her terrible father and slimy cousin without complaint. She'd killed her cousin herself when he'd tried to hurt her. She'd raised a kid alone to protect him. She was brave in a way few could be.

She walked into the room first. It smelled like crayons and chicken nuggets. She walked to the end cubicle. She couldn't afford a private room for our son. It hit me deep inside. Because of Antonio De Sanctis, Leo had suffered more than he had to. If I'd known everything, Kirill would have provided the best care in the world for him. Instead, Sofia had toiled away to do what she could. One day soon, Antonio would pay for every day she'd struggled without me. He'd answer for every tear my family had shed.

"Leo? I've got a visitor for you," Sofia was saying before me.

She pulled back a curtain. His bed was near the window, and a view of the woods, and beyond, the sea, filled my vision. A tiny figure sat on the bed. He wore dinosaur pajamas, navy and red. His gray eyes locked on to me with interest.

"A visitor! Who is he?"

Sofia took a seat on the edge of the bed, leaving the chair beside Leo free.

"His name is Nikolai," she said and nodded toward the seat.

I found myself sitting in it before I'd even realized I'd moved. I was having an out-of-body experience.

"Nikolai?" Leo scrunched up his little face. It was like looking at a mirror image of myself at his age. It was uncanny. "Like the name inside your ring?"

The name inside her ring? I looked to Sofia, but she avoided my eyes and simply nodded.

The boy considered her answer for a moment before twisting to me, crossing his legs on the covers and sticking out a skinny hand. "I'm Leo."

"Hello, Leo. It's good to meet you." His little bones felt as fragile as a bird's in my grip.

"Nice to meet you, too. You have an accent. Are you Russian?"

I blinked between him and Sofia. "I am. How did you know?"

"I'm learning Russian. Well, my mom tried to teach me some, but she's bad at it. Will you teach it to me?"

"If you want."

"Cool! Do you know Dumoulin?"

"The hockey player?"

Leo nodded enthusiastically. "He's from Maine. He's so amazing. After I have my operation, I'm going to try out for the school team. In Hade Harbor, there's a really good team at the high school where my mom works. Cayden West is the best."

"Is that right? Do you know how to skate?"

Leo's face fell. "No, not yet. Mom thinks it's too dangerous, and I could slip and fall, also *Zio* Angelo can't stay on his feet. If you're Russian, does that mean you know how to skate? It snows there a lot."

I could barely keep up with the swerves in the conversation. "I know how to skate." I tried to keep to the pertinent question. "I can teach you, if your mom doesn't mind… after your operation."

Leo smiled at me. That terrible confusion in my chest, like the winds of madness that had been blowing for years, suddenly died. His smile was like the dawn, just like his mother's.

"Promise? Pinky swear?" He held his hand out, pinky up.

I fit mine around his, and he solemnly shook our joined hands.

"Pinky swear."

"Now it has to happen. You can't break a pinky swear. It's for life," he explained in a hushed, reverent tone.

A laugh bubbled up in my chest. It wasn't mocking or sarcastic. It wasn't jaded in anyway. It was new. I didn't know what to make of it. The calm inside me continued. "That's fine by me."

I could feel Sofia's eyes on my face.

"Leo, we're going to go home today, but the tests you did were very important. Well done."

"I'm not having the operation?"

"You maybe are. We don't know yet. We have to check a couple more things."

Leo was quiet, studying his mother. "Did the man change his mind about helping me?"

Sofia wrapped an arm around his little shoulders. "No, sweetie, but there are a lot of factors involved."

He stared at his mother for a long time. I knew that look. I'd given my own mother that look many times. It was the look of a kid who is desperately trying to make the world a little better, for the person who loves them the most.

"Don't worry, Leo. Your mom told me about the operation. I'm going to help, if I can, however I can." *You're not alone anymore.*

Leo turned to me. He looked serious for a moment, and then he smiled. The look just about gave my wasted black heart an attack.

"Okay, sounds good. Do you know the book about the Ugly Dinosaur?"

"Er, I don't, but you can tell me about it, if you want."

Leo nodded and stretched to grab a hardcover book by his bedside. "I'll read it to you." He leaned closer to me, looking like he was about to share a secret. "I can't read all the words, but I can remember them."

"Good, that's good. Having a good memory is important," I found myself whispering back.

Leo nodded. "My mom says that, too. She always says that memories are the only way she can see my dad."

My eyes flew to Sofia's. I was caught in her chocolate-brown stare. It was official. Something weird was happening inside me, and I had no frame of reference to cope with it.

"Is that right?"

Leo nodded and then opened his book. "I'm going to read now. If you have questions, wait until the end, that's the rule."

"Clever."

He grinned and started to read.

"SHE'S NEARLY DONE. Your little man is something else. Congratulations, brother." Bran dropped onto the chair next to me. "Let's see the new ink." He tutted as he inspected my hand. "I'd love to say that it's great work, but I'd be lying."

"They aren't supposed to be pretty."

"Well, they certainly aren't. Will they be a problem for the kidney thing?"

"I hope not. As long as there is no infection, it should be okay, if I'm a match."

I was sitting on a bed in a private room. Directly below me, Sofia was filling out the discharge papers to take Leo home. It felt like a piece of me was downstairs with them. Twice in my life I had experienced love at first sight. First when I'd walked into an underground poker hall in New York, at the tender age of nineteen, and seen Sofia De Sanctis sitting at the bar. And now, the moment I'd seen that little boy smile up at me.

I was a goner.

I'd burn the entire world down to keep them safe.

My family.

My everything.

"I read up about these things. Sometimes they don't last forever, and you need another one, eventually."

I leaned back and tried to arrange the IV from my hand to be more comfortable. "That's fine. He can have the other one when he needs it, if I'm a match."

"You know you need to keep one, unless you want to die."

"I'm aware."

Bran snorted and changed the subject. "People have been asking about Sloane. His secretary is looking for him and his men. What should I do?"

"Nothing. When I get out of here, I'll speak to the Russians. They're the backbone of the business. It won't be too much work to take it over."

"And this *vory* business. Now that you have the title, do you get paid or something?"

"No, not at all. Being *vor* isn't about money."

'What's it about then?"

"It's about power. The power to keep my family safe."

Bran stared and then chuckled, running a hand up his arm. "Man, that just gave me shivers, like when a wolf protects its cub instead of eating it. So unexpected. So, what's the plan now?"

"Take Sofia and Leo home. Watch them. Don't let them out of your sight, until I can get there later. Nothing matters more than making sure they're safe. Antonio De Sanctis won't let this lie. He's planning his move. We've got to be ready for him."

"Got it, brother. I've got it."

26

SOFIA

I set the steaming casserole dish on the table and called upstairs to Leo. It was his first home-cooked meal in a week, and I'd made his favorite. *Pasta al forno*. A pasta dish, with tomatoes, baked in the oven until the cheese was melted to perfection. I tossed a salad and set it in the middle.

"There's room for one more, isn't there? Don't break my heart," a lilting Irish brogue murmured just behind me.

I turned to find Bran looking longingly at the food. The man had been sitting outside on the porch for an hour, after I'd chased him out of the kitchen.

"There's plenty. I'm having guests."

"Hmm, is it the bodyguard and his bride? How exciting." Bran leaned an elbow on the counter and stole a radish from the chopping board. "How did you end up here together? Nikolai told me a little of what went down at the end of his time with your family."

"It was terrible in the way that only my father can be responsible for. The only good thing to come from the entire thing was how Nikolai's brother, Kirill, made sure Angelo and Chiara got money to start over. He never asked them where they were going. He just equipped them to escape."

"Kirill is a good *pakhan*, according to Nikolai."

"Yeah, except for that time when he handed him over to my father." I gave Bran a wry grin.

"Maybe so, but you wouldn't be here, and Leo wouldn't be either if he hadn't. Sometimes, fate has plans for us." Bran smiled at me.

"Well, fate didn't bring Angelo and Chiara to Maine. It was me. She managed to contact me through our college emails, since I didn't have a phone she could call or the ability to see anyone I knew. She'd offered to come where I was. I jumped at the chance. I was so scared of being pregnant and alone, without any money or place to go... It was pretty selfish of me."

"That doesn't sound selfish to me. It sounds like you found your people, and they found you. Maybe they needed you, too. One person they didn't have to lie about their identities in front of. One person who really knew them. It's important."

"I never thought of it like that. So, do you have lots of people who really know you?"

Bran chuckled. "I have three siblings, so pretty much. Killian, Quinn, and Ronan."

The name finally clicked. "Wait a minute, you mean to tell me you're Bran O'Connor. From the notorious O'Connor family? I knew I'd heard your name. So, you and Nikolai bonded over hating my father?"

Bran laughed. "A little, maybe."

I tapped my lip, considering everything I knew about that family. "Your brother Ronan is a criminal defense attorney, right?"

"The best."

"And your eldest brother, Killian. Isn't he in prison?"

"He is and has been for a while. He doesn't play well with others. Ronan is working on getting him out, though. I'm sure we'll all be sitting around eating dinner again soon enough."

"And your sister?"

"My sister's only twenty-one. You'd think that'd be too young to cause problems, but she's the real troublemaker in the family. You'd like her."

"Is that right?"

Bran nodded. "And how's your brother? Renato De Sanctis... does he sleep well at night, considering what happened to you and Leo?"

I glanced at Bran. There was judgment in his eyes that I couldn't face. "No. Neither of us do, but it doesn't change anything. You wouldn't understand, unless you grew up with my family. Honor, respect for your father, for the don, knowing your place... it's ingrained in us from birth. Written in the blood. Italians don't go against blood easily."

Bran nodded. "You're blood, too. Leo's blood."

I swallowed hard. I had no way to make him understand the number that Antonio had done on Renato. How he'd taught him to push people away, to stay cold and aloof, and locked inside. People were a weakness, and the only way to avoid that weakness was not to care about anyone. My brother was fucked in the head, just as much as I'd been, the little bird with clipped wings. Renato was worse, probably, because he'd been around it longer.

"Well, what is it Nikolai says? Happy families are all alike; every unhappy family is unhappy in its own way."

I smiled. "It's Tolstoy, from *Anna Karenina*."

Bran sighed. "Figured it would be some depressed Russian, writing that shit. I've never seen someone read as much as Nikolai. It was all he did in prison. Well, that and wreaked havoc on the gen pop."

"Naturally." I found myself smiling at the very thought of Nikolai, reading away the time, escaping into books like he had when he was young.

The doorbell chimed softly, and Bran straightened. "I'll get it. Let's see if daddy Angelo believes you have a new boyfriend."

He disappeared through the house just as Leo came down the stairs.

"Dinner. Wash your hands."

"I already did!" He got into his little chair at the end of the table.

Chiara rushed into the kitchen. "Holy hell, girl. When you do something, you really do it. I thought you'd clean your pipes with the hot Irishman, not bring him home to Leo."

She pulled me close and kissed me on both cheeks. Her eyes widened dramatically as she held on to my shoulders. "Is he as hot in bed as he looks like he'd be? Blink twice for yes."

"*Zia* Chiara!" Leo called, waving from the dining area of the open-plan kitchen.

She turned and plastered an innocent smile on her face and waved to Leo.

"Hello, *tesoro*, I've missed your cheeky face."

Angelo appeared, looking back over his shoulder as he went. Suspicion and caution were written across his features as he stared hard at Bran.

The man himself ambled toward me and draped an arm across my shoulders. "Well, love, have you told them all about us?"

"Hilarious."

"Who is this?" Angelo asked, eyeing Bran with a dangerous look. He might have stopped being paid to be my bodyguard seven years ago, but he'd never really given up the role. He was as overprotective as ever, over me and Leo.

"You wouldn't believe me if I told you," I muttered, juggling the hot dinner plates and the casserole dish. "Are you really eating with us?" I directed the last to Bran.

"Damn right. It smells amazing. I love a woman who can cook. How does your lady stack up in that department?"

He grinned at Angelo, who looked like he wanted to tear Bran's head off his neck.

"Tell me who you are, or you're not staying."

"For dinner?" Bran wondered.

"In Maine," Angelo growled, his huge shoulders bunched up.

"Don't worry, big guy. He's with me."

The newcomer spoke from the doorway, and the voice was enough to freeze us all to the spot, well, all except Leo and Bran. Bran leaned back, smiling at his friend, while Leo perked up, sitting up in his chair and casting curious eyes at the man lounging in the doorway.

Nikolai leaned against the doorjamb, his eyes fixing on Angelo. My former bodyguard stood slowly, his chair scraping noisily across the floor.

"Oh my god, what the hell! Girl, you've been holding out on me so hard," Chiara squealed.

"What is it, what is it!" Leo demanded.

Bran patted him on the shoulder. "Just old friends catching up."

"Okay." Leo smiled at the scene around him, happy to have a full house.

Angelo had crossed the room to Nikolai. The two sized each other up. A wave of nerves traveled across me as I watched them. What if Nikolai blamed Angelo for keeping me a secret? What if the room was about to turn into a bloodbath? No. He wouldn't do that. Not with Leo here. I knew it without a doubt, somehow.

Nikolai's serious expression suddenly morphed into a wicked grin. "Come here, big guy. Long time no see."

He pulled Angelo into him and wrapped an arm around his shoulders. Angelo jerked with surprise at first and then relaxed. He slapped Nikolai's back, and the two split apart, smiling.

"Holy shit, that was hot," Chiara said, gaze riveted to her husband and Nikolai, a piece of garlic bread halfway to her mouth.

"*Zia cattiva*! You said a swear!" Leo held out his hand. "A dollar fine."

Chiara slapped a ten into his hand. "This dinner requires an advance payment. Go nuts, kid."

"They let you out? This whole country's gone to pot," Angelo grinned.

Bran cackled. "Classic dad joke."

"Hey, don't you call my husband old," Chiara quipped, pointing at him across the table.

"Look, you, don't forget who first called your husband daddy, eh? Let's get our facts straight."

I tore my attention away from Chiara and Bran, squabbling across the table like siblings.

Nikolai approached me as Angelo returned to his seat.

"Good evening, Ms. Rossi," he said quietly, his hands landing on my hip. He leaned in to kiss me hello, and his lips brushing across my cheek felt far too intentional and slow to be a greeting.

I flushed.

"Good evening. Are you okay?"

He leaned back, resting against the counter and crossing his arms. "Believe it or not, I'm a big boy and don't get scared of needles. Getting a sticker was fun, though."

"Very funny. I mean... are you okay really?" I didn't really know what I was asking, only that Nikolai seemed calmer than I'd seen him since he'd returned to my life. There was a contentedness about him that made me feel soothed inside.

We both looked at the full, noisy table.

Nikolai discreetly took my hand, lacing his fingers through mine. "A month ago, I'd have said no, and seriously doubt if I ever would be again. Now... Yes. I'm okay. *Budet zima, budet leto.* There will be winter, there will be summer."

"Meaning?"

People called us to join them. Leo was laughing, and Bran and Chiara were arguing, while Angelo poured wine liberally into glasses.

"Meaning, you, Sofia... are my summer."

I didn't know what to say to that. Like always, he stole my words and my heart at the same time.

"Nikolai!" Leo's voice carried across the din. "You can sit next to me."

Nikolai immediately turned toward the sound of his son's voice. "With pleasure."

He squeezed my hip and headed to the end of the table, where Leo was grinning at him madly.

Finally, everyone had a plate, a drink, and was ready to eat.

"Can I propose a toast?" Bran said, rising to his feet. "It'll be short, because this food is too good not to eat immediately."

"Go head then," Nikolai said and waved to his friend. "He won't stop until he's done it," he explained.

"To friends, old and new. To good health and many more dinners to come. To family, wherever you find it, no matter the distance or time apart." Bran's words seemed to hold us all spellbound for a second.

"*Slainte!*' Bran grinned and raised his glass.

"*Salute*," Angelo followed, kissing Chiara on the forehead as she clinked her glass against his.

I turned to Nikolai. "Cheers."

"*Na Zdorovie*," Nikolai raised his glass to mine.

27
NIKOLAI

I slept with Sofia. She didn't seem worried that Leo would wonder why someone was sharing her room. I took my cue from her.

When dawn was just peaking over the horizon, with my beloved held tightly in my arms, I heard the soft sound of the door creaking open. My hand closed around the pistol under my pillow. Thankfully, before I could level it at whoever had come in, a tiny voice reached my ears.

"Psst, Nikolai! Wake up!"

Releasing my grip on the hidden gun, I shifted carefully and sat up. Leo stood in the doorway, his hair tousled and adorable. He waved at me. I waved back. My heart tightened painfully.

He beckoned me with a mischievous grin. The kid looked like trouble. I couldn't wait to see what he was up to. I followed him quietly. He took us downstairs to the kitchen.

"Let's make my mom breakfast. She never stays in bed late."

"Okay, let's do it. What do you want to make her?"

Leo considered it for a moment. "Toast?"

"Toast? I think we can do better than that. What about *blinchiki*? Pancakes."

"Can you make them?"

"I'm the pancake king, but I'll need your help."

"Okay! I can help."

I gave him a list of ingredients, and he scampered off to get them. I washed my hands, staring out at the water beyond the window. The ocean rolled softly past the dock at the end of the street. The silence felt deep, and salt and pine hung in the air. My *lastochka* had picked a good place to make a home.

"Are you going to be sleeping over every night?" Leo asked once we were deep in the mixing and measuring of the pancakes.

"Is that a problem?" Evasion came naturally to me.

He shrugged. "Sometimes *Zia* Chiara sleeps over."

"Anyone else?"

Leo shook his head. I was ridiculously happy to hear it.

"I think my mom likes it when you stay. She's smiling all the time lately."

"Is she?"

Leo nodded. "I hope you stay so she keeps smiling. What's your last name?"

"Chernov."

"Chernov. Are you my dad?"

I stared at him, all thoughts startled out of my head. His gray eyes stared at me, unblinking. It was like looking in a mirror, except I couldn't remember being as young and unspoiled by the world as Leo was.

"Why do you think that?"

"Your name is inside mom's ring. She said that ring was for my dad. So… you must be my dad."

"I'm sure there is more than one Nikolai in the world." *Fuck*. I wished I'd thought about how I was going to handle this.

Leo narrowed his eyes at me. "But you're the only one in our lives."

"Right, you're right. You're really smart, did anyone ever tell you that?"

"Yes, my mom tells me all the time."

"Well, she's really smart, too." I blew out a breath and pulled a chair out, sitting so I was at the same height as Leo. Nothing in my life had ever made me as nervous as this conversation had.

"If I was your dad, would that be a good thing?" I couldn't swallow suddenly.

Leo considered my question and then slowly nodded. The relief of his small, hesitant smile hit me like a ten-ton truck.

Then a small frown crossed his face.

"What is it?"

"I just wonder why you took so long to come to us?"

It was official, this was the most difficult conversation of my life. I was sweating.

"Sometimes we don't have a choice in these things, Leo. Believe me when I say I wanted to come. If I could have come, I'd have run the whole way here. Also believe me when I say that I will never, ever leave you and your mom again. I'm here to stay. I missed you before I even met you."

Leo studied me and then stuck out his little hand, holding his pinky up again.

"You know how important a pinky swear is."

I nodded solemnly. "Yes, I remember."

"Do you pinky swear that you won't ever leave us again?"

"I swear." I took his tiny finger and shook it. His hand was small next to my large, tattooed one.

"Also, you'll teach me how to skate? You didn't forget?"

"I didn't forget."

A clatter overhead announced Sofia had gotten up. Leo squealed.

"She's up too quick. She's going to ruin the surprise!"

"You go and stall her, I'll cook these."

Leo nodded solemnly. "Good plan."

Then he turned on his little dinosaur slippers and disappeared up the stairs, leaving me with the half-made batter and a heart that felt too big for my damn chest.

Two minutes later, Sofia strolled into the kitchen. She wore an oversized t-shirt, her feet were bare, and her short hair was like a puffball around her face. I couldn't stop staring.

"Wow, Leo was telling the truth. You're really cooking."

"I've fed you plenty of times, if you care to recall." I caged her against the counter and kissed her neck.

"Yet I've never seen you cook." She looked up at me steadily. "How did the tests go last night? We didn't get to speak."

That's right. We didn't get to speak because as soon as the guests left and Leo was in bed, I tugged Sofia into her room, locked the door, and fell on her.

I'd lost count of the number of times I came hard inside her, our bodies sticking together with sweat and juices.

"They went well. Though with the way you wore me out last night, I need to go back in to replenish vital fluids."

"Nikolai," she breathed out, exasperated. "Can't you be serious for a second?"

"I'm being serious, very, very serious. I'll see to Leo's problem, one way or another. Nothing is more serious to me. I am also very serious about getting to the bottom of something."

I had the ring off her finger before she could stop me. I turned it, holding it up to the light. Sofia made an attempt to grab it, and I pinned her hands behind me.

There it was, in the smallest cursive, engraved on the inside.

Nikolai Chernov

"Why didn't you tell me?"

"Tell you what?"

"That you've always been waiting for me?"

Sofia was silent for a long moment and then shrugged. "I guess I didn't know how."

"I would have gone easier on you." I thought back to chasing her through the woods and pinning her to the ground, fucking her with her own knife, and locking her in the coffin.

"Would you really?" She raised an eyebrow at me.

"I don't know." It was an honest answer. "The demons inside aren't easily placated. They wanted a blood sacrifice."

She brought a hand to my chest, pressing just over my heart, the place where the swallow was tattooed. "And now?"

"And now, I don't know. They're quiet, for the first time in years. I feel... calm."

"If you're trying to call me boring to be around, it won't go down well," she warned.

I chuckled at that. "When you've lived the life I have, calm is precious, rare. Calm has to be cherished, just like you."

"Hmm, you're pretty romantic in the morning."

The sound of hurrying little feet raced above us. "I'd love to get a whole lot more romantic right here on this counter—"

"But you're about to get a crash course in life with a kid, so brace yourself." Sofia stepped away so it didn't look quite like I'd been about to sit her ass on the counter and eat it for hours.

I took her hand and slid her ring back on. "This needs to be official as soon as possible."

She blinked at me. "Are you asking me to marry you?"

"No." I shook my head, smiling at Leo as he raced down the stairs toward us. "I'm telling you we're getting married, and soon."

"You're such an asshole," she murmured to me, smiling at the incoming shape rocketing toward us.

"True, but I'm the asshole who will be your husband before the week's out."

I FOUND the Russians in Portland. Bran and I had been watching their movements. The operation itself was frighteningly simple. Drugs, arms, and people were moved out of Canada, through Maine, and down into Boston, where they spread out all across the East Coast. Edward Sloane had relied on exiled bratva members to do the dirty, dangerous work for him, while he paid the police and customs to look the other way.

There were five Russians who had worked for Sloane. The leader of the group was a man called Andrei.

He was sitting eating with his men when I arrived at the bar.

It was dimly lit, despite being daytime. A woman was singing on stage. The entire place smelled like greasy fries.

Bran waited outside in case another car full of them should roll by. I made my way across the room toward them. They went quiet as I approached. I swung myself into the free seat across from the leader.

Dark stares fixed on me.

"And you are?"

"Nikolai. Nikolai Chernov."

The stares only turned darker. One of them reached for his gun under the table.

"Don't turn this into an argument, *bratan*. I'm not here to argue. I heard you were looking for your boss."

Andrei took his time to answer. He nodded. His answer was about as forthcoming as I expected from Russians.

"Well, you're looking at him. Sloane's operation is mine now. If we get along, then your jobs are safe. If you think that you'd like to be boss over me, you can join Sloane."

Andrei's gaze fell to my hand. The new tattoo from the *vor* stood out against more faded ink.

"*Palach*. We've heard of you."

"Stop, you'll make me blush."

"Why would Kirill Chernov's brother, a *vor* in his own right, the *palach*, want to take over a two-bit operation here?"

"New York is over, *bratan*, didn't you hear? My reasons aren't important, and it won't be a two-bit operation by the time I'm finished. We're done with moving people, though. It's not my wheelhouse, and I don't like it for our brand."

The men exchanged cautious looks at my glib humor.

"I don't know who you are, or what you did to be forced from your bratva, and I don't care. From today, you have a shiny clean slate with me. If you work well and prove yourself, you'll be given more responsibility."

"Is the Chernov bratva expanding up here?"

"Maybe. If you want to belong to a brotherhood again, this is your chance. Take it or leave it. But we do things my way. I'm going to live here, and we have to respect it. Clean, honest drugs and arms running. That's the plan."

"Clean and honest drugs and arms running? You really are as crazy as they say," Andrei said, finally cracking a smile.

"I sure am. We'll work it out, if you're with me."

Andrei looked around at his men one by one. They communicated without speaking.

He turned to me and nodded solemnly. "It'll be an honor to be brothers with the *palach*."

2 8
SOFIA

*M*onday at school felt like a dream. It was too normal after everything that had happened in the last forty-eight hours. My students didn't get on my nerves, and the sun was shining. The sky was blue above the woods outside the back of the school.

Best of all, there was a car waiting for me by the door, in direct defiance of the strict no-parking rule. Nikolai Chernov, as always, had never met a rule he didn't want to break.

He was leaning against the door when I left the main entrance and straightened up as I approached. He was drawing even more stares than Bran had. I could only imagine the interesting rumors that had to be flying around the student body by this point.

No one looked like Nikolai Chernov. In full daylight, I was finally about to see the changes that had happened in the seven years we'd been apart.

He was broader. His body had been lethal, even then, but seven years ago there had been a leanness to him that whispered of the remnants of youth. That was long gone. His hair was shorn close to the scalp. I'd always loved his tumbling dark waves. They softened a dangerous man. Now, there was no softness left to hold on to. His tattoos were dark against his golden skin, licking up his neck.

"Good afternoon, prom queen."

I abandoned all hope of killing the rumors when Nikolai snagged my hip and pulled me close to him, kissing me deeply.

"That is not a workplace-approved kiss," I reprimanded him.

He only grinned. "It's after work. I've been counting the minutes. Besides, I'd say we've done worse on school grounds."

"Oh my god," I muttered, trying my best not to blush like I was a teenager myself. I felt like one. I'd never felt so light. I turned my attention to the car that sat at the curb. It was shiny and new, not to mention top of the line. "New ride?"

Nikolai nodded. "It's for you. I already had the other one towed."

"You did what?"

"Had it towed. Do you think I'm going to let the mother of my child, and my only son, drive around in an unsafe car? The only other option is that I simply drive you every-where. I don't want to put you back in a cage, Sofia. Be free, but be safe." He tossed me the keys. "Here, you're driving."

We got into the new car. It was nice. Luxurious as hell. I melted into the leathery seat and pressed the ignition button. It purred smoothly beneath us.

"Do you really mean that? No security... nothing changing?"

"I can't promise no security, but I don't want you to live the life you hated with your father."

"Life has been quiet without you, except for Edward Sloane, that is."

"Hmm, you are quite the danger magnet, as always. It'll get more dangerous, just through the fact of me being with you, but that will also make it safer. We will need to move, though."

"Move? I like my little house in the middle of nowhere."

"I like it, too, but we need something bigger, more rooms, and able to be properly secured."

I drove us through downtown. The fall light was fading earlier and earlier these days, and a cold wind promised that we were on the cusp of winter. A new season, a fresh, white slate.

"More rooms?"

Nikolai smirked. He was leaning an arm along the window, and the warm sunlight cut slices over his tattooed skin. I didn't want to stop looking at him.

"Leo needs siblings, don't you think?"

I stopped at a light and finally got to look at him. "Are you serious? We've been... back together... for a week, and you're talking kids?"

"Exactly, it's already been a week, and you're not pregnant yet. We aren't trying hard enough. We have seven years to make up for, prom queen."

"Niko," I trailed off, unsure what I wanted to say next. I couldn't pretend I didn't want to have another child. I had dreamed of giving Leo a sibling, but I'd given up hope that it would happen. Now, the future felt wide open and dauntingly full of hope. It made me anxious to feel so light. Something bad was surely on its way to balance the feeling.

"Hmm?" His voice was lazy. He had settled a hand on my knee and slid it up my leg, under my skirt.

"You're distracting me."

"If you think this is distracting, you've not seen anything yet," he murmured, his gray eyes dancing with wicked amusement.

"Stop. We've got to go and get Leo. He'll be tired after his first day back at school."

"It's already done."

"It is? By who?"

"Bran."

"Oh, okay. Well, in that case, put your hand right back where it was."

Nikolai chuckled. "Just try and stop me."

THE NEXT DAY, while Leo was having his routine dialysis, I met with Dr. Evans.

"So far, not to get ahead of ourselves, but the preliminary tests look good for a match between Leo's father and him."

I gripped the edge of my chair so hard it creaked. "Really?"

"Really. Same blood type, tissue type. Now we have to check on Mr. Chernov's overall health and ability to recover from an organ extraction, though something tells me he wouldn't let an operation slow him down."

"You've got that right. He's determined, as long as he's a match."

Dr. Evans nodded. "If we get the green light, then I want to do it as soon as possible. Mr. Chernov has assured me that insurance isn't an issue and he's willing to pay out of pocket for a quick surgery date. Given Leo's age and the severity of his condition, there's a good chance that we could be doing this first thing in the new year, maybe even before."

"Before?" I was dumbstruck. It was November. In a year, we could be going skating together out on the pond at the edge of town, a simple pleasure that Leo had been longing to partake in for years.

Dr. Evans nodded. "Now, the aftercare is important, as you know. Mr. Chernov mentioned getting nurses at home to help out."

"I guess. I can probably handle it."

"You also have a job, and Mr. Chernov himself will be inca-pacitated. Don't underestimate how hard all of this is, Miss Rossi. We don't need any heroes here. Take the help, and take care of yourself."

. . .

THAT NIGHT, Chiara came over for dinner and ended up falling asleep with Leo, in his bed, while reading endless bedtime stories.

When I went downstairs, Nikolai was putting a jacket on. I still couldn't get used to the sight of him in my little house. It was like seeing a dangerous wild animal in a cozy, domestic setting, without even a leash to keep the people in the house safe. Bran was lounging on the sofa, watching TV. With the two of them in such a small space, it felt a little much. There was a lethal quality in the air that was vaguely unsettling. I hadn't asked Nikolai exactly why he had his friend watching over me and Leo whenever he couldn't. I didn't want to know right now. I wanted to keep my head firmly in the sand and ignore the world for a little more.

"Come on. We're going out for a bit."

He held my jacket out for me, and I slipped my arms in. We went out onto the porch, and Nikolai locked the door behind us.

"Where are we going?"

"Not far."

He walked me to the edge of the porch and held out a hand while I stepped down the stairs, before turning us toward the garage and my little studio.

Inside, the familiar smells of my oil paints and turps met my nose. I hadn't been in here since I was trying to finish up Edward Sloane's portrait of his mother. That was one piece that would never need finishing.

There had to be something wrong with me, because the certainty that Nikolai had killed the local hotshot and set it up in a way that hadn't brought the cops to our door should be frightening. It wasn't, though. After all, I was a woman who had grown up around violence. A woman who had cut the throat of her own cousin.

Nikolai was right, in the end. We weren't so different, deep down inside. Maybe I'd be him, if I'd lived the life he had.

"So, show me," Nikolai called to me from farther into the studio. He was standing at my covered canvases. The ones of him.

I hurried toward him, suddenly shy to reveal the truth of my years-long obsession with this man.

"No, they're bad. Amateur, really."

"Doubtful. Show me, prom queen."

I shook my head stubbornly. He moved quicker than I could properly see in the dim light. His hand snatched the cloth off the painting sitting on the easel. He stilled as he took it in.

It was the one I'd been working on for a while. A dark forest ringed a puzzle piece of night sky. Stars winked in the darkness like scattered diamonds on velvet. A dark head was tilted back, enjoying the view. Only the back of the head was visible.

Nikolai stared at it for a long time.

"It's the story. The one you told me that day... in the basement."

He nodded, not needing more explanation than that. Our shared past thrummed in the air between us.

"Once upon a time, because that's how all the good stories begin, there was a boy. He was a child of the woods, and the trees were his only friend. At night, he lay in the loam and counted the stars. He was a wild thing, and sometimes, he seriously considered walking farther into the woods and never returning to the world of men. In the end, he couldn't, though."

"Why not?"

"Because the boy wasn't as whole as the animals he played with in the forest. He had a cage around his heart... one without a key. He could smile, and laugh, and pretend to be a real boy, but deep inside, he wasn't. There was a hole inside him, inside that locked-up place, where he couldn't reach it."

"You shouldn't tell sad tales as bedtime stories."

"Ah, but this story isn't sad. One day, when the boy became a man, and his heart was blacker than the purest tar, he met a girl. One who once stared at the stars at night and dreamed of being loved, too. It didn't matter how terribly he had lived his pathetic life. When she smiled at him, it felt like the fucking sun had finally risen for the first time in his life. He could feel the light on his face when she looked at him."

Then Nikolai was turning to me and pulling me close. He kissed me lightly at first, smoothing my hair back.

"You destroy me, you know that? No one understands me like you. No one has ever tried to."

"Yeah, well, ditto. You saw me, even when I was drowning. You saved me," I whispered against his lips.

It was the quiet, intimate conversation that we should have had, all those years ago, after everything that had happened at Casa Nera. But we had been robbed of so much.

"You saved yourself, Sofia. Your life here, Leo's happy childhood, your job, your home… you saved yourself, and our son."

He walked me back toward the table behind me, pressing his hips against mine. He was hard; the man was utterly insatiable.

"Tell me you love me," he commanded.

"I love you."

"Tell me you'll never leave me." Another command, one that made me smile.

"I'll never leave you."

"Good, because I'll never let you. Now, lift up that little skirt, bend over this table, and let me love you. You showered this morning, and I need to make you smell like me again."

"Nikolai!"

LATER, when I was spent and tingling with pleasure, we headed back to the house. His hand took mine, and we walked across the grass toward home. Nikolai stiffened when he turned toward the porch. The tender, intimate atmosphere evaporated as tension radiated from his every move. He let go of my hand and pulled a gun from his belt. Fear laced up my spine.

"What's wrong?" I asked.

He held a finger to his lips, indicating for me to be quiet, and jerked his head toward the door. I hadn't noticed the small black gap down the side.

It was ajar.

29

SOFIA

I started forward before I could help myself.

"Leo!"

Nikolai's arms went around my middle, and he held me back, clamping a hand over my mouth. "Shh, they might still be inside. Stay behind me. And take this."

He set me down, releasing my mouth and pressing a wicked-looking knife into my hand. Where exactly he'd had it on him, I had no idea, but now the feel of it in my hand was reassuring.

I followed him to the porch, Leo's name trapped behind my lips. I felt wild with worry. Nikolai led the way first, his gun ready to shoot and ask questions later. I edged in behind him. We got to the sitting room. The first thing I saw was red on the white sofa cushions. So much red.

I stifled a sob as I took in Bran, lying in front of the sofa.

"*Yebat.*" Nikolai was tense as hell as he approached, his gun trained on the corners of the room.

My mind seemed to detach itself from my body at the sight of the blood. Blood here, in my little humble house. Blood splattered on Leo's coloring book that he'd forgotten on the sofa when he'd gone to bed.

I was running up the stairs before I could stop myself. Nikolai hissed my name, but I couldn't stop. Nothing would stop me from going to Leo. Nothing.

I ran down the hall and burst into his bedroom, my knife hot in my hand. I'd kill them. If anyone had touched him, I'd kill them myself, and I wouldn't need a weapon to do it. My bare hands would more than do.

I came to a stop just inside the room as Nikolai caught up with me.

The room was empty. The bedside light was toppled over, and a glass was broken beside it. The empty bed was rumpled.

Chiara and Leo. Both gone.

I turned wordlessly to Nikolai, my entire world dissolving. I couldn't stand up straight. I couldn't see. I couldn't do anything.

Nikolai's arms surrounded me, and he held me when my knees failed.

"Sofia, I'll get them back. I promise. No matter what, I'll get them back," he said quietly into my ear. "I need to call an ambulance for Bran."

"He's alive?"

Nikolai nodded. His words felt like they were coming from very far away, like I was sinking underwater.

"How are you going to get them back? Is this because of Edward Sloane?"

Nikolai shook his head and smoothed his fingers under my eyes, just as I realized I was crying.

"No, prom queen, it's nothing to do with that. This is more personal than that."

Horror dawned through me.

"It's Antonio, isn't it? It's my father. He's making good on his threat." My face was going numb. My entire body was following. Only Nikolai's hold on me kept me upright.

Nikolai nodded. "It's time for me to go back to Casa Nera, Sofia. It's time to finish what we started seven years ago."

"He'll kill you. He'll kill Leo, and then you, too." I was babbling.

"No, he won't. He won't get the chance. Do you trust me?"

His question broke through the screaming chaos in my head.

"Yes."

I knew the answer without having to think about it.

"I'll get our son back, unharmed. Antonio doesn't want him, he wants me."

"So, what are you going to do?"

"Whatever I have to."

"You'll die. He'll kill you."

He pulled me close and kissed my cheeks. "Don't forget, prom queen. It's better to die than do nothing."

I WENT in the ambulance with Bran. Nikolai followed behind us. The paramedic in charge didn't like my rapid breathing and paleness. He was checking my blood pressure when I passed out. I couldn't help it. I hadn't seen someone hurt, really hurt, in a long time. Bran's face was pale and bloodless, and his abdomen was a mess. He'd been shot in the stomach. I could only guess that it had been with a silencer, since Nikolai and I hadn't heard anything. We'd only been feet away in the garage, and we'd missed it all.

Guilt choked me, and the sight of Bran's dark blood welling up and dripping to the floor of the ambulance made me think of Leo. I fell into the darkness gratefully.

When I woke up, a stranger was sitting beside my bed. I shot up, and he flinched.

"Who are you?"

"I'm Andrei. I work for your husband," he said, voice gravelly.

Worked for Nikolai? He only got to town a week ago.

"Where is he?"

Andrei was silent, a muscle ticking in his jaw. Alarm pushed me upright.

"Where is he?" I demanded.

"He has gone to take care of the problem."

Cold dread struck me. Nikolai, and probably Angelo, had both gone and left me here. They were pursuing the men who'd taken Leo and Chiara. They were on their way to Casa Nera.

I pushed back the covers. "I have to go."

"No, you're to stay here. The doctor said."

"I don't care what the doctor said!"

"Fine, but the *palach* said the same. I can't let you leave."

"I don't care what he said. My son is gone. My son! If you think I'm going to lie here and rest, eating Jell-O, while they go after him, you're wrong."

"You have no choice," Andrei told me.

That's what you think. I took a deep breath and tried to calm my racing heart. Panicking wouldn't get me on the road to New Jersey any faster. I had to be smart.

"I want to see Bran. How is he?"

"Stable. He's out of surgery and asleep."

"Take me to see him. I can relax if I see him."

Andrei stared hard at me, clearly unconvinced.

"Take me to see him, or I'll scream this place down and tell everyone passing by that you attacked me."

He blinked at me, sitting back. "I'll take the chance."

"Okay, fine. When I see Nikolai next, I'll tell him you touched me. Explain that to your *palach*."

A look of unease drifted over Andrei's blunt features. He sighed.

"Fine. I'll take you to see the Irishman, but then you have to agree to come back here."

"Thank you," I muttered. It would be a cold day in Hell when I thanked a man for controlling me, but Andrei didn't know that. I was getting out of here and going to Casa Nera, and no one was going to stop me.

I got out of bed. I was still wearing my clothes, thank goodness. I put my sneakers on and walked beside Andrei as he led me to Bran's floor.

"Are you all right? You're not dizzy?"

I put a hand to my forehead. "Only a little." I wasn't sure how I was going to get away from Andrei, but it seemed best to keep my options open.

He brought an arm up, as though he was going to support me, and then blanched, no doubt remembering my promise to tell Nikolai that he'd touched me. Andrei looked over his shoulder.

"I should get you a wheelchair."

"No, there's no need, I can manage. Thank you," I said, taking his arm and leaning on it. I might be laying it on a little thick, but thankfully this man didn't know me. He had no idea what my normal looked like.

We got to Bran's room. A nurse was just coming out.

"Mr. O'Connor can't have visitors. He's just out of surgery."

"Oh, I just wanted to check on him. Can you tell us how it went?"

"It went well. He needs to sleep now, and the doctor will be seeing him soon."

The nurse looked at the inpatient band on my wrist. "Are you ok? Do you need help getting back to your room?"

Here it was, my opportunity. I swayed a little against Andrei, who looked at me in alarm.

"Maybe. I am a little lightheaded."

"No problem." The nurse directed me to a seat. She started up the hall. "If you come with me, I'll give you a wheelchair to take her up in." She directed the last to Andrei, who looked torn about leaving me.

I forced a yawn and rested my head back against the wall. "I'm so tired, you're right. I need to lie down, before I fall down."

He nodded and seemed to decide I wasn't a flight risk anymore , taking off after the nurse.

I was up and running toward the elevators as soon as he'd turned the corner. I didn't know how much time I had until he came looking for me.

As I ran out, a voice called to me. It was Dr. Evans. She was standing at a vending machine, her wallet in hand, waiting for a candy bar to drop down.

I veered toward her.

"Sophie? This is a late visit to the hospital. I hope everything is okay with Leo?"

"It is, thanks." Forcing the words out made me want to cry. "My friend got hurt, so I'm just checking on him."

Dr. Evans nodded. "I'm sorry to hear that." She turned as the candy bar got caught before dropping down and tutted. "Isn't that always the way. Just a moment."

She set her wallet down on the side and leaned down to try to work her hands into the thin slot of the machine.

I had her wallet in my hand and was out the front doors of the hospital before I could see if she'd gotten her late-night snack or not. I sent a silent apology to her. I'd pay her back.

I jumped into the nearest taxi and gave him Chiara and Angelo's address. I couldn't risk going back to my house to get my car. If I was right, Angelo would have gone with Nikolai and Chiara's car would be sitting in the driveway. I knew where she hid her house keys and where her car key was inside.

Nikolai might think he could handle whatever happened at Casa Nera, but this was my family, and I wasn't sitting it out. I wasn't going to let the man I loved hand himself over for Leo. I wasn't going to let either of them be hurt. I finally had a life worth fighting for. I finally had hope. I wasn't the same woman I'd been when I'd last seen my father.

This time, I wasn't running away.

30

NIKOLAI

"*A*re you serious? You couldn't hold on to her for one night?"

"She... she tricked me. She's not an easy woman to keep hold off." Andrei sounded anxious.

"Tell me about it. What about Bran?"

I was sitting in the passenger seat, and Angelo was driving. We were flying down the highway toward Casa Nera. Fear threatened to overcome me when I thought about Leo in the callous, arrogant clutches of his grandfather, but I forced it down with cold hard logic. Antonio wanted me. He might want to kill Leo, too, but he'd wait until I could witness it. Even in his revenge plans, he was unoriginal and predictable.

"Bran is out of surgery, the nurse said it went well."

Something released in my chest at the knowledge. Bran had become a brother to me during our time inside, and the thought that he'd died protecting my son had threatened to send me off the deep end. No matter what I wanted to do, I couldn't walk into Casa Nera with a machine gun and waste every single De Sanctis there. That wasn't the deal.

Antonio had made his move sooner than I'd expected. I'd known since that day in the woods that he'd make a move. It had been obvious. His anger and spite had been so much more potent than I'd have predicted, after all this time. Things weren't going well for the De Sanctis family in New York, and not even deals with my brother could help them. Kirill did what was needed but nothing more. No relationships had formed, and without a beautiful virgin daughter to sell off for an alliance, Antonio was no doubt watching his empire crumble. He should have stepped down and handed it over to his son, but he suffered the same hubris as my own father, Viktor. He had underestimated his sons until the bitter end.

"Good, keep an eye on him. Don't worry about Sofia, I'm sure I'll see her before you do."

I hung up on Andrei and looked to Angelo. The gentle giant's hands were so tight on the steering wheel, he was in serious danger of bending it.

"Keep calm. We'll get her back."

"In one piece?"

"In one piece. Don't forget, she grew up with De Sanctis men. Her father is still alive, I believe?"

Angelo nodded.

"Good." I checked the tracker app on my phone. The little blinking dot had made it to New Jersey. Leo was about to meet his grandfather for the first time. Putting a tracker inside his favorite stuffed toy, the dinosaur with the missing foot, was one of the first things I'd done. He and Sofia were my family, and I'd stop at nothing to keep them safe.

You shouldn't have snuck out to fuck Sofia in the studio last night. It would all have gone differently if you'd been home. I dismissed the thoughts. They were useless to me now. This confrontation was always going to come, and I had waited for it for a long time. I wanted it over. I needed Antonio dead so we could finally live free of his shadow.

"Looking forward to going home, Angelo?"

He grunted. "That's not my home, neither is Maine. Chiara is my home. If she's hurt…"

"If she's hurt, I'll help you burn the place down myself. You have my word."

It was nearly daybreak when we finally reached New Jersey and the quiet little neighborhood that housed Casa Nera. In a lot of ways, my time in that house had defined me. It had left a lasting mark. In a dark and twisted way, it was like coming home.

We stopped at a location I had pinned on my phone. Getting out on the dark street, Angelo looked around.

"Are you sure this is the right place?"

"Sure."

Sofia's former bodyguard went to the trunk and strapped on an arsenal. Angelo hadn't come to play. He finished strapping a knife to his thigh, just as a shiny black SUV pulled up behind us.

"Are you sure about this plan?"

"No, but we're going with it. We have no choice. Remember, Antonio doesn't want to hurt anyone except me."

"Hurting Leo would hurt you," Angelo rightly pointed out.

"He won't get the chance." I offered my old friend my hand to shake. "Good luck, just in case I don't see you again."

"Christ, don't say that." Nonetheless, he held out his hand to shake mine.

Three shadowed figures got out of the car down the street. They started toward us.

"Thank you. I never had a chance to say it until now. Thank you for being there for Sofia and Leo while I was inside, and before. You've always watched over her."

"She's more like a little sister to me than anything else. She'd be hurt if you died, so try not to."

I laughed. "At least it's not doing nothing. If I should die… make sure Leo gets what he needs from me. Kidneys have an expiry of twenty-four to thirty-six hours for extraction."

"You didn't seriously just ask me to harvest your kidneys to give to your son, did you?"

I chuckled. "Of course not. Ask a doctor to do it." I slapped Angelo on the shoulder. I turned to the figure whose silhouette was as familiar as my own.

"You're cutting it a little close, aren't you? Now's not the time to be fashionably late."

Kirill cut me a terse smile. "Are you sure about this? We can still change the plan and take every single Chernov in there, guns blazing."

"Would you do that if Ruslan and Kira were inside?"

He let out a long breath. Beside him, his right-hand men shifted. Max and Ivan were bratva and had been by my brother's side since I could remember. The fact that they were here meant that they understood how important this was. It wasn't just business. It was personal. Despite never meeting him, my brother was ready to protect his nephew at all costs. I didn't know how to feel about that.

The three men were armed to the hilt and ready to go. How much stronger I'd feel walking into the compound with that might and muscle at my back, but the plan didn't work that way.

I had to go alone.

I took a step away from them along the dark road, heading into the middle of the quiet, residential street. Dawn was only just spreading her pale tendrils across the sky, and the air was fresh. "Time to go. Once more unto the breach."

Angelo saluted me, his expression torn between worry and determination. Kirill only nodded. Max and Ivan were expressionless. We all knew what was at stake. Not everyone could laugh in the face of death. Not everyone was as intimately acquainted with it as I was.

With a parting grin, I turned on my heel and left my allies to the dark and difficult journey through the secret tunnels to Casa Nera, the one that only Renato De Sanctis remembered the way through. Thankfully, he'd been willing to share.

I headed toward the main gates.

The compound was bustling. Every light was blazing in the place, and men with machine guns patrolled the gates. I strolled toward them.

As soon as they caught sight of me, they leveled their guns, shouting instructions at me. I raised my hands slowly. The men surrounded me, looking behind me cautiously. Clearly, they hadn't expected me to be ambling into their clutches without a fight. Antonio had probably expected my brother to be by my side, and the might of the Chernov bratva descending on Casa Nera.

Antonio lacked originality in every way. He was stunningly mediocre. How he had managed to spawn a fascinating woman like Sofia was a miracle.

"Hands up, Chernov!" one of the guards shouted at me.

I raised my eyebrow at him. "Forgive me if I'm wrong, but I have them up, I believe. Surely you want to check me for weapons first?" I reminded them.

Silence met that question, and then one of the men came forward. He was sweating bullets. He felt around my ankles and patted down my legs.

"Psst, it's not down there," I whispered to him mockingly.

He stood and looked me square in the eye.

"Try my chest."

His hand moved over my pockets, and he pulled my phone out. "He's clean." He tucked my phone away in his own pocket and jerked his head toward the gates. "Hurry up." He pressed his gun between my shoulders and pushed me forward. His radio chirped, and he spoke into it. "We've got him. We're on our way."

"Let me guess, you can't hit me because Antonio wants that pleasure for himself?"

The men were silent as they led me up the dark driveway. We walked past the spot where Sofia had killed her cousin and I'd taken the blame. We continued to the green where I'd shot poor ol' Gino, the bumbling, good-natured security guard who had tried to prevent me from taking Sofia hostage all those years ago.

Casa Nera looked different in the rising light. Scaffolding hid the right side from me. There was a general air of disrepair that had never been present before. A classic sign that a capo had held on to the keys of the kingdom too long.

We entered the building, and a flood of memories washed over me. It had the same Gothic style that Sofia had hated when growing up there. Dark oppressive wood and low ceilings pressed down on me. Intricate, dark oil paintings hung on the walls, and the lights were low inside. We didn't go down to the basement, I was happy to find.

Instead, I was led through to what seemed like a great hall of some kind. Maybe, in the past, the room was used as a grand dining room, perhaps there was dancing after dinner and an orchestra played. Now, it seemed that Antonio De Sanctis had set it up as his own throne room - a place where he could play king.

A single ornate chair sat before a huge fireplace. A hearty blaze burned within it, some of the flames rising nearly as tall as me.

Men lined the walls, all armed, their dark eyes trained on me. I stopped just inside the door, my eyes meeting Antonio's. He was sitting on his little fake throne. Pathetic.

"If you wanted to ask me for dinner, Tony, you could have just called."

Antonio raised his hand and gestured, ignoring my goading words completely. "Bring him."

We walked farther into the room. My eyes found Renato. He was standing to the right, just behind his father's shoulder. His eyes, so like Sofia's, met mine. There was no flicker of recognition. None at all.

"Well, Nikolai? I'm sure you knew it would come to this?" Antonio's voice was grand, speaking to his own sense of self-importance.

His words made me chuckle. "I did, and the fact that it was so obvious to both of us only makes what you did even more ironic."

"Meaning?"

"Meaning, if you thought I'd expect you to kidnap my son… you surely must have guessed that I'd take precautions?"

Antonio nodded slowly. He didn't look nearly riled enough. "I did expect that. A tracker in the soft toy. Hardly inventive."

"Well, we can't all be brilliant like you."

"No, you can't. The only thing I'm surprised about is that you didn't bring my daughter along to bargain with."

"This is between us."

"Between us. Between men. I guess that includes little Leo now, doesn't it?"

I fought the urge to surge forward and attempt to kill Antonio, despite the guns trained on me. I simply shrugged. The De Sanctis patriarch didn't like that. He wanted a reaction from me, and this wasn't it.

"Maybe we should hear from the boy." He jerked his head toward Renato. "Bring the bastard in here."

My eyes connected with Renato's, just before he turned away and strode from the room.

Antonio stood and shuffled toward me. "You know the problem with you, Chernov. You are too confident in your abilities. Sure, you can kill a few men in prison, but really, you don't rate next to a well-organized, loyal family."

"Loyal, you say? I don't think loyalty is something you have any authority to speak on."

"I inspire the kind of loyalty you can only dream about."

"We'll see." I clasped my hands behind my back and turned to check out exactly how many men we were dealing with in here.

The men in the room with us were older than those with Renato. A typical scenario where the younger generation supported the heir, while the older were dedicated to the aging *capo*, even if his methods had become too old-school to make sense anymore. Just the state of the house revealed that the De Sanctis family wasn't the force it had once been.

Antonio confirmed my suspicions when he leaned forward and stabbed a finger toward one of the men watching me from the sidelines, a gun clasped in his hand.

"Every single man in this room would die for me. That's loyalty."

"Is it? Sounds like a death wish to me."

The room had an inner balcony that ran around the entire second floor, leaving a gallery below. Now, I stared up at the men poised around the gallery at even intervals. Not so many. About twenty, at most. Renato De Sanctis wouldn't find it too hard to take over the family, if this was the total number of men who were loyal, diehard Antonio supporters.

Silence stretched between us. I ambled around the small circle in the middle of the armed men, whistling softly. Antonio scowled. I wasn't afraid enough for him. For a while, there was only the sound of my obnoxiously cheerful tune and my boots scuffing against the parquet floor.

While I was physically here, my mind was far away, traveling the passages into the compound with Kirill and Angelo. Were they already in the house? Had Angelo found Leo and Chiara? Every second that Renato took to go and check on Leo, the better. We needed time to get into place.

The door at the top of the hall opened, and Renato appeared, nearly ducking to get through the old-fashioned, low doorway. He was alone.

"Well? Where is the brat?" Antonio snapped at his son.

"I don't know. He's gone." Renato's powerful voice froze his father to the spot for a second. He crossed to his father and handed him a soft toy. A stuffed dinosaur. It was familiar-looking, except for the fact that it had four feet instead of three.

Antonio blinked at it with fury.

"This was all that was left."

Antonio stood, crushing the soft toy in a death grip. "Find him, now! Search the house. This Russian swine didn't come alone!" His voice thundered around the room.

His men split in two, and half left the room.

"I'll help," Renato said, backing away from his father.

Antonio spun toward his son and pointed at him with an accusing finger. "Your men did a piss-poor job of watching your sister's bastard, and now you volunteer to go and help them? You're a disgrace, Renato."

Renato didn't flinch from his father's words but merely nodded. "As you say, Father."

"You wanted to keep the boy in comfort. You didn't like seeing his tears. You're weak. Love for your sister and your sister's whelp is disappointing. You'll never learn, and this is exactly why you're not ready to be capo. Maybe you never will be."

Renato's hands curled into fists, but his face was impassive.

"If you're having a spat, I can always come back later."

Antonio's head snapped toward me. "You can shut your mouth, or I'll have your tongue cut out before I kill you."

I rocked back on my heels and shrugged. "Whatever floats your boat."

Antonio opened his mouth to retort, just as a loud, electronic tone cut through the tension.

The sound repeated again and again, and the remaining men in the room looked at each other. It was a phone ringing, and no one wanted to take responsibility for it.

"Oh, my bad. That's mine. Can I take it? We're not doing anything else, right?" I grinned at Antonio, sending his face an even deeper shade of tomato.

Antonio turned to stare at the man who'd patted me down outside and taken my phone. I wandered toward him. Antonio held his hand up to stop me.

"Don't even think about it, Chernov. Renato, *via,*" he snapped at his son.

Renato headed toward the man holding my flashing phone in his hand.

Time seemed to slow. I was holding my breath without realizing it. Antonio watched his son head toward the ringing phone. Renato reached the man and took the phone from him. He stared a down at it for a moment before raising his head and looking at his father.

"It's not a call." His voice was flat, impersonal.

I admired his poker face.

He dropped the flashing phone into a pocket. "It's an alarm."

A countdown started in my head.

Antonio frowned. "An alarm?"

I smacked my forehead and stepped back from Antonio. "Of course, silly me. I forgot. If I didn't set an alarm, I'd forget my head. Did you know that trackers aren't the only things you can put in stuffed toys?"

I was still backing away, and Renato was doing the same.

Antonio glared at me, and then my words dawned. His scowl transformed to horror as he looked down at the dinosaur toy still clutched in his hand. The very one I'd bought as a duplicate, had Artur work his magic on, and given to Renato on my way back from New York.

"Three, two, one… boom." I grinned at him.

Before he could drop the rigged device, it went off. The bang wasn't as loud as it could have been, but still, it scared the unsuspecting men in the room shitless. Smoke filled the air, obscuring the view. Antonio was howling in pain. With the amount of power that Artur was able to pack into his little devices, Antonio De Sanctis should have at least lost an arm, if not more.

Chaos rose around me as the first gunshots rang out. Bullets were being fired in the gallery. Kirill and his men had reached us.

The men below returned fire, ricocheting shots pinging wildly around in the smoky air. I rolled over, narrowly missing a bullet, which embedded in the floor beside me.

"Here," Renato said, appearing at my shoulder as I stood. He pressed a gun into my hand.

"Leo?"

"Gone. I've held up my end of the deal," Renato said.

I slapped him on the shoulder. "Yes, you have. Now it's my turn."

I'd gotten the explosive put inside the decoy toy after my *vor* initiation. Artur had enjoyed the challenge. Meeting Renato on my way out of town had been a stroke of luck. He'd had the toy ready to go for a week. Antonio had moved faster than I'd expected, but luckily, we'd been ready.

I moved through the large room, squinting up at the gallery. Kirill, Max, and Ivan had put down the men on the balcony first. Now they were shooting down at the ones remaining on the lower level. Those who were below had found places to take cover by now and were more difficult to pick off. I avoided gunshots as I walked toward the place where Antonio had fallen. The floor was black and burned. I could make out his body lying in the center of the blast zone. His white shirt was so bloody, it looked completely red.

I was hit with the macabre sight of the remains of his arm, lying several feet away. I stepped over the limb and crouched beside him. He was barely breathing. I met his eyes.

"Well, Tony. What do you have to say about loyalty now?"

He tried to speak, but I couldn't hear him over the shoot-out that seemed like it was never going to end.

"Speak up, old man. Or if you're thinking about confessing your sins and asking for mercy, here, at the end, don't waste your breath. They'll be no mercy for you, here or in the afterlife."

"You... you devil..." he managed to get out, past the red foaming from his lips.

I simply nodded. "You're right, Tony, I've seen Hell, and there's a nice, toasty place in it, for men like you. Before you die, know this. Your son hates you and conspired to kill you. Your daughter will forget you and never mention your name again. All the legacy you've built around honor and respect is a lie that only you ever believed. No one will remember you, no one will burn a candle in your memory. You leave no legacy. You leave nothing. I'll bury you in an unmarked grave and salt the earth once I'm done."

Antonio's mouth moved silently now. His time for words was gone. He'd never speak again. My gaze fixed to his, and I savored the moment when the life faded from the man who'd caused nothing but loss and pain in my life. Despite the whirling madness around us, I felt calm. Despite the bullets flying, I was at peace.

Renato appeared from the thick of it and looked down at his father's body. I stood and left him to it. Whirling, I brought my gun up and took out two of Antonio's men who were hunkered down behind a pillar, shooting upward at my brother. Dodging a bullet with my name on it, I rolled across the scarred floor and took out another who had just leveled his gun at the higher level, fixed on Max, Kirill's right-hand man. The shot was the last that sounded.

"I think we're good!" My voice echoed around the suddenly quiet room. The smell of gunpowder and blood filled my nose.

My brother appeared above, looking over the edge of the gallery. "And Leo?"

"Gone. Angelo took him and Chiara out through the tunnel." Renato sounded somber and as expressionless as ever.

I knew what it was to see your own father lying in a pool of blood. I knew how it turned the world dark and thinned the veil between this world and the next.

Unfortunately for Renato, he didn't have time to worry about it.

"Are you ready?" I asked him.

He nodded.

I turned toward the doors and whatever lay beyond. "The king is dead. Long live the king."

31

SOFIA

I drove like a woman possessed. I barely noticed the cars passing or the horns blaring at me. I had to have run a hundred speed cameras. I didn't care. Nothing mattered more than getting to Casa Nera. Home. No, it wasn't home, it had never been a home to me. It had only ever been a house I'd lived in for a while.

The sun was up by the time I reached an all-too-familiar road. Just down it, to the right, lay the gates of Casa Nera and Leo.

I was more than ready to drive the car right through those gates if I had to.

Then I saw it.

A collection of black cars parked by the side of the road.

I knew this place. It was one of Renato's secret entrances. When we were kids, he'd always been obsessed with finding ways in and out of the compound that no one else knew about. Casa Nera was old enough to have plenty of those. He'd kept his findings a secret from everyone, including me. I'd once spent several days poking around looking for possible entrances on the street and never finding anything.

I slowed as I drew level with the cars. A tall figure stood there, his head bent over, his face locked with concentration.

Angelo.

I slammed on the brakes. The car had barely stopped before I was out of it.

He was hurt. His arm was streaked with blood. I ran toward him, terror making it hard to breathe.

"Angelo!"

He looked up at my sudden cry. I slid to a stop on the road as I took in the person standing just behind him, a bandage in her hand.

Chiara.

They both tensed at my cry, clearly still on edge from whatever had gone down. I looked madly to the side. They were alone.

"Where is he? Where is Leo?"

I stood frozen to the spot, I couldn't move. I was too scared. I'd never been so terrified.

The silence felt deafening. There was a roaring in my ears that I couldn't hear them over.

One voice cut through the sound.

"Mom?"

I jerked my head from Chiara and Angelo and looked to one of the SUVs. A small, tousled head poked out of the back window.

"Leo?"

I stumbled as I went for him. It felt like someone had swept my legs out from under me. Nothing seemed to work right. Despite my uncooperative body, I was moving. I wrenched the car door open and fell on Leo. He laughed, falling backward in the seat as I pulled him close to me, pressing my face against his head, breathing him in, feeling the hot, wiggly strength of his little body.

"Mom! You're squeezing me like a lemon!"

"Sorry. I'm sorry. I've just missed you so much," I muttered, easing back enough to check him over carefully. "Are you hurt?"

Leo shook his head. "Just tired. I stayed up all night, and I met my uncle!"

"Did you?"

Leo nodded enthusiastically. "He was so nice. He took me to meet Angelo, and we came out of a secret tunnel, like in the movies."

"That's amazing… and what about your uncle now? Where is he?"

"He stayed behind at the house."

I jumped when Chiara put a hand on my shoulder. Releasing Leo, I pulled her close to me and breathed in her perfume.

"Thank God you're okay. You're okay, aren't you?"

She nodded. "I'm okay. It's all okay. It wasn't that bad."

"Agree to disagree. I've died ten times over since it happened. But I felt stronger, knowing you were with him." I pulled back, more tears falling. I stroked my best friend's hair. "Thank you for being with him."

"It's my honor. Don't thank me. Like I'd let them take my little lion and not fight to go with them?"

I hugged her close, my face hidden in her hair. After a long moment, I knew I couldn't put off asking what I needed to know for one more second.

Angelo was stroking Chiara's back.

"Are you okay?" I looked at his arm.

"It's just a scratch. You should see the other guy."

"I take it he's dead."

"Damn straight."

"How did you know about the tunnel? Did Renato help you?"

Angelo nodded. "He met Nikolai nearly a week ago, and they planned for this. Sofia, I'm pretty sure your father is dead by now."

I swallowed hard and asked the question that terrified me. "And Nikolai? Where is he?"

Angelo's long exhale made my anxiety only worse.

"At the house. My role wasn't to help him, it was to get Chiara and Leo out. I had to protect them. I don't know what happened after... if the plan worked out, he's alive and well."

"If not?"

Angelo jerked his head toward the cars. "If not, we need to get in the car, start driving, and not stop until we reach the West Coast."

"No. I'm not running away from my father again. I won't." Violent menace coated my words. "I'm going up there to see what happened to Nikolai and Renato."

"Sofia, you need to keep Leo safe," Angelo started and stopped as his phone rang. He cut off to answer.

Chiara pulled me close again. "Don't worry. You think Antonio can stack up against Ren and Nikolai combined?"

Angelo turned back, hanging up the call. "He couldn't. That was your brother. Let's go."

"Where?"

"Home, to Casa Nera."

THE FIRST STEP on De Sanctis property felt like standing on a volcano about to erupt. Nothing could have prepared me for the sight I encountered when I got out of the car.

De Sanctis men were kneeling on the lawn. More De Sanctis men were standing behind them, guns trained on the back of their heads. Renato stalked the line of captives. Behind him stood three men.

I hadn't seen Kirill Chernov in over seven years. He was still as huge and deadly as he had been then. His men flanked him. Kirill was lounging against the bumper of a car, watching the oncoming bloodbath like it was a Sunday matinee. He straightened up when he saw me, nodding a silent greeting.

My gaze couldn't stay on Kirill, though. Not when my heart was aching. I spun around, searching, always searching.

I felt like I'd spent my entire life searching for Nikolai, and whenever he was about to be mine, he was torn away, time and again.

Fresh tears fell from my eyes as I failed to make him out in the mass of men gathered in the courtyard. His distinctive profile was nowhere to be seen. Renato's eyes met mine. He was still pacing the line of De Sanctis men whose new allegiance hadn't been pledged.

An argument broke out, someone tried to run, and Renato strode toward them, taking his gun in hand and leveling it at the man, right between his eyes.

"Don't look, *lastochka*. Don't take that evil inside you." Warm hands landed on my waist and turned me.

Before I could register what was happening, Nikolai had pressed me into his chest and turned me away from the sight of my brother executing those who he couldn't trust. Their bones would join the rest under the ground of Casa Nera.

"Only my evil is allowed inside you, prom queen."

"Nikolai?" My breath hitched. All the anxiety I felt crashed around me like waves washing hard against rocks. Only he endured. Only he remained unbroken by the storm.

"Yes?"

"You're not dead."

"No, not yet, though I'm sure you have something to say about leaving you behind. Lay it on me."

I leaned back and slapped him just as the first gunshot sounded, renting the night. I jerked, and he pulled me back against him, turning my head into his chest and tucking it between his shoulder and neck. A little spot that fit only me.

"How's Leo?" His voice was tired, but content. Only he could be content when we were standing on a battlefield.

"Safe. Safe, thanks to you." I pulled away as silence fell over the courtyard. It seemed that the De Sanctis made men were done doubting my brother's determination to be capo.

"I hate you," I whispered vehemently to Nikolai.

He only nodded. "I know."

"You left me behind."

He nodded.

"I thought you were dead!"

The bastard chuckled. "I know. I guess we are well and truly even now, prom queen."

"You're sick."

He smirked. How the man could smile after everything that had happened, I had no idea, but somehow, the sight warmed me.

"Yes, but I think I might be a little less sick than before. It turns out that there's a cure for my madness." He put a firm finger to my jaw and tilted my head back so I could see his eyes burning into mine.

His gaze tracked across my face, drinking me in. "It's you, Sofia. For me, there's only you who can save me from the darkness inside. You're still, and always will be, the sun on my face. After the endless winter, there is you... and it's all I've ever wanted."

His words stunned me. I couldn't answer him. I had no words that could match his beautiful honesty. So I said the only thing I could think of. The only thing that felt right.

"Your son is tired. He's had an exciting night. I'm tired, too. I want to be at home, with my family."

Nikolai smiled widely. "I could listen to you talking about our family all day long."

"Will you take us? Take us home, Nikolai."

EPILOGUE

SOFIA

*A*fter a kidney transplant, it can take up to a year for the body to recover. Maybe it was because it was such a good match, or maybe it was because he was determined enough to get well enough to ice skate with his father, but Leo exceeded all expectations. His father also made a speedy recovery, like Nikolai Chernov would ever let a little pain or invasive surgery stop him.

I watched them out on the ice. Miller's Pond froze over every winter. This year, a whole twelve months after the death of my father, for the very first time, Leo got to skate, just like he'd always dreamed of.

"Here, hot chocolate with a little something something," Chiara said, plopping herself down next to me. She sighed as she leaned her body back. Her winter coat was tight around her growing bump.

"Something we're allowed?"

She gave me her patented wicked smirk, then laughed. "Relax, it's just a little peppermint syrup."

I sipped the sweet, frothy drink. It warmed me like all the gloves and feather down coats couldn't. I took a deeper drink and settled back in the chair Nikolai had carted out to the pond, just so I could take the pressure off my feet while watching Leo's first skating lesson. Being pregnant was definitely easier this time around, with an overprotective, at times overbearing, and utterly devoted husband around to wait on me hand and foot. While I mostly enjoyed it, sometimes it could be maddening. Nikolai was still Nikolai, and he didn't do anything by halves. He had it in his head that it was dangerous for me to shower alone, given my advanced stage of pregnancy. Therefore, he insisted on showering with me. Of course, that ended up being distracting for both of us.

"Go on, *tesoro*! You can do it!" Chiara yelled beside me.

I followed her gaze. "Are you shouting at Leo? I don't think he heard you."

"No, Angelo. That man can do a lot of things well, believe me, but skating isn't one of them. He's gonna fall and bruise his balls. I can't wait," Chiara chortled.

"How sweet of you."

"I'm planning on kissing them better. He prefers that to sweetness, believe me."

Smiling, I looked out over the pond. It was a brisk winter day. Christmas was just around the corner. School was going well, and I'd dropped down to teaching part time. I was painting more than ever. Nikolai wanted me to give up teaching horny teenage hockey players and teach adults, or better yet, paint to my heart's content and fill our house with kids. For the lonely boy who had looked at the stars and dreamed of being loved one day, there wasn't such a thing as too many kids.

We had moved to a new house. Edward Sloane's house was even more fabulous when you owned it. If I had any kind of conscience, maybe I should have felt bad about living in the house of the man who my husband had killed.

I didn't.

Nikolai had told me a little more about the kind of man Edward had been, all while pretending to be a local golden boy. He'd played in our world, just enough to get filthy rich, while still thinking himself above it. It didn't work that way. Once you were part of it, you accepted its rules. In the world I had grown up in, it was survival of the fittest. Edward had been no match for a true predator.

Honestly, I'd forgotten he'd ever lived there after a month. I wasn't the moral police. I had no authority to act like one. Nikolai and I had done what we'd needed to do to survive, and we'd keep doing it to keep our family safe. There was no judgment between us, only teamwork.

Nikolai effortlessly crossed the ice, skating with a natural-born grace. He helped Angelo to venture further onto the ice. I couldn't help but laugh as the burly bodyguard clung to his support.

"Ladies, who are we laughing at?" a cheerful voice spoke from behind us. Bran picked up the nearest empty chair and plopped it down next to me. The charming Irishman came to visit often, despite his responsibilities in New York.

"Angelo, the abominable snowman."

"Right, of course."

Bran was carrying his own hot chocolate, and I could smell from here that he'd added something other than peppermint.

"So, how was physical therapy?"

Technically speaking, Bran didn't need it anymore. He'd recovered well from his injury, but there was a therapist at the hospital who he liked. I didn't think the terminally fun playboy would ever be able to settle down.

A twinge deep in my belly pulled my attention from the ice, just as my eyes met Nikolai's. Angelo was standing with Leo now, and the two were moving at a glacial pace, hand in hand. A sharp kick inside me made me wriggle in my seat.

Only seconds later, the sound of cutting ice came from in front of me, and Nikolai was crouching, his hand pushing mine out of the way to place it firmly over my distended belly.

"Did she kick? Did I miss it?"

Another kick came just as he spoke. His mouth curved in a devastating smile. "There she is."

"You know you don't have to catch every kick, right?"

"I already told you, I'm not missing a thing this time. I already missed too much."

"Hmm, I don't think you're in danger of missing anything, considering I can't even take a shower alone anymore."

Nikolai laughed and slid a hand up my body, gripping my chin in a firm hold. He tilted my head down, until his gray eyes stared into mine.

"That's nothing to do with being pregnant, and everything to do with the fact that you're mine. My prize. That's just your life now. Get used to it."

"You're joking. You'll get tired of it eventually."

He chuckled. "When are you going to understand, my intentions for you are only just getting started, now that I have our son at home, a baby in your belly, and my ring on your finger. This is just the beginning of my obsession with you…"

My breath caught, and my heart pounded. Like always, I couldn't tell if it was excitement or nerves.

He studied me, as if deciding how far to reveal his possessive madness. "The only thing I've ever wanted in my life… was you, prom queen, and now, I've got you. There's no escape." He smiled, a dark, hungry thing.

In the end, I really was as crazy as he was, because I knew exactly how he felt.

"Stop making it sound like a challenge. You'll make me want to test you."

Nikolai threw his head back and laughed. "Test away, I like a good game. I've already pursued you when you were dead to the world, and I'll pursue you in your next life, too. I'll never stop catching you, and you'll never stop letting me."

I ran a finger down the faint scar that I'd left across his face, so long ago. "You're crazy, you know that?"

Nikolai turned his face into my palm, pressing his lips against the silvery N carved there. "About you? Always."

THE END

BONUS SCENE

It's Nikolai and Sofia's wedding…
Click read here to get it by email
https://www.milakane.com/extras

Join my reader group to get ARC opportunities, news
about new books, cover reveals and more!
Mila's Minxes

MILA KANE

I'm obsessed with cats, coffee, and anti-heroes just the right side of insane.

I write dark and dirty romance with the alpha-holes of your most filthy nightmares.

I only write SAFE stories, there is never a place for another woman in my heroes sights, once he's caught the scent of the heroine, and there will always be, no matter how dark and twisted the story might be... a HEA guarantee xx

Check out my books, deleted scenes, character profiles and more at
milakane.com

ALSO BY MILA KANE

Vicious Vengeance Duet

Wicked Heir

Savage Throne